THE SAILOR IN THE BOTTLE

THE SAILOR
IN THE BOTTLE

MANFRED BIELER

*Translated from the German
by James Clark*

NEW YORK
E. P. DUTTON & CO., INC.
1966

First published in the U.S.A. 1966 by E. P. Dutton & Co., Inc.

The characters in this book are entirely imaginary and bear no relation to any living person.

First published in Germany under the title
Bonifaz oder Der Matrose in Der Flasche
Copyright © 1963 by Aufbau-Verlag Berlin

English translation under the title
The Sailor in the Bottle
Copyright © 1965 by Hodder and Stoughton Ltd
and E. P. Dutton & Co. Inc.

First Printing   January 1966
Second Printing January 1966

Library of Congress Catalog Card Number: 65-19956

THE SAILOR IN THE BOTTLE

1

HERE is where you came out of the woods and went down the slope, though of course in the old days you could avoid doing this and follow the footpath, but ever since the Reverend Leverentz's little halfwits stopped up the brook and it overflowed there hadn't been a footpath. It had now been dark some time and the meadows and the cart ruts were frozen hard and I slipped, slithered and jumped all the way to the wooden steps in front of the Moravian Brothers' Home.

"Brother Leverentz!" I shouted. A couple of sparrows took off from the gutters and cut interlocking figures in the air, fluttering over the snow, and then settled down in front of the stable and waited for Messiah.

"It's Brother Bonifaz!" I shouted and rattled my blue knuckles on the door to the tune of a drum roll from the Finland Cavalry March. At long last Leverentz pulled the window open with heavy sashcords steeped in paraffin against frost, sat up in bed while the mountainous pillows slipped down behind him, and sighed, "The Lord be with you! Have the Russians arrived?"

Well, he's still alive, I thought, as the steam of his breath flew outwards in speech balloons into the cold air. "No, Brother Leverentz, not yet," I shouted.

"Then get home! I'm freezing." He stuck his hand in the loop of the stick beside his bed, propped his left elbow on his bony knee and shoved the window shut again.

Dutch clogs thundered down the staircase inside the house, crashed on to the hallway floor and then appeared in the door, 'twixt lock and hinge.

"I'm the Holy Ghost," said Helmfried, but I already knew that. Somebody or other had got to look after old Leverentz. Helmfried and Ernst were the last pupils in the home. Their parents were on the run or dead; whatever the reason, they had been unwilling to fetch their children home, mentally retarded and undersized as they were.

I walked past Helmfried; he blew me a whiff of fried onion. I went upstairs into the Reverend Leverentz's room, he had now been in Paradise for three years. As the rule is among the Moravians, the word Paradise had been painted on every object in the room, on the basin, on the night pot, on the coat stand. The room the children lived in was called Resurrection, and the box-room was called Nazareth, while the bottled fruit (when we used to have them these were pumpkins, plums, black-currants, beans, cucumbers, morellos, pears) and the rose-hip wine were kept in a cellar called Golgotha.

"What are the Russians waiting for?" asked Leverentz when I appeared in his doorway. There was a crease down both sides of his nose and he was used to blaming things on other people. But I had already asked Enno the same question, and even he had been unable to make the Russians materialise.

"Although they're used to the winter," I said, only I could not think of the rest of the sentence.

"Wouldn't it be just as well for us to nail a plank on top of the crucifix, above the head of God the Son, the Most Blessed?"

"The next thing will be that the Americans get here first, and then the timber will have gone for nothing."

"Bonifaz," whispered Leverentz, "I feel sure the Russians will be first. They're using little Mongolian ponies and there's more counting on animals than on machines. If it wasn't for being so dangerous, I'd have let my hair grow. I want the Believers among them to know that here with me they're at home, and they'll find a stable too. But you never know when a Nazi might come this way through the woods and spot me wearing a Greek-style beard. A change of religion is mighty hard for the likes of us."

Helmfried and Ernst came into the room and huddled together against the cold, opening their nostrils wide.

"Get us some of the rose-hip wine," requested the Reverend Leverentz, "but take the chill off it, and don't forget to wet your own throats." Alarmed by their slamming of doors and shattering clog

6

steps, he called after them, "And don't get drunk, you greedy pigs." And then, as if to reassure me, he added, "They don't really understand any of it, the dear souls." We had a long wait. I numbered off the letters in Paradise, and dreamt "The Russians Are Here"—that makes eighteen letters—and then they had gone away again, and I was boss of the German Reich: German Reichs-Boss. I always did want to be number one. Leverentz could be Suffragan Bishop of Garmisch-Partenkirchen. There are eight letters in Paradise and they are written in gold and blue, like the Swedish flag, and I daresay Paradise is situated over in Sweden: they're neutral, for a start. And the same goes for me, as a matter of fact. This thought was enough to pull me together again.

Leverentz's chin and neck sank deep into pillows stuffed with the down of Pomeranian geese which the community had brought over unplucked from the east in times long ago.

2

WAR is exhausting, even for the spectator. I had had to fetch the milk just like on any other afternoon. I quickly got to Reuthen. I picked up the aluminium can and walked ten paces from my little house to the corner, turned left along the highway, walked through the snow for two hours to the spot where the road turns down towards Reuthen. Provided artillery wasn't being towed along the highway, it was only children's knees that picked up the gravel in summertime, and then in autumn it stretched, red as mountain ash, up hill and down dale and it was not until the end of November, when the peasants were as fed up with potatoes as their barrows were full of them, that they let down nets of drizzling rain between the trees, kept out of sight, and played blind man's buff in their warm cowsheds or cock-a-peekie in the draughty henhouse.

7

I got the milk at the third farmstead. In exchange for curds I gave postage stamps. Iraqi fils, Afghan puls, Rumanian bani and Turkish kurusa got us our cream. I used to let the village cobbler sniff his way through the perforated indigo scraps and occasionally gave him money as well, although war is a time to suit cobblers well, what with their double-welted temperaments. I wandered back again along my own meandering track, past the gooseberry bushes looking like sponge cakes laden with crystallised sugar and from there I liked cutting home across the hill, so I scooped up some snow and flung it in the air, playing snowstorms. Up in the heights a moderate winter gale was blowing and I lit myself a cigar, using my lighter and the glowing end for recognition practice of the world's principal harbour lights, took my bearings on Rio and Bremerhaven, Murmansk and Muckle Flugga, and after that dropped down to the valley again.

In the summer there is a footpath and in the winter there is nothing at all. In the summer there is a stream, broom, elders, geese and the redskins from down in the village. In the autumn long lines stretch overhead, marked out with scraps of paper or chips of wood, the smallest of them no higher than the tide gauge in the Weser estuary or the Kiel Canal. In the winter it is all ice, snow and thin tree trunks and since last week there had also been a knocked-out tank by the stream, where the hedge-hopper had surprised it. Beyond the tank lay the common, the rat pond, the highway. By this time I was well on my way home and could see my house. It counted as part of the town of Tesch, whose fame mainly derived from some famous variety artistes who had settled there. I need only mention King Schwapp, Aunt Galupo, Pipi and Speranza, or Sergio and his great bottle-top trick, or the dwarf Enno, turning his elephant into a mosquito, right there by the regulars' table at Schamofsky's, which my friend Maiko had actually seen done, one of the times when he was not in clink. The dwarf's elephant had perished and Speranza, the ex-giantess, got Ration Book D. This was the winter of 1945 and the whole town was still in place, and fifteen thousand women, invalids, old folks and children were preparing to defend it.

When I was within a quarter of a mile I could see a crowd of people

8

round my house, so I set a skirting course, as they were digging holes in the footpath on either side of the road, throwing picks into the frozen soil, shovelling out lumpy sods, ramming in planks which they propped up with stones, and filling in the trenches again. A man in blue earmits, lending a hand everywhere, some sort of foreman it seemed, caught sight of me and shouted, "You there—trying to sneak out on the job?"

I brought myself to attention and barked back so that he would not understand me: "On my way to make milk soup!"

Blue-earmits waved me off and I did an about face. From my doorstep I shouted back: "No repatriated person shall be employed on active military service. Article Seventy-Four of the Geneva Convention of July 27th, 1929."

You have to know that sort of thing by heart when you're directly affected. Then I went inside my house, opened the kitchen door, took the milk saucepan down from the shelf above the range and poured in the milk. My wife was sitting by the range warming her feet, with strands of hair pushed underneath the bows of her glasses, as she always did when in a gloomy mood.

"You could at least shoot from the window," she said. I pushed the milk onto the hotplate and drew off my boots. Why don't the Swiss give their women the vote? Why indeed? A true-blue German woman always votes National Socialist, Maiko used to say, but he had gone and hanged himself.

"You know perfectly well," I said, "that I had to give my word of honour to Captain Moosbaker in Lobito that I would stay neutral!" Emma, my wife, picked up a splinter of wood, and ran it along the row of white enamel jugs and pans, making music of a sort.

"But supposing," she said, "you just tossed down a hand-grenade from the attic, without the enemy knowing you were neutral?"

I drew the striped curtain aside, and scratched a hole in the ice-flower patterns on the window-pane with my fingernail. For pity's sake —they were still at their burrowing.

"Things look different in Africa," said Emma.

"My dear Emma," I said, "you may be in the Party, but there are

9

some things which you do not understand. If the Tsar of Russia, the King of England, and the German Kaiser sign something, it means that the thing stays put, come what may."

"Come what may, we've got ten bazookas and three lads from the Hitler Youth to hold the first assault with."

"It's much too cold anyway," I said, so as not to hurt her feelings. Through the hole in the ice-blossoms I could see the town's defenders dancing around the ram blocks, thrashing their arms, clenching their toes, screwing up their eyes and then, at a whistle, dashing over to the opposite side of the road. Put a searchlight behind the group and they would have performed a perfect shadow theatre against my gable-end. It was quite dark now.

"You and your Africa," said Emma.

They were rolling up heavy fir trunks, and in no time had ingeniously rigged up a ramp, over which they shoved the timber as far as the gaps between the planks. It all looked like a perfect force diagram on the physics teacher's blackboard—$f \times distance \times \sin \alpha$. How many cubic feet of timber does a member of the German Volkssturm support during construction of a tank obstacle if the angle α equals thirty-eight degrees? If at the same time he is singing *Dobrze Dobrze Tra la la, Violinka wire kaputt*? If he receives Ration Book C with supplementary tickets for T.B.? Blue-earmits pinched his finger, letting out a screech. He could not see me laughing. My little monkeys were bobbing above the kitchen range, spinning out as far as both ovens. The elephant and the wire giraffe are swaying next to my grandmother's eightieth-birthday photo. My oil lamp was underneath them, the one I take out onto the terrace in summer, and on which the moths cannot burn themselves. The neighbours' dog howls, the barren hens cluck in their sleep, and when I stand up I can see the moon rising over the clump of Jerusalem artichokes. And I'm sick of the scent of elders.

The milk is boiling. The milk is boiling over. I jump up in my socks to get to the range, pull the saucepan away from the heat with my index finger and blow into the white foam.

"Seeing that you've dodged the theoretical course," said Sergeant Mayerbär, who had silently opened the door leading out into the yard, "may I remind you that a bazooka is by no means the same as a penny firecracker? So leave as much open space behind you as possible when firing, if you possibly can. Otherwise you'll blow yourself up."

"That must be the miracle weapon we're expecting," I said, licking the finger that had now got a blister on it. Sergeant Mayerbär signalled to three Hitler Youths. In they came with half a dozen bazookas which they laid in my kitchen with infinite care, peering left and right as if hiding Easter eggs. The smallest of the three managed to catch the sights of one in his steel helmet and dropped his bomb, at which Herr Mayerbär, Emma, the two other Hitler Youths and myself held our breath. The little chap himself, however, put his hands up.

"Well, well," commanded Herr Mayerbär after a general pause, "you'd better put them in the bedroom, so that nobody can get at them. The softest pillow is a quiet conscience. *Heil Hitler!*"

"Herr Mayerbär," I asked, "are you aware of Chapter Three of the Hague Convention on the right of capture in maritime war, signed on October 18th, 1907?"

"What?"

"Aren't you aware that I'm neutral?"

"You're mad but not neutral."

"Herr Mayerbär, when I was exchanged for a British naval prisoner of war on board the *Robinson*, 2698 gross register tons, I was obliged to make a formal promise to His Britannic Majesty's Captain Moosbaker that I would not undertake any service connected with the operations of the war. This promise is endorsed by the signatures of the Tsar of Russia, the German Kaiser, the King of Rumania and the Japanese Son of Heaven!"

Sergeant Mayerbär stared at me. "The Japanese Son of Heaven? Was he in your ship?"

"Of course not! They signed it in 1907. The year I was born. Consequently . . ."

"I suggest," interrupted Mayerbär, "that you think about Germany for a change. Don't forget which is your country."

"My country is somewhere else, sergeant. This place here is more like a flea—it just tickles me. It gives me the giggles and I can't catch it. I catch up with it on my belly and the next moment it's running up my back."

"Blasted drivel," said Mayerbär and glanced at the Hitler Youths to see whether they were listening in while the grown-ups picked a bone. "You'll have to form a hedgehog position."

"That's right," said Emma, "we'll form a hedgehog."

"I hereby appoint you warden of the tank barrier," said Mayerbär and snapped his boot heels together, while Emma answered "Right!"

He stepped to the window and tried to rub away the ice-blossoms with his fist. "Look through here," he commanded, but it was a view I had already seen.

"Take up your post at the window tonight and keep your eyes on the tank barrier. In the event of an attack . . ."

"I shall form a hedgehog."

"Rubbish!"

The three Hitler Youths snickered happily. "You will fire one round. If possible two rounds. We shall then proceed to your assistance. Understood?"

"I served in the *Robinson* for three years and she wasn't a man-of-war, just an honest freighter, so supposing I was even capable of firing one, not to mention two, shots, how can I be sure that you'll come, sergeant? —No, please, let me finish: at the critical moment you might be down in the cellar or in bed. Nobody would think of your being asleep on a night like this. Wouldn't it be much better if I set fire to my house? A wind's blowing up tonight and a first-class blaze against the low clouds would be an absolutely positive signal."

But Mayerbär shook his helmet so hard that the chin-strap creaked in its rings.

"So now you want to light up the battlefield for the enemy's benefit? We have one advantage: attack under cover of darkness."

A pumpkin-shaped drum stood in the corner of my kitchen.

"That's my tom-tom, it comes from Angola," I explained. "If you'll remove your helmet and cock your ears, I'll give you a signal. Like this: dom!—one tank."

Dom. Dom.

"Two tanks," interpreted Sergeant Mayerbär.

Using thumb and little finger I produced a high staccato.

"Infantry?" asked Mayerbär.

"You're the man to have with me in the jungle. Now listen to this."

I slapped my palms alternately on the tom-tom: the rumble of artillery interspersed with the crackling arpeggios of machine-guns and pistols, aided by my fist and my knee, until Herr Mayerbär shouted "Stop!"

"So you see, I'd have had it. By then I'd be, as they say in the papers, in Valhalla."

"Show more trust!" said Mayerbär.

My milk had cooled off enough. I drank it straight out of the saucepan and spoke my next sentence into its interior, so that the sound boomed in my ears: "Ten years ago, Herr Mayerbär, you went and threw cowpats down the chimney of Herr Eisenberg because he didn't have a foreskin, although two Christmases earlier you'd married his daughter. Trust is a big word."

Mayerbär leapt over the bazookas and came close up to me. His eyebrows made a V on his forehead and his lips were drawn back over his teeth, so that I actually felt quite sorry for him. If he had sat up and begged I would have given him a bone.

"Say that again," he barked.

"I can write it out for you if you like, but I can see you'd do better to have the dentist fit you up with a bridge after the war's been won. If you can't bite properly the best of steaks come out the same way as they go in. Just think of when Schamofsky serves his Songs Without Words again, that glorious meat platter of his! Good teeth make good digestion."

"You're a defeatist," snapped Sergeant Mayerbär.

"I don't know what that is, but if it means that I'm a gourmet, well, I can only agree with you."

"You know my orders."

"Sure, sure," I said.

"Party Comrade Emma," said Mayerbär to my gloomy wife,

13

warming her feet by the range, "we'll be waiting for you at eleven p.m. in the Party building. That is, unless you think you ought to assist your husband in the defence of the tank barrier?"

"Oh, I'll manage on my own," I assured him.

"The Winter Help contribution lists need checking."

"I'm a dead accurate book-keeper," nodded Emma.

"Fine," said Mayerbär and added "*Heil!*" and then to the Hitler Youths: "Dismiss!"

For me he had no parting word. He left me there to fight on alone, deprived of my last handshake and martial exhortation. Just the silhouette of his steel helmet from outside against the curtains, and there I was on my own with Emma and six bazookas. Emma went off to the Party building. Before going she pulled the hair out from underneath her glasses, looked at me through the thick lenses and said, "Leave some milk for me."

3

LEVERENTZ'S wine looked yellow in the smoky glasses it was served in, they must have been warmed over candles. The stuff oozed tepid and oily over one's teeth and trickled down the uvula into one's throat. We hummed and hahed, Leverentz seeking some pious remark for the occasion. He failed, at any rate he contented himself with rolling hallelujah eyeballs and left it at that. Nothing suited me better. Who wants to do a deal with the parson and to speak of the Lord withal? I poured out another round.

"I should like to get you a little timber, Reverend Brother."

"You'll be asking a shameless price for it," said Leverentz. "We're only a little community living in momentous times. Last year you had my little children over to pluck grass for your goat. And from the churchyard at that "

"The goat perished of starvation, Your Reverence. God alone knows your part in that guilt."

"He can't know anything of the sort . . ."

"He numbereth every hair, ever single hair, and is it not written in the Epistle of the Blessed Apostle . . ."

"Spare me your scripture! Are you or am I the clergyman here? How much does the wood cost?"

"It's good spruce."

"How much?"

"Two hundred marks."

Some people sniff hard, others stop twisting their thumbs, a third type drops his eyelids. Only a truly recollected man has complete mastery over himself.

"The wood will be wet."

"Dry as the Saviour's bones."

"Where is it?"

"I shall need Helmfried and Ernst to help me bring it down. This very night. Tomorrow I shall be over the hills and far away."

"There's something very fishy about all this, Bonifaz."

I had to reassure him. By tomorrow wrong was going to be right, and right a crime.

"Fir trees true and slender they are, like in Mendelssohn's *Wer-hat-dich-du-schöner-Wald*."

Leverentz reflected. The room became very quiet. He had let his hands relax on the sheet. Now and again he lifted a finger as if to see whether it had not yet frozen stiff with the cold. This made a shadow crocodile on the wall, for the third and little fingers would not separate. Then he said what sounded like "hoppla", having once upon a time been to a horse show.

"And how would it be with an advance, Reverend Brother?"

"I shall let you have something. No," he added at once, "not money. Far better than money." Leverentz puffed out his lips and screwed up his eyes.

"Heartburn again," he said. The folds of his eyelids stretched from his fur cap to the bridge of his sharp white nose.

15

"Assuming I could grant you your wish, what would you like to be?" asked Leverentz.

"Don't try and take me in. After all, you aren't a saint. What's the point of an old trick like that if you don't want to give me the money?"

But Leverentz simply parted his lips to let out his breath and said nothing.

"Well, all right then, it's getting on toward midnight," I said, "but if you insist: what I'd most like to be is a white four-master with yards a housetop high and a broad red hull-line and a full wind astern, inside a nice green Jamaica rum bottle."

"Yes," said Leverentz, "but not so loud."

"And then afterwards with the moon sailing through the Northern Lights, and the bowsprit drawing white streaks over the belly of the sea, the ice going south into the whisky, and when I'm lonely, I'll throw out a line with my heart on it for any bites I can get."

4

"I'LL give you something," began Leverentz, not very clearly but I could understand him, "that will make your way easier. You'll seem a nice person in the eyes of others, as far as anyone can in times like these. Not for your whole life. But they'll feel close to the hand that you break bread with and carve little birds out of soft wood for children with. They'll thank you for your affection and friendship, though not for very long, and in fact only very slightly longer than they do to others. But in the span between little and a little more lies your advantage. Then there'll come the day when you see the sea again. When you cross through the woods in the spring you'll go as far as the outskirts of the towns, up to the first houses, with their sheltered gardens and their ant rings on the trees. Don't stop there, but go for the main roads. All roads lead to the sea. Stand outside the factory gates when the shifts go in, when they march inside pink, clean and shaved, but don't miss the bleached-out, tired and hurrying ones coming out. Crowd into the trams and buses with them, dance with them, drink with them. But never forget; no one will ever wait for you at the corner with a child in the crook of her arm. Your bed will be empty. Your table will be set, but there'll be no one to wait on you. You can gulp down the biggest helping, and who shall say to you: eat up! or: that's enough! Everyone will be friendly to you, everyone. But that won't be enough for you. One day, there's no hurry, you'll want them to love you. They'll look at you as though you'd made an improper suggestion. For they take you to be happy. They'll laugh at you. That will be their excuse. To them you'd always been the happy vagabond, the salesman in lucky charms, the good-cheer merchant, the sailor in the bottle, the man with the lucky touch who always lands on his feet, the sort who finds a seamstress to love him even after giving his last shirt away. You'll make a long voyage and yet there'll come the day when you'll lean your head against the window and look out into the dark street and you'll know no more . . ."

"But the sea, Brother Leverentz?"

"It's there, behind it all," said Leverentz.

Handle incense or onions and you're marked for life. Preachers are all the same. They make it sound so lofty but in the end you're left with nothing but fine words. The Reverend Brother's face now lay on the pillow-case absolutely alone, while on and off his hands still practised getting up.

5

I LEFT the room, creaked down the stairs to where the children lived and pushed the door open. Helmfried and Ernst were squatting glassy-eyed beside the cast-iron stove. They were drinking rose-hip wine from tin mugs that they set on the stove between sips.

"Get your coats on, we're going for timber. I'm the sailor in the bottle now."

"And I'm the Holy Ghost," said Helmfried.

"Then we're made for each other."

"And I'm Churchill," said Ernst.

I took down two fur caps with Resurrection labels inside them and popped them on the two boys' heads to save time, and then we went out by the farmyard door. I nearly fell over a snowman whose nose dropped off, and Helmfried and Ernst went to fetch Messiah the horse from the stable and attached two chains to his collar. The four of us set off across the meadow and up the slope, puffing four clouds ahead of us, the biggest of which was Messiah's.

We came out of the municipal woodland onto the highway which runs from Rossbach to Tesch and I blew out the oil lantern. Messiah had no calks on his shoes and was slithering on the snow-covered surface. Helmfried and Ernst had to pick up the chains in their hands so as not to wake up the town defences. I nearly fell over the tank barrier in the darkness.

Emma must already have gone off to the Party building, for as I passed through my kitchen into the toolroom to get my crosscut saw I noticed that the milk had been finished and that the ever-chilled feet were no longer propped in front of the oven door. I wiped the saw blade down with an oily rag, tried the teeth with palm and thumb, picked up a wedge and hammer and walked out of the house again.

6

THE night was moonless and our neighbours had drawn their blackout curtains. Helmfried and Ernst tied Messiah to the fence. The first thing to do was to saw through the upright planks.

The boys knew how to handle a saw, put their shoulders to it and kept a nice straight cut, reducing the sound of the grating and squeaking of the blade. Once I had knocked the wedge into the cut things went faster, and after a couple of minutes we fetched Messiah, knotted the chains around the plank and led the horse away. We levelled another two planks in the same way, and then we got Messiah to draw out the long tree-trunks. As they came away from their holes they scraped noisily over the planks and bounced onto the road.

Helmfried and Ernst kept looking around, so I reassured them, to the sawyer's rhythm: "Tonight they're all dreaming—of the cannibals arriving—Tonight they're wondering—if a dishcloth's big enough—to do for a white flag—or have they got to get out—the best damask tablecloth—and hang it from the flowerbox—when the moment comes? —Tonight they're all wondering—what it's going to be like—when they give up lifting their right hands—and use them to shake with again—Tonight they're practising—handshakes in bed—shaking hands till their palms sweat—and then drop to sleep again."

Helmfried nodded as I spoke, and Ernst and Messiah trotted off easily with the first log towards the municipal woodland. Helmfried came into the house with me. He sat down at the corner of the stove, in Emma's place, pressed the back of his hands against the warm stove-top, pressed his stomach and thighs against the tiles and did not look up. I relit the oil lantern.

"Are you hungry?" I asked him, but he did not answer. I left the lantern by the range and went into the next room. I got myself a pair of warm trousers out of the clothes chest and put them on. "The warden of a tank barrier must have trust, that's what Sergeant Mayerbär said!"

Helmfried lifted his head and smiled.

"Before I became neutral I once worked in a slaughterhouse. That's the place for trust, I can tell you. Then I was overseer of a plantation in Africa."

"The Reverend Leverentz has set us a punishment," said Helmfried.

"Then you know where you stand."

"We've got to copy out the first three books of Moses, for smoking."

"How far have you got?"

Helmfried laid a finger on his brow and recited: "The Lord shall give you of the dew of Heaven and of the fat of the land and corn and wine in abundance."

"The Israelites went in for having trust, too. Once when I was on the Sydney run I read the whole Bible right through. One fine day God went and showered all the Jews with shit—because of their having married the wrong lot of women."

I fastened my braces and came back into the kitchen.

"I'm the Holy Ghost," said Helmfried.

"Well, that makes it easier for you."

I took the boy's hand and led him back into the next room where the wardrobe stood. "I'll let you have something as a parting gift," I said. I showed him Emma's dresses and my summer overcoat.

"Look!" said Helmfried. I reached up to the top shelf and fetched down the top hat for him. Ten years ago Emma had bought it for me to go to church in. I put my hand into the hollow of it and spun it round on my middle finger. I stroked the cardboard with a little brush and added a final polish with the sleeve of my winter overcoat. Then I crammed it over Helmfried's ears. For myself I took down the sailor's cap with its blue ribbons and stood behind him, so that we could both get a view in the mirror. The highlights of my wedding hat shone in the oil lantern's glimmer, and Helmfried's eyes beneath the narrow, gaily curving brim turned serious.

"Now you really do look like the Holy Ghost," I said.

"Brother Leverentz . . ." said a voice from the door and in the glass I saw the gesture by which Ernst made known the death of the reverend brother; dropping his chin onto his chest, he spread his arms out wide, fluttered his little leather mittens, and stationed himself behind Helmfried, so that I had to move out of the way.

"No more copying," said Helmfried, shoving back the top hat.

"Now we can smoke," said Ernst.

I went back through the kitchen with the boys and out into the street. I put the chains round the second tree trunk, gave Messiah a smack on the crupper and led the children away. Along the highway we went, past the biscuit works at the back of the municipal woodland, down the slope and up to the front door of the Moravian Brothers.

20

7

BROTHER LEVERENTZ was staring at the ceiling with his mouth wide
open. The index finger of his right hand was stuck in the air, as if it
had frozen there with his last living gesture. Helmfried and Ernst
followed me into the room and the top hat came into its own.

"Leverentz is dead," I said, superfluously. Helmfried and Ernst
knelt by the bed and sang:

> *Spread thy welcoming pinions wide,*
> *Jesu, Lord, my joy.*

After that they sang the deceased's favourite song, and I joined in:

> *Merry May is here,*
> *The trees do dress in green.*

While we were singing the bit about the clo-houds up ther-here in the
hea-ea-eavenly dome, I noticed that there was a paper bag at the
bottom end of the bed which had not been in the room previously.
Letting Helmfried and Ernst, who were getting into the swing of it
and warming up with fast breathing, repeat the first stanza, I opened
it. Inside there was salt, coarse, granular, crunchy salt, the kind you
can rub between your fingers, and it got under my nails the deeper I
probed. So Leverentz must have got out of bed again and fished out
the salt to pay for the wood with. Two hundred marks, which I needed
for my fare? Not a bit of it. Leverentz must have stood the ladder
against the trapdoor in the ceiling and have crawled up it in the old
morning coat which he draped over his shoulders in lawcourt style.
He kept his salt in a dry place and in the old days he had occasionally
taken me up with him under the roof, and while we talked about
holy wars and the cost of beef we wetted our fingers and stuck them in
the sack of salt and then licked them with prehensile tongues. We
praised the salt of the earth, the heavenly salt, the salinity of the oceans

and the salt in our blood; we exchanged stories about goats licking up the crystals, about salt-pan workers buried alive, about salt deserts and salt lakes. And now there was salt by the cold feet of the Reverend Leverentz, and I was both irritated and thankful at the same time.

I knew that Leverentz had a little library in the next room which could be quite useful. If it hadn't already been well past midnight I might have sold the timber to King Schwapp or Pipi: they would have the necessary put aside. But where do you find a taker for a tank barrier at this time of night? Even if it's built of nothing but finest spruce? Underneath the dusty bookcase I found a stack of pious booklets dating back to the time when Leverentz was still a Catholic. There was one brochure entitled *Some Quills from the Wings of the Holy Archangel Gabriel*, another was devoted to the *Swaddling Bands of the Holy Child Jesus*, and there was a third concerned with the *Means of Preserving the Clamour of the Bells to Which Our Blessed Saviour Entered Jerusalem*. I tore up the pages to make little cornets, wrote the recipients' names on them and filled them up with the saline bequest. At that time salt was well worth a blasphemy in Tesch, where they pickle pork so merrily and relish their bacon. So I wrote the name FRANZ KUTSCHMANN in good thick block capitals upon the *Tidings of the Incarnate Sighs St. Joseph Uttered during the Planing of Knotty Planks*, shook a pound of salt into the cornet and put it down on one side. For ERNA WICHORSKI, who worked in the hand-grenade factory and had four children, I filled the *Blessed Breeches of Saint Anthony* with salt, and for HERR FLECK, accountant to the Church Assembly, I poured a quarter into *The Sudarium of St. Veronica*. I even scraped a few ounces together for my wife—Party Comrade Emma—and bequeathed them to her in the *Homily upon the Scissors Delilah used to Shear Samson's Hair*.

Coming back into Leverentz's room, I saw that Helmfried had fallen asleep at the side of the bed. His elbows were on the bedclothes, and the top hat had slid off his head to find a stand in Leverentz's erect forefinger. I stuffed the cornets into my coat and jacket pockets, piled the rest in the crook of my arm and blew out the light.

Ernst stood on the staircase outside, looking out through a dormer window.

"Milord is out on the tiles," he said.

"What lord?" I asked.

"Our black cat."

When I got down to the yard outside and looked up to the dormer window, I saw a hand reach out and pull the cat back in. Milord was no longer walking the tiles. Milord was staying indoors.

8

I PUT Emma's cornet down outside my front door. I didn't even go in. Emma had once been the lovely blonde Emma, the lovely blonde Emma who danced on top of the counter. Emma had grown pale, weary and preternaturally grave. I had written to her twice from Africa but she refused to believe that I really was a P.O.W., for the photo which I sent her showed girls with nothing over their breasts and there was I in my shorts right in the middle of them, smoking. My left hand was behind my back, and Emma maintained that this was only to hide a bottle of gin. True enough. So then she went and joined the Party, and when four years later I was repatriated she was sitting there by the stove, with grey strands of hair held down by her glasses, warming her feet.

I left three little bags outside the big iron-studded door of the tenement block with its one-room dwellings, and thus took my leave of the red-haired collier's carter and his seven children, from my friend Maiko's widow—Maiko who had hanged himself by his braces in Rossbach woods—and from the broad-whiskered policeman Crapper, whose application for a change of name by court order was lodged deep in enemy-occupied territory and who would now bear his distasteful name to the end of his life, writing it beneath charges of burglary, unlawful slaughtering and trespass. The tobacconist Teichmann also received his share, the small-beer and hot drinks caterer Schamofsky would be able to pickle his floating kidneys, and the street-sweeper Barth would be able to spice his rabbit-dripping with the reverend brother's salt while meditating upon the innocence of the basin in which Pilate washed his hands. I wrote a message for Aunt Galupo: "In lieu of a kiss we send Your Highness this little purse of salt, beseeching you, in the spirit of the great affection that exists between us, to deign to celebrate herewith, you and your brothers."

I did not forget Pipi and Speranzo and Serpio and the Dwarf Enno either, and thus I took leave of the town, for I wanted to reach the sea, and as the salt left my pockets so my heart grew lighter, and with every cornet that I laid at a door I lost a friend, and memories of morning and night, of baptisms and wakes, and only when I was putting down the last bag in front of the house where the cemetery keeper lived did I remember Leverentz. On a piece of paper I wrote down the death of my friend in the old wood-built Home. My last man could be relied upon. He was up to the ears in work, with corpses being unloaded and left behind every time a refugee convoy trekked through the town. But I was sure that he would have a box and a corner to spare for Leverentz. I looked across the cemetery: rank on rank of hero's sons and mothers' boys, thin ones, fat ones, chesty ones and those with stomach cancer, the Stag-in-the-Glen artists, the chair-leg turners, the women in childbed, and the chemist, the waitresses and the brewer's drayman. I knew them all, and I had had enough of the whole little world of these half-timbered souls. I turned about. I never wanted to come back. I snapped out of my ambling pace and kicked my shoes into the snow so that the flakes whirled around me. It had got lighter since Leverentz's death. I hurried over the Hitler-Platz, down the Herder-Strasse, noticed lights still on in the Party building—meaning Emma was now bent over the contribution lists, running up and down the columns with her red pencil—past the statue of Roland at the town hall with a snowball lodged on his nose, hurried on and on and on until the town lay behind me. I slowed down only when I was on the forest trail to the south-west and saw the trees over my head moving backwards and forwards and stepped out of the darkness into the clearing that lay between Rossbach and Tesch.

But the town would not let me go so easily. Sergeant Mayerbär approached across the snow. A horse bestrode him. A sensational act: a horse was riding him, urging him on with his hoof, seeming to anticipate the juicy crunch of Mayerbär babies, Mayerbär granny, Mayerbär missus. What a big mouth you've got—all the better for eating you with!

"Good morning, Herr Mayerbär. Where are you taking that horse?"

"I can't give any away. It's only a quarter of a horse."

"You can keep it."

"Man thirsts, horse eats, they say—it's the other way round for once, and anyhow, what brings you here out into No Man's Land?"

"I'm going away, Herr Mayerbär."

"I detailed you as warden of the tank barrier."

"I know. But I'd had enough. I've sold the tank barrier."

The shock brought the horse's quarter tumbling down. The hoof described an arc in the air and then lay motionless in the snow.

"You ought to put a bullet through your head," said Mayerbär.

"You can't even rely on the pistols nowadays."

"I've got a wonderful .08 at home. I could finish you off in a wink with it."

"I'm not going with you, though," I said, for I did not intend to get myself shot.

"What, may I ask, did you get for the tank barrier?"

"Two hundred," I replied.

"Yes," said Sergeant Mayerbär, "it was good timber. Well, come along now."

"I'm not going; I'm neutral. Anyhow, I'm the one who's got his face turned towards the foe. I'm not staying to surrender, so I'll leave you to commune with your Fatherland for a while."

"Now you listen to me, when I was in the police I picked up a few judo holds. I'd have you on the ground before you could say Jack Robinson."

"I don't doubt it, Herr Mayerbär, but will you still be able to keep a hold on your horse?"

Mayerbär swung his skull from me to the bloodstains on the back of his hand. Which is harder to bear, hunger or the love of justice? The cries of the children or the tears of the fatherland?

"I'm a-horse at the head of my troop," I assured him. "I shall strap my body to another steed and let me tell you that it'll be no lame mare like your old piece of carrion there. I'm not giving up hope. Spring's on the way; I m going to sea."

"And what about your family?" he persisted.

"Tell Emma from me that she's to take our flag and pick off the white part with the big black mark on it and use the red background on its own for the next twenty years. Get me?"

"We shall shoot your wife in your place."

"Emma always was in favour of family hostages," I was just saying, when we both harkened to the eastward. A long-drawn-out, soft booming came from over in that direction, like all the towers of the land striking up a dead-man's chorale, to an accompaniment of ghosts from the barrow graves: *Lott is dot, Lott is dot, Jule liecht im Sterben* . . . Russian guns.

"Spring's on the way, Herr Mayerbär."

"Oh, well, many's the bullet without a billet," he said.

"If one ever finds you, though, I'll know something . . ."

"What's that?" asked Mayerbär.

"I'll know there'll be leaves on the trees again, and the schools will be full of children instead of casualties. If one ever finds you, Herr Mayerbär, then I'll sit upon my rooftop and hoist the Blue Peter. Fair passage for clouds and an Indian summer."

"It's nice being alive, eh?" Mayerbär asked me and stared at me with his big, miserable eyes.

"Yes," I said, "life's wonderful."

"It's a pity people are so bad," he said and punched my face with his fat cold fist, so that tears came into my eyes.

I dashed down the frozen track, along the trail of blood. At a bend I turned round to look for him. Because of the tears I couldn't see anything, but I kept saying to myself: "The snow will have to be swept off the eaves. There's a thaw coming."

I quit the blood trail, crossed the road to Rossbach and went up a forest path as far as the top of the steep part, from where I could see the tower of Reuthen church. I felt my two broad blue sailor cap ribbons flapping on the back of my neck.

9

IF the snow kept off and there was no one on the road I could go on up by the footpath and would not have to heave my heavy and soaking shoes through the undergrowth. I stopped to listen ahead now and again but there was no machine-gun nest, and the snipers were at work somewhere else. This was an open flank; no wonder I felt safer. I fell into step, stuck my hands in my coat pockets and reflected: The crocodile's a greedy creature, but seldom eats enough—he'll even eat the mission father, though he's both thin and tough. And afterwards: *Stumpfsinn*, three-quarter time, *du mein Vergnügen*, but I was already asleep, and the Vienna Boys' Choir took it up for me, or it may have been the Regensburg Choristers, or the men of Hitler's bodyguard, whistling it for the Sunday radio request concert. My friend Maiko had once had a dream on the march, which was that as soon as the Nazis had gone out of business all the biggest crooks were getting back in the saddle again, but dressed in civvies and minus all their old decorations. Which only goes to show what rubbish you can dream up on the march. A man in his senses can part with everything he has barring his decorations.

I came to with a sudden start, by my head colliding with stone. How on earth could I have forgotten! A wall of rocky ringlets rose before me, even, regular ringlets, but each one of them an average of two yards across! Luckily I found the ladder, so I did not have to make a detour.

Up on the plateau, by the glimmer of dawn, I could clearly make out the big pyramid that was the nose and the pits of the eyes, though the breasts were still hidden by the mist. Not to mention the knees and feet. I waited for a while on Freya's granite brow, slippery with thin snow. I was in the mood for putting my feet on our Teutonic Venus. Occasionally it does one good to be able to trample around on a person without any immediate consequences. I stood my right foot on her left eyebrow and took my bearings. From what I knew, Professor Wollgast had now set up his studio in Freya's left nostril, while his artistic assistants were quartered in the right one. Freya was actually supposed to have been erected for the Führer's birthday on April 20th, but even in Tesch it was not known whether this deadline would really be met. I decided to pay a call on Professor Wollgast, so I stroked my skinned knees, cooled the bump on my head with some snow, and proceeded between the eyebrows towards the nose, taking care not to climb the great beak in this weather, making my way instead down the narrow track which led round it to the nostrils. I deliberately avoided looking into the deep white hollows of the eyes. It is only too easy to take a fall that way.

At the edge of the left nostril I looked cautiously round the corner, but seeing only single tracks in the snow inferred with assurance that Professor Wollgast must be by himself. To tease him, I yelled: "*Batsko! Buri! Dabatsko! Stoï! Urrá!*" Whereupon a white flag emerged from the wooden cabin that filled the nostril.

"Professor Wollgast!" I called.

"*Da, da, da-da-da-da-da!*" came from behind the door.

"So you're expecting your extra rations again as soon as the Russians arrive?" I asked him. He was standing behind the door, in a brown velvet jacket. He had let his hair grow and had combed it romantically over his ears.

"Come in," he said, "it's cold."

On his studio wall there were sketches for two big new projects: Stalin and Roosevelt.

"What do you want me to do!" he said, "I can't just throw up my life's work. I've been working on Freya for ten years. Six months ago I completed the second breast. All I now need is to make a few repairs to a couple of toes. I'm ready—and now we have to lose the war!"

"And what are those," I asked, pointing to the sketches, "new life's works?"

Professor Wollgast got into a fur coat and shook his head. "First come, first painted. If I took off Freya's breasts and hung something between her legs, she'd pass for a man. The only thing that bothers me is the Stalin moustache, and also I'm not sure whether Roosevelt would be a likeness without glasses. But where on earth am I to get the wire I'd need at a time like this? Have a cigarette?"

We put our heads together.

"Look, Bonifaz," explained Professor Wollgast, "art has an element of unpredictability in it, particularly in something that takes as much time as sculpture. For God's sake, who could possibly have imagined ten years ago that the day was coming when Freya, our splendid, ageless Germanic female, would be out of date? We entreat thee—*Thu biguolen Friia*—but it's no good—spells, prayers, nothing works any more—Roosevelt *ante portas*!"

"And Stalin *cum katyushas*."

"Where are you going, Bonifaz?" he asked me, but he did not seem to be very interested in my reply, for he walked over to the charcoal sketch of the American president and touched in a bit more twinkle.

"To the sea," I said. "Please don't let me disturb you, Professor. I'll be on my way."

"To the sea?" he asked. "What do you want to do there?"

I stubbed the cigarette out in the ashtray and left by the nostril. I would have fallen asleep at the table otherwise; he wasn't any sort of company for me. A suspension bridge crossed the line of the mouth because the workers had been complaining about the long trek round it, and I let myself down from the chin to the bosom by the little cable service. A basket carried me across to Freya's enormous left mammary, Professor Wollgast's demonstration to the world of how much a proper German woman could achieve by putting patriotism first. It was quite some object that he exposed to view—not pornography, of course, but one's head spun at the mere thought. An investigation among the artistic assistants had revealed that ninety-five per cent of the married ones now wanted to leave their wives, while the unmarried ones complained without exception of losing their responses. I clambered on to the nipple and had a look round. Well, no wonder! Professor Wollgast would need a good ten years to make any sort of man out of Freya and then there was always the uncertainty—was everything going to stay as it was at the moment? Supposing Roosevelt was on the downgrade too? I strolled over Freya's belly, skirted round her snow-filled navel, continued my way down her thigh to th knee and then lowered myself to the road again.

10

I REACHED the terminus of the tramway from Tesch. The girl driver and the conductress were sitting on a bench beside the lines.

"Good morning," I greeted them. "How's the war getting on here?"

"Oh, thanks," said the conductress, "we aren't running any more. Ever since they painted us over with camouflage people think they're sitting in a tank and offer half fares. They try bargaining for their tickets. Have you ever heard the like of that on a German tram?"

"Well you see, war spoils everyone," said the driver. "And where have you come from? An able-bodied fellow like you not at the front?"

I brushed a bit of snow off my shoulders. "The front's coming along behind me. As a matter of fact I *am* the front."

The conductress and the girl driver stood up and began to button their dark grey uniforms with the green facings.

"How far away are they?"

"Here any moment."

"Were there any blacks?"

"Sure," I said, "President Roosevelt has occupied Tesch with nothing but Negroes, and one battalion of extra-blacks is marching on Rossbach this morning. They've got their eyes on the girls."

The conductress and the girl driver gave each other a quick look, grasped each other's hand and took to their heels in a flurry of snow. "Hey!" I called after them. "Your tram! You can't just run off and abandon your tram!"

But they ran and ran. They had totally forgotten their tram. It might be worse, I thought, and climbed into the front car. I took my station in the driver's compartment and tugged at the lever. The tram tugged back in reply and then got under way. I turned the lever round to zero and the tram halted.

I got out and walked once round both cars. Then once again. "Anyone inside?" I shouted. No answer. "All aboard! Fares please!"

There was no sign of life except for sandwich papers in the corners and on the narrow wooden benches. "Hold tight!" I turned the lever through one, two and three, and away we went. A hundred yards down the line I overtook the girl driver and the conductress. Their felt boots struck out in step from beneath their long uniform overcoats, the wind blew their crimped hair against their peaked caps, the conductress clung to the coin machine on her chest with one free hand, and the driver held her mittened right hand over her mouth.

I put my foot on the bell push, swung the lever back to one and shouted: "Keep running girls! The black man's after me! He wants to count your pennies! He's going to make mincemeat of everything! Run, run, run, girls!"

For a moment they glanced sideways with screwed-up eyes. They had completely forgotten about their tram, and could not make head or tail of the man in a sailor's cap standing on the front platform treading on the bell button with his left foot. All they heard was "black man" and "run", and that was enough for them.

The tram was gathering speed, for we were now on the down grade to Rossbach. I looked for the brake; I'd have liked to give the girls a lift. But I could not find it. I threw the lever over to zero—the tram headed down the valley with ever increasing speed. My distance from the two females also increased. I leant out of the front entrance.

"Where's the brake?" I shrieked. The girls kept running, looking straight ahead, and gave no answer.

"The brake!" I yelled, putting my arm out and pulling it in again, jerking my shoulders, raising my eyebrows and working my mouth. "The brake," I whispered, for it was now too late.

11

IF I had not been so scared, and had worried less about the brake and more about the view, I should have noticed, on the opposite side of the valley and also approaching Rossbach, Major Yevgeniy Yurievich Sapunov with his spearhead of tanks and horse-drawn column. On his side, Yevgeniy Yurievich had his glass trained precisely on the line down which my tram and I were rolling. I had taken the lever off the knob and had gone aft to the other driver's compartment. I fitted the lever there and turned it to one. There was a shower of sparks from the overhead cable and the shock of the second car crashing into the leader threw me through the door into the interior. I came to my senses again holding the lever in one hand while the tram still plunged on its course to Rossbach.

Yevgeniy Yurievich saw the flash, closed his hatch and said to his driver *via* the throat mike, "Hold tight, Vanya!"

12

I PICKED up my cap, straightened the ribbons and went forward. I laid the lever on the deck and slid the glass window open. I was getting hot.

"Blessed Cap'n Bommalaria," I prayed. "What the hell did I sign

on with this bloody Never-Come-Back-Line for? I'll go on fog watch
for the rest of my life, I'll never touch a drop again, just anything you
send me, all I'll do is scrub the side, if that's what you want, and
I'll shake hands with every ordinary seaman who wants to. I'll never
shoot another gull, and if you insist I'll even leave the chicks alone. But
don't let me die in this tram!"

13

YEVGENIY YURIEVICH opened his hatch again and observed the
descent of the grey-green-brown-daubed carriages. "Madman," he
said and gave orders: "We'll hold the road. It doesn't look as if we're
in for much of a reception. Keep your eyes on that vehicle. It's heading
for the town. Over."

14

I FELT seasick, for our velocity on the curves nearly threw me out of the
entrance. I never can stand a swell. I have to try singing:

> *As we heave around the pawl, boys,*
> *We will sing our well-known song:*
> *Up aloft amid the rigging,*
> *Up amid the howling gale,*
> *We will furl our big main-topsail . . .*

But I couldn't manage as far as *Rolling Home*. No Old England, no
bright smiles for me. Just the green jimjams as the tram took the curves.

I had a last look behind. The two girls were still hopping over the snowdrifts down the cold avenue of trees. Oh, to be able to foot it again—to be ashore! Every man has got his own little hurricane coming, as we used to say, dipping a finger in the rum, but even that is bound to blow itself out in the end.

I went and sat down on one of the double seats behind the sliding door and just as we came past the first houses in Rossbach I was sick on the deck. I wish it didn't always give me tears in the eyes. I was shivering with cold and fright, for all my manly years. The market square, sloping upwards in the centre of the town, brought my tram to a halt and so ended my sweet chariot's swing.

15

I LAID the lever on the driver's seat, and started to get out. But a couple of boys with bazookas ran up to me. Holy Bommalaria, I thought, you've got it in for me today.

"Comrade," said the pack leader, "we thank you for your devotion to duty. We thought the trams had stopped running. Here's a real soldier," he called out to his boys, "have a look, he's a sailor!"

"Oh, please," I said, "don't mention it. I see that you're armed. Don't let me get in your way."

The Werewolves goggled at my blue and white cap with its dejected ribbons, at my winter coat worn through at the elbows, at my wide-bottomed dark trousers and my vomit-spattered shoes.

"Which command are you from?" the pack leader asked.

"I belong to a neutral command," I replied.

"On special assignment?"

"Yes," I said, "I've got to get a proper blowout here, and then make a getaway."

"Tiedke!" bellowed the pack leader. "Mess tin!—I'm afraid we

34

haven't got anything to drink, but the two of us could have a look in the Ratskeller when it's getting dark."

"That could be arranged," I said and helped myself to a slice of bread and jam from Werewolf Tiedke's mess tin.

"After we've fired off our bazookas," announced the pack leader, "we can still sling paving-stones at them. What do you think of Leonidas?"

"Do you mean the shoe polish?"

"No—"

"Oh, because if you did, I'd have had to warn you against it. Don't worry, I see you're thinking of that fellow who wouldn't let the mob from Persia through. Well, that was a long time ago. Don't you want to eat some?"

The pack leader declined, and the fourteen-year-old Werewolves stared with embarrassment into their mess tins. The pack leader came closer to me.

"One of the Werewolves' mothers says the Führer is dead."

"You mustn't believe anything like that," I said. "However did she get the idea! Well, and if? There was a lovely poem once in the *Völkischer Beobachter* which said: the Führer cannot die, because he lives in everything. Strictly speaking, of course, that would mean that he's not only living in the woods and in the clouds and in the guns, which we all know, but for example in my jam slice as well, with the result that I am eating him up at this moment."

The pack leader stared at me with bulging eyes.

"But as a matter of fact we can also derive consolation from the same verse, for if he lives in all and everything, he also lives in my teeth, perhaps even in the gold filling I had made by Dr. Reinig at Frankfurt-on-the-Oder, so that he's therefore in a way also eating himself. I don't mean Dr. Reinig; he's already dead, but the Führer of course. It's possible that he's in my stomach somewhere or in my appendix—no, he can't be there, I had it out in 1932. I consider the statement that the Führer is dead to be completely unmeaningful. The woman in question has probably never read the poem to which I refer, or she may take a different newspaper. She may be a reader of the *Alsatian and Sheepdog*

Gazette, but you'll find they have poems about the Führer too from time to time, because what he loves most of all is Alsatians. No doubt you are aware of that already?"

The pack leader shifted from one foot to the other.

"I think you should be getting on your way, comrade. It sounded like some firing just now."

"Guns that bark don't bite."

I pressed the empty mess tin into his hand. He flung it away and stood up. "We're going to move down the road to Petzau. Strong armoured formations were reported to be heading from there this morning. Get on board."

"In the tram? But I can't drive."

"Don't talk nonsense! You arrived by tram!"

"But I'm not a properly trained tram driver. It was only by accident. I don't even know where the brake is." He refused to believe me. "Attention everyone!" he yelled. "You too! Stand up!"

The Werewolves formed up, aimed their bazookas at me and placed their soft walking shoes all at the regulation angle. I was about to point out that no repatriated person shall be employed on active military service, but I was not at all sure that the pack leader would understand this, so I got in instead. That gave me another idea, I got out of the opposite entrance and walked round the tram until I was back with the pack leader.

"Pack Leader, sir," I said. "I have a tactical proposal to make."

"Okay," he said, and folded his arms across his chest in the pose of his favourite Luftwaffe marshal.

"You know I'm a sailor. Now, like you, I want to get the whole business over quickly, but I think you may not be aware of the relevant transport regulations. In peace as in war, any vessel with ammunition on board is obliged while in port to fly the red pennant, which means 'I am loading or unloading explosives'. The reason for this is for people ashore to get the message and say to themselves, 'What-ho! No smoking!' Now, in the wider sense, both ships and tramways come under the general heading of transport. Whatever rightly applies to seagoing craft applies equally to vehicles on shore. So the question for us is, where can we get hold of a red pennant, so that we can let the enemy know that we're travelling with bazookas aboard and aren't out on a pleasure trip?"

"You won't find any red flags here," said the pack leader.

"Well," I said, "there'll be a change coming. Let's face it: already we're stuck without one."

"To hell with the regulations," said the pack leader.

"Bravo," I said approvingly. "But wait until you get to my age. I grew up in this place."

"I'll take the responsibility," said the pack leader and drummed his fingertips on his sleeves.

"I'm not questioning that. But everything has its weak point, the same as with the girls. You, sir, are still at the happy age when you've got to hold yourself down in your trouser pocket when the subject is only even mentioned, but . . ."

"You can stuff all your drivel up your arse!"

"Supposing we put the bazookas in the trailer and only get them out when we really need them? Like that we won't need the red flag, as our explosives wouldn't be in the front car at all, but in the trailer, and we'd still be obeying the rules. What do we care about what goes on in the trailer? Yes, well, I suppose if we were taken to court, we'd want a pretty smart lawyer, but I feel sure we could successfully plead the emergency in mitigation."

"Okay, okay, okay," growled the pack leader. "I've had as much as I can stand. Bazookas aboard the trailer! And then full speed ahead!"

They stacked the bazookas on the forward platform of the trailer and climbed into the leading car.

Meanwhile I was examining the coupling between the two cars, unhooked the trailer and separated the cables.

"Forward!" bellowed the pack leader from the front. "Armour ahead!"

"Not so fast," I said, shoving myself onto the driver's seat beside the pack leader. "Stand here beside me," I told him. "This is where you get the best view."

I turned the lever to one, and the tram jerked forward. The trailer with the bazookas remained standing at the market square fare stage. The windows were blacked-out with cardboard, apart from small peep-holes, and all the Werewolves sat with eyes front, to where the street dropped down towards the edge of town.

16

YEVGENIY YURIEVICH SAPUNOV and his tanks had just reached the first green-painted railings in the suburbs where white sheets were dutifully hanging from the windows, and the snow-laden hedges concealed no sharpshooting patriots. Yevgeniy Yurievich, who held the tram in view for only so long as he was on the opposing level, drove ahead over the cobbles of the main road, leaving two tanks to cover the approaches to the town.

"The cable's shaking," said his driver. Yevgeniy Yurievich opened the hatch and looked up. Sure enough, it was shaking.

"Perhaps they've already begun stringing themselves up on it, if they've run out of lamp-posts," he said, but about two hundred yards farther up the road, just where it made its final bend toward the market square, my tram came squealing and shuddering round the corner, riding the curve on two wheels and then crashing back onto the rails with relief and thundering down at Yevegniy Yurievich's column.

"Halt!" bellowed the pack leader. But I shook my head.

"No good," I said.

"Why not?" he shrieked and clutched hold of me.

"I'd like to," I shouted back, "but I don't know where the brake is."

I jammed the lever on zero. "Come on, son," I said to the white-faced pack leader, took him by the arm and dragged him back into the passengers' compartment. Tram and tank rammed each other head on, telescoped and came to a standstill. We were all piled forwards on the wooden seats and lay trembling against the sliding door.

Yevgeniy Yurievich shouted: "Get out!"

The pack leader whispered to me: "Now for the bazookas!"

I tapped my head with a finger.

"Get out or I shoot!" shouted Yevgeniy Yurievich. I stood up, still rather dazed, pushed the Werewolves out of my way and got down from the tram, not forgetting to straighten my cap as I went.

"Hands up!" ordered Yevgeniy Yurievich. I raised them to the level of my chin. "Me neutral," I said, "me nix soldier."

Yevgeniy Yurievich's face appeared, dark eyes and a black moustache. "You sellor?" he asked.

"I am neutral," I said.

Yevgeniy Yurievich shook his head. "Neutral—is nonsense!"

The pack leader was leaning out from the rear steps.

"Where's the trailer?"

"At the market square," I answered without turning round.

"Kho else in there?" asked Yevgeniy Yurievich. "Everybody outside or we shoot."

The Werewolves clambered out with wobbling knees and fell in behind me. Their mess tins clashed together. Yevgeniy Yurievich swung his turret round so that he covered the group with the gun barrel.

"Put up khands," he said.

The Werewolves obeyed. Yevgeniy Yurievich leaped out of the hatch and waved the other tank crews forward. He came up to me and pushed my hands down to my sides. "Good," he said, "enough! Where is town commandant?"

"I'm not sure, but I suspect we don't have one any more."

"Where you going wit tram?" asked Yevgeniy Yurievich.

"We thought we'd come and meet you, because you wouldn't know your way about, and what's the point of your having to go the long way round? It's easy to get on the wrong road here. You only need to miss the turning to Tesch at the crossroads and take the one to Essig and you're in a pickle right away."

"Why you not stop?"

"I'm afraid I've not been trained as a tram driver, major. I apologise for the dent on your tank. I couldn't find the brake."

39

He looked me in the eyes, then turned to face the tanks which had closed up behind and had opened their hatches. He called something to them in Russian. A grinning face appeared from every hatch.

"What name your ship?" he asked.

"The *Robinson*," I answered, bringing my heels together, "two thousand six hundred and ninety-eight gross registered tons, but at present she's manned by the forces of His Britannic Majesty. I was repatriated in exchange for an Englishman."

"You Communist?"

"I'm from a little town twenty kilometres away from here and there used to be two Communists there before the Nazis. They went over to Geilsheim for their meetings. That's a village near Tesch. The tavern keeper there, named Moser, was a Communist too, and they'd hold their meetings with him, for as they said, you need at least three gathered together to make a meeting, which seems perfectly reasonable to me, because otherwise what do you talk about if you get just two fellows sitting together? Sex and booze, that's all. You wouldn't have got me over to Geilsheim with wild horses—the tavern keeper was an out-and-out mixer, which means the proportion of water he mingled with his beer was beyond enduring. Anyhow, in 1933 this Moser had second thoughts about the whole Communism business. Not that he gave up mixing, of course! He went into the Storm Troopers and personally helped to hang his two friends in Geilsheim Wood. You know the way it is with country folk."

"And on ship?" asked Yevgeniy Yurievich.

"My word of honour, major! I wasn't a Communist on ship either. Really I wasn't! I swear I wasn't."

"All right, good," he said, "today you mayor of Rossbach."

"Commie!" hissed the pack leader, who was standing behind me. I turned round and slapped his face.

"I regret," I said to Yevgeniy Yurievich, "that my first official function has to be a sock in the face, but it was unavoidable."

"Good, good," he said. I wiped my hand with my overcoat, and we shook on it.

When we got to the market square, where the tram with the bazookas was standing, the boys were sent home. I accompanied Major Sapunov into the town hall. A man with glasses balanced on his nose was standing in the main door, waving a white flag. I tapped his shoulder and said, "Good morning. My name is Bonifaz. I'm the new big white chief around here."

"Pleased to meet you, Mr. Mayor. I am Bogumil."

He propped the flag against the town hall portal. "I am keeper of the town archives. I have in my charge several military relics of the Thirty Years War, including two muskets, the actual trunk-hose belonging to Count Rossbach, and a morning-star."

"The muskets and the morning-star are confiscated," I ordered, "the trunk-hose you may keep for yourself."

"Thank you, Mr. Mayor," said Bogumil.

"We go inside," said Yevgeniy Yurievich. "Tonight we stay khere. Americans already in Tesch. For us war finished."

We entered the mayor's panelled parlour, and between us unhooked the portrait from the wall and stood it in the corner, moustache to the wall. The three of us sat down at the conference table and Yevgeniy Yurievich said, "we need telephone and straw. You need water, electric and food. You responsible, mayor."

"Give me one of your tanks and I'll go over to the waterworks," I said.

"Hold it!" cried Bogumil, "my son-in-law has a job at the water-works. I'll have a word with him. Don't let's all shoot at once!"

He dashed out of the room.

"I now go into town," said Yevgeniy Yurievich. "My soldiers stay in town khall. But first we make check-up. You find out people khelping you, and tonight we celebrate."

I heard his steps going down the corridor and the next thing I knew was that I was sitting there all on my own, as mayor. A quarter of an hour later Bogumil came back; the taps were running again.

Mayor was one thing I had never been before. "What we are in need of," I said to Bogumil, "is a policy. There's not much good in just governing away into the blue."

"Quite so," said Bogumil.

41

"To start with, I shall appoint you my deputy."

"I appreciate your trust," said Bogumil.

"Do you have a pencil on you?"

"Certainly, Mr. Mayor," said Bogumil, spreading a large sheet of paper on the table and poising himself to write.

"What shall we call this?" I asked him.

"Shall we say 'Mayoral Pronouncement'?" he suggested.

"That sounds a bit petty to me."

"What about 'Decree', then? Or 'Ordinance'? Or 'Order'?"

"No, no! No orders, please! I want to sweep the people along. You understand? Now write down: 'Manifesto'. That's what I want, 'Manifesto'."

'What comes next?"

I pulled myself upright in my chair.

"Article One: Above and Below are hereby abolished."

"But Mr. Mayor!" groaned Bogumil.

"You are already infringing the first paragraph of my manifesto," I cautioned him. "The title of mayor is abolished under Article One. The form of address to be adopted in future will cease to be 'Herr Direktor Meier', but will instead be 'Humanbeing Meier'. Put this down! This directive applies to all persons of male, female or neuter sex."

Somebody knocked on the door. Bogumil looked at me inquiringly, I nodded, and he went out. After a moment, during which I was drafting Article Two in my mind, he returned and announced: "Humanbeing Walluseck asks if he may speak to you."

"Who?"

"Humanbeing Walluseck, the postmaster, asks if he may speak to you."

"Certainly!" I said, feeling enormously satisfied that my titles-reform was already in operation. Bogumil let in a gaunt man whose eyes seemed to pop out of his head when he saw me sitting behind the conference table in my sailor's cap.

"Humanbeing Walluseck," I said as kindly as possible, "what can I do for you?"

42

"I am, that is to say, I was or I am about, as I hope, to be, once more, little as I want to, the—as I was saying—postmaster. You know: the post office, the place the letters go, where your letters fly away from to places all over the world, just because of us post office folk in there, sticking and stamping away."

"That's funny, I always thought the post office was where cakes were made," I said.

"No, Humanbeing Bonifaz," he insisted, "that's a mistake. The post office is a big house where all the little birdies come with little letters in their beakies, bearing sweethearts' greetings far and wide."

"When will the telephones be in order again?" I asked him. He smiled.

"Naughty, naughty," he said, "now that's asking! Tomorrow, if necessary, or the day after tomorrow."

"Tomorrow," I said. "You may go now."

Bogumil accompanied him to the door, and returned, shaking his head.

"I'm not at all sure that it'll catch on," he said.

"What won't?"

"The new style of address, Humanbeing Bonifaz. You mustn't be in too much of a hurry. I wonder if we oughtn't to start by letting them say 'Herr Meier', before we go right over to 'Humanbeing Meier'. The Herr Postmaster—I mean, the Herr Humanbeing Walluseck—was completely bewildered when I explained this business about the new Humanbeing before he came into the room. Didn't you notice it?"

I waved him away. "The main thing is that we shall be able to use the telephone."

Bogumil sat down at the table again and raised his pencil.

"Article Two," I dictated. "Money is abolished."

"How are you going to do that?"

"You'll see. Write down: all banknotes are to be heaped in a bonfire on the market square and burnt. All Humanbeings will attend, to the tune, *Jimmy Crack Corn and I don't care*—"

Another knock. I nodded. Bogumil went out.

"Humanbeing Leupold," he announced. This was a red-nosed man who followed him into the room.

"Humanbeing Leupold has been working up to the present moment as manager of the Commercial Bank."

"Aha," I said, "Humanbeing Leupold, please sit down. I'm just in the process of dictating our manifesto. I don't want to lose the thread. Please sit there for a moment!"

Leupold sat down on a leather chair quite near me, stared at me and then, without saying a word, began to polish his glasses.

"A public contest," I dictated to Bogumil, "in ducks and drakes will be instituted, making use of the coinage as counters. It shall take place over still water, and the winner will be whoever succeeds in scoring ninety-nine ricochets with a penny piece. In the event of no one scoring this number, no winner will be declared—or would you say," I asked turning to Leupold, "that ninety-nine is setting it too high?"

He pursed his lips and tilted his head.

"That depends on whether you are asking me as a Humanbeing or as a banker," he said eventually. "Speaking as a Humanbeing, I would say: too high. As a banker, however, I would say: what on earth would induce anyone to throw their small change into the lake?"

"Money is being abolished," said Bogumil.

"In that event I would appear to be superfluous here," said Leupold and rose to his feet, but sat down again immediately, as there was another knock on the door. Bogumil admitted the pastor, the hospital chairman and two butchers, one of whom dealt in horsemeat.

These people took their places at the conference table, and Bogumil read aloud to them those parts of the manifesto which were already in existence. The pastor had the impertinence to enquire whether he might continue to send up prayers with the address "Lord God" or would he now have to say "Humanbeing God"?

"I may have to close the church. We haven't enough kindergartens."

"The church is far too cold for that," objected the doctor.

"Go on writing," I said to Bogumil. "Article Three: forced labour is abolished."

44

"What?" they all said at once, and Leupold added "The basis of civilised life!"

The pastor: "Remember the parable of the forced labourers in the vineyard."

The doctor: "Forced labour is healthy."

The horse-knacker: "Does everything have to be topsy-turvy at once?"

Only Bogumil looked at me and nodded.

"Each shall work as much as he can," I continued, "and if he can't, he can't, but everyone who's working can take two helpings."

"As a matter of fact I brought along a liver sausage for you," said the butcher, unwrapping a piece of paper from round a sausage ring with a triumphant expression on his face. I handed the sausage to Bogumil.

"Article Four: the national anthem is abolished," I said.

"One saw it coming," observed the bank manager.

"Article Five: marriage is abolished."

"Sodom and Gomorrah," sighed the pastor, "just as I expected."

"Existing wedlock," I added, "is dissolved, alternatively will constitute sexual cohabitation at a joint address."

The horse-knacker whinnied as the hospital chairman dug him in the ribs.

"Children," I went on, "will be cared for in the kindergarten, where every Humanbeing shall go and play at least one hour per week, and which he may not enter without foodstuffs sufficient for three children's dinners—that takes care of the most important points. Have any of you any questions?"

"Actually, I had come here to see you on the question of a currency reform," said the bank manager, "but it may be that you're right and that the best thing is literally to throw one's property away. The only thing I ask myself then is, what am I going to do with myself? The only thing I've ever learned is counting money. I do know a few games of chance, but I can see you'll be banning roulette next. Perhaps I ought to let my wife keep me?"

"You haven't got a wife any more," needled the pastor. "The mayor has this moment separated you from her!"

"For all I care, the gentlemen can remove their own appendixes from now on," said the doctor.

"What makes you say that?" asked the horse-knacker.

"Each shall work as much as he can. I've done enough."

"Are we to address the Russian commandant as 'Humanbeing', too?" asked the butcher.

"I could possibly get a brothel going in your church," said Leupold, "I'll have to make a living somehow."

"I've had much the same idea already," said the pastor, "but as you've already been told, the House of God is too cold even for a kindergarten."

"How about taking *A Night in Monte Carlo* as our new national anthem?" asked the butcher.

"I'd prefer *Once Beside the Rhine*," suggested the pastor.

"*Cornflower Blue*," intoned the bank manager.

"One moment!" I said. "The manifesto still needs to be approved by Major Sapunov. I assume that the signature will take place this evening on the occasion of the victory celebrations."

"Oh, I see," said the butcher, reflecting for a moment and then reaching out for the liver sausage which I had pushed over to Bogumil. "So you aren't the proper mayor yet after all?"

"And we all thought that this manifesto was being issued in the name of the commandant," said the minister regretfully.

"I think we can go again," said the hospital chairman.

"Do I throw my money away or don't I?" asked the banker.

"I would advise," said the horse-knacker, "that you hold on to it until tomorrow at least."

They all stood up and prepared to go, but Bogumil ran round them like a sheepdog and kept them away from the door. "Your Reverence!" he exclaimed.

"Humanbeing Siebert, please!" he protested, with a glance at me.

"I think you could prepare a list jointly with Humanbeing Heinemann, the hospital chairman, showing essential needs for the next few days. Humanbeing Leupold, would you be good enough to prepare an extract of all accounts and report on current transactions, together with a statement of your liquid assets? Humanbeing Salinger, you as the butcher will work out a plan in conjunction with the ration office to see to it that we are kept supplied with meat. Details of bread rationing will be announced tomorrow. Humanbeing Grumach, you will open a soup kitchen in your horsemeat shop. If we run out of pigs . . ."

"There'll be refugee horse," finished the knacker.

"That's all for today," said Bogumil. "We expect you for the next meeting at nine tomorrow morning."

"That's when I'm doing my rounds of the wards," said Dr. Heinemann.

"Then you can come an hour later," said Bogumil.

"What about the manifesto?" Leupold asked again.

"Tomorrow, Humanbeing Leupold, tomorrow," said Bogumil.

They all shook Bogumil and me by the hand and left. Bogumil had made a big impression on them, although I thought that my manifesto might have done more good to some of them. Anyhow, there was going to be time to decide about that in the evening when Yevgeniy Yurievich held his victory celebration. Bogumil wrote down all the instructions he had given them in his minute book and asked me to sign the page. And so to this day my signature is preserved in the Rossbach municipal archives beneath a mayoral proclamation of the year 1945.

17

I THEN made a formal announcement: Bogumil and Bonifaz will carry out an inspection of the commune.

The houses were dressed all over with white sheets. Filled by the wind from the hills, fine linen and cotton twill bulged in classless equality, flapped and collapsed, as if the whole town were shaking out the dust. We looked into the tram trailer: it had been evacuated and disarmed, and I told Bogumil about how I had made the journey to Rossbach.

The Werewolves peeped through their windows and sulked at being kept indoors. Their heads disappeared when they saw us go by. The poster in front of the cinema showed a girl on skates—*The White Dream*. We went inside. A refugee column was quartered there.

They had unscrewed and taken out the seats and piled them against the walls in front of the exits. The babies had been put in the centre on hay and straw and on padded seats from the boxes, some of them swaddled in strips of the dark red velvet. We gave these people the horse-butcher's address and told them that they could collect warm food from him. They nodded but didn't move from where they sat on the tip-up seats in their heavy overcoats, scarves tied round their heads and shoulders, propped against one another, exhausted by their long trek.

"Humanbeing Bonifaz," said Bogumil when we were in the street again, "I'm afraid we're knocking our heads against a brick wall."

"Not at all, not at all," I said. "The day's coming when we're going to get matches again, and cigarettes, and real coffee, and Schnapps. And fat men selling frankfurters at street corners. And you'll go into a shop and ask for a hat, and instead of being handed a steel helmet you'll get a soft round felt or a stiff-brimmed homburg or just an ordinary cap."

"I can scarcely believe it," said Bogumil. "I'm afraid the grass will be growing on the roofs, and sheep and goats running wild in the streets, and the rabbits will soon be the pest they are in Australia if it goes on like this."

"What makes you think so?" I asked him.

Bogumil looked at me sideways but did not seem to want to answer, shoving his hands deeper into his coat pockets and stamping with his thin shoes on the frozen puddles in our path.

"Come on, out with it!" I begged him. "We can trust each other."

"It's like this, Humanbeing Bonifaz," he began at last, "I'm looking forward to matches and hats again as much as you; I want the barracks turned into schools, and I want to be awakened in the morning by a plain alarm clock and not by bugles and drums. But the thing with your

48

manifesto—although it's got its good points, I'm not questioning that—is that if you tell people that Above and Below have been abolished and that it's left to them to decide when they'll work and for how long, the result will be—well, what do you think? They'll sit on their backsides next to the stove, creep into bed, and when they've got through all the provisions, they'll start eating each other up. Human beings need some sort of order, and it's one of the elements of order, people being what they are, that there's an Above and, er—Below. How are you going to find out whether you can take the tram to Petzau if the driver hasn't made up his mind whether he feels like working today? Where will the planes take off for, who'll run up the shutters at the butchers, who'll build houses out of the ruins, and what plate will you eat out of, if there's nobody there to press the tinplate, slaughter the pigs and mix the cement?"

"You're just a goddam pragmatist, Humanbeing Bogumil," I said. "Haven't you any feeling for higher things?"

"You're a neutral, Humanbeing Bonifaz, that's the difference between us: you can afford the higher things, the rest of us can't."

We saw an old man with a fur cap on his head coming towards us. He was pulling a handcart with a long bundle on it that at first glance looked like a corpse with rugs wrapped around it. We did not want to bother him, but he stopped and asked us where he should go to hand in weapons.

"What sort of weapon?" I asked.

"I've got a torpedo here," he said, "I farm twelve acres in Wünschs-dorf. People are saying the war's over. About time too. I've never had much of a head for figures, just all right for the milk deliveries and the land tax, but by the time a war's being going on for thirty years, even the likes of us begin to take notice."

"What do you mean, thirty years?" I asked.

"From '14 to '45," he answered in an aggrieved tone, and then counted off on his fingers and said: "That's it. Thirty one. You were right. So where do I go with the torpedo?"

He pointed to his handcart. "As good as new, give it its due, though I've had it these six-and-twenty years."

"Where did you get it from?" I wanted to know. But he shook his head and gave me a sly look.

"Military secret," he whispered.

"Put it down in front of the town hall," I said, and he wavered on his way.

A patrol of three Russian soldiers approached, with tommy-guns slung round them. They were talking and smoking and did not seem to notice us. But when we came level with them they would not let us go any farther.

"Going where?" asked the elder one.

"To the town hall," replied Bogumil.

"Why?"

"This is—" said Bogumil and pointed to me, but I stopped him.

"I am Humanbeing Bonifaz," I said to the soldiers.

"Ah," he said, "Khumanbeing. I see. Show me documents!"

"Humanbeing Bonifaz has abolished documents," explained Bogumil. "No more Above and no more Below. Document nix, Humanbeing everything, understand?"

"I understand," said the soldier, "come wit me!"

"Actually, we were on our way to the town hall," said Bogumil and turned round, but one of the soldiers hit him in the back, and he started forward again.

"Nix Town Khall, nix document, everybody Khumanbeing," said the older one.

"Why don't you say you're the mayor here?" whispered Bogumil.

"Nix talking," said the soldiers.

We were taken at a quite dashing pace past the cinema with its *White Dream*, but instead of turning in the direction of the town hall we went the opposite way. At one point we met the postmaster, who was also stopped but, as he could produce papers, was allowed to go. Curiously enough, he gave no sign of recognising either Bogumil or myself.

Night had now fallen, but it was still light enough to see that we were on our way to the jail. One of the soldiers banged on the gate with the butt of his tommy-gun, a door was opened and we were taken into a cell where fifteen or twenty other men were already waiting.

"Everybody Khumanbeing," said the soldier with a grin and locked the door behind us.

"Herr Bogumil," whispered a fat man in a loden-cloth jacket. "It can't be you! What brings you here?"

Bogumil took no notice, and passed the fat man on his left.

"Who's that?" I asked Bogumil in a discreet whisper.

"Your predecessor," he said loud enough for all to hear.

The only light came from a little forty-watt bulb hanging in a wire basket from the ceiling, but I noticed that suddenly everyone was looking at me.

"It can't be true!" said a man who was busy hammering his belt buckle on the floor with an iron-tipped shoe-heel, in an attempt to obliterate the embossed swastika.

"It was a misunderstanding, Herr Ortsgruppenführer," stated Bogumil.

"I wish you the best of luck in your mayoralty," said the former mayor to me. "But I see you have already run into some difficulties."

Everybody laughed and stared at me to the point where I almost began to feel embarrassed.

"What have you been brought here for?" asked one of them, who was pointed out to me by Bogumil as the former prison governor. I did not answer.

"Too grand to talk to us, is that your trouble?" asked the Ortsgruppenführer. "They'll put the whole lot of us up against the wall tonight, anyway. We might as well relax while we can. Do you happen to have a cigarette on you?"

"No," I said, while I wondered whether they would execute me too. Being shot is bad enough, but not knowing the reason makes it worse.

Like most of the rest of them we sat down on a couple of crate-lids with our backs to the wall, stretched out our legs and drooped our heads.

The prisoners were rehearsing for their interrogations. They were polishing up their answers.

"When they ask you," said the Ortsgruppenführer, turning to the ex-prison governor, "why eleven politicals had their heads chopped off in your establishment, what will you say?"

The ex-prison governor rubbed his nose with two fingers and replied: "Those were my orders—but then perhaps they will ask you why you were in the front row to witness the executions and why you brought along your whole family, although it was strictly forbidden?"

"Gentlemen, please," pacified the ex-mayor, "surely they're not going to pursue matters like these with us. After all, *we* didn't chop anybody's head off."

"Oh no, that was Herr Dannecker from Wilhelmsberg who came over to do it for us," said a voice from the corner

"Well, there you are," said the ex-mayor.

"You didn't say anything in your manifesto about closing the prisons and penitentiaries," said Bogumil suddenly. "Did you forget them, or would it be automatic?"

I did not feel this was the right place for us to discuss the subject freely.

"What's your view?" asked the ex-prison governor amiably. "Will the Russians let us go?"

"I don't know," answered Bogumil on my behalf. "Humanbeing Bonifaz proposes, according to his manifesto, to abolish Above and Below."

"A manifesto?" exclaimed everybody at once. "Have we got a policy already?"

"It strikes me as being a far from negligible idea," observed the Ortsgruppenführer. "Human nature is disposed towards a certain degree of equality. What's the value of these distinctions? Above and Below certainly ought to be abolished."

"Very true," said the ex-mayor, "our needs are all the same: eat, drink and sleep."

"Hear, hear," said someone from the corner, "no one has the right to look down on anyone else. We're all born equal, in our cots we're naked and the same—let's remain that way!"

"We'd need to wear something, though, doctor," said the Ortsgruppenführer, "we oughtn't to offend against common decency."

52

"Fiddlededee," said the voice in the corner, "where health and beauty are combined, there's no need to."

"I should like to know," said the ex-prison governor to Bogumil in an imploring tone, "whether our new mayor happens to have been incarcerated on account of this manifesto?"

"No," replied Bogumil and gave me an amused look through his glasses. "The mayor, or should I say, Humanbeing Bonifaz, finds himself in this company on account of having renounced the title of mayor, and for wanting to be a human being plain and simple!"

He declaimed the last few words in a rising tone, describing a horizontal arc with his right hand.

"There's real nobility of soul," agreed the Ortsgruppenführer, beating away at his belt buckle.

"A master spirit," said the ex-prison governor.

"It's people like that we need in times like these," said the ex-mayor. "A human Humanbeing."

"I'd go through thick and thin with you," called the doctor in the corner. I closed my coat collar over my face and shoved my blue cap down over it. Another prisoner was brought in, so I stood up and spoke to the soldiers: "Please go and tell Major Yevgeniy Yurievich Sapunov that I'm the mayor Bonifaz. This is my deputy, Bogumil."

He smiled.

Two hours later Major Sapunov looked into the cell.

"Sellor!" he shouted.

Bogumil and I stood up and went to the door.

"Remember us, Humanbeing Bonifaz," said my predecessor.

"I certainly shan't forget any of you," I promised and bowed to them all. "I shall remember the executions in particular, and the fact that it was customary to take the children along. I want to thank you for letting me know that."

We went out, climbed onto the truck in which Yevgeniy Yurievich had arrived, and drove to the Town Hall. Bogumil sat beside me on the wooden bench and didn't speak. He just chewed the cardboard tube of the cigarette that Yevgeniy Yurievich had given him. The wheels

53

shuddered in and out of potholes. We were shaken together and our heads collided.

"Did you think they were going to shoot you, too, tonight?" I asked him. He shook his head.

"Nobody's going to be shot," he said, "they could never shoot everybody who ought to be shot."

"You know what, Bogumil," I said, "I have decided on something."

"Really?" asked Bogumil. "And what is that?"

"I'm taking to the road again. You carry on being the mayor here. You know more about it."

"And what about you?"

The truck stopped. I pulled the pin out of the ring, dropped the tailboard and jumped out first. Then I reached my hand out to Bogumil and caught him.

"Yevgeniy Yurievich," I said when I got wind of his *makhorka*, "Bogumil is the mayor now."

"Why?" he asked.

"I'm a sailor, and what's more, I'm neutral."

"Crezzy is what you are," said Yevgeniy Yurievich. "You say to peasant, khe put torpedo outside town khall. If exploding, everybody dead. Understand?"

18

THE soldiers had pushed the tables together in the Ratskeller and judging by the racket it wasn't lemonade they had in their field flasks.

Yevgeniy Yurievich walked around the long table with us. As we passed the soldiers they looked at us with a moment's surprise and suspicion, but the major was right behind us and they turned back again. A shaved-head sergeant was dancing on one table. He whipped from heel to toe and back again and whirled round on one leg, spinning the other one over his comrades' heads.

Four basses and a leader were standing at the bar, arms around each other, singing so loud that sweat poured down over the tightly-buttoned collars of their uniforms. There were many in pairs at the long table, one with an arm over his mate's shoulder, looking into each other's eyes, drinking, and mostly not speaking. Somewhere there was always one weeping, with the other to take his head to his breast as if lulling the man to sleep and to forgetting it all at last. Next to Yevgeniy Yurievich's chair there was a blond young officer nursing a guitar and plinking it with his thumb.

"Zis Captain Petrov," said Yevgeniy Yurievich by way of introduction. "I do not know if we can disturb him. Khe tenor. Before war khe singing in Moscow, in operetta."

I got out of my coat and draped it over the chair that the major offered me.

Petrov stopped playing. He looked at me and asked: "You sellor?"

"Yes," said Yevgeniy Yurievich on my behalf and added something in Russian.

Petrov laughed and handed me the guitar. "You play—sellor songs."

He handed me his field flask and I took a pull at the stuff. It tasted like rat bane in boiled snow. Blessed Captain Bommalaria, that'll keep the old globe spinning, and I saw the Aurora Borealis come dancing down from the Lofotens right into my eyes, and a Biscay gale blew straight up my nose, and my old tom-tom of a heart throbbed the good news from Mecca to Medina.

"Cape Horn!" I shouted and strummed my fingers across the strings, and started off softly with the old sieve from Hamburg across the sea, then I warmed up with the loud exalting gale and the thousand miles behind us and the thousand miles before, until I was properly carried away, up aloft amid the rigging, up amid the howling gale.

They hummed the chorus with me, even the others right down the table behind us, rolling home for ten and three.

When I was through, I noticed something. I was standing on the

55

chair, and the earth was revolving in a decidedly un-Copernican manner, the equator was off on its own, the Greenwich meridian was looped round the North Pole and the Great Bear had hopped into his motor and driven over to see the Little Bear.

"Bogumil," I whispered, "catch me."

"You eat somesing," said Petrov, "zis your ration."

He pointed to what was on the table in front of me.

"Gift from our company," he said.

I put my hand out to catch the white mess that was swaying in front of my eyes. It was sprinkled with black spots and as I thought they were flies I flapped my hand in the air above it.

"Is not flying away," said Yevgeniy Yurievich, "is *korinka*."

Salt pork and currants. The pork was no longer fresh, but that was what the currants were for. First you taste the fat, slimy pork, then the dry, sweet currants, and after that a gulp of vodka. A repast to revive the dead. If I was Stalin instead of a sailor, I said to myself, I'd make all the Fritzes eat salt pork and currants and chase it down with a little vodka for the good of their souls.

But I think they must have given me more than was good for me, for I found myself standing on the chair again:

> *Boys, we've been the whole world over,*
> *Via Paree and Holy Rome,*
> *Our souls we've upped right over the gun'le—*
> *Keep a watch down Sydney way*
> *And you'll see 'em floating home!*

The soldiers had warmed up now. At first they sang as if their corns had just been stamped on and the agony of it was uncontainable, stretching their mouths to wide that you could see all their magnificent teeth, but that seemed to be their style, for once they had got the beat together the troika was well away: Petrov let his voice fly up, drawing us all with him, and round about us silver birches shimmered in a lilac haze, onion domes and horse waggons, white headkerchiefs along the river bank, great green markets with awnings and melons, high chimneys with long red flags attached, and the last thing I saw was a forest, and a sailor swimming through it. Deep breath now! We're shouting all together: Ay, ay, ay! and the post-sleigh is away with us all, too late to get out, if you can't fly you'll have to learn, the chair is wobbling, I'm spreading my wings and stretching my legs, my feet strike together in time: Baikal the beautiful, I drink to you! You've won the war and I haven't lost it! I am Bonifaz the neutral, and if the postmaster needs a head for the new stamps, he's welcome to my bottom. I say this to Petrov too. He's a tenor at the Opera Comique and he'll understand, and I sing into his ear:

> Come, child, cease to ponder, I do implore:
> kiss me at once and our love will be sure!

But this isn't Petrov's ear. It's Bogumil's ear, and in need of a wash. As is obvious even by candlelight. So Bogumil laid me down on a mattress in the mayor's parlour, with the portrait of Hitler still standing in the corner, and Bogumil said, "Goodnight—the Council meeting commences at nine a.m.!'

I shake my head. Goodbye, Yevgeniy Yurievich! Goodbye Captain Petrov! Goodbye, Humanbeing Bogumil! You'll have to make out on your own with your historic muskets, your Right Honourable trunk-hose and your morning-star.

Now Bogumil knows that tomorrow morning I shall not be in Ross-bach, but somewhere—or other.

19

I was on the run day and night. Keeping to the forests by daylight. I lost my way. I was hungry. I squatted on my heels and the hem of my overcoat lay in the snow. Gradually the cold rose up to my knees and froze my buttocks stiff, but I kept my balance, for five minutes, for half an hour. Rigid, I stared at the entrance to the cave, which at times shrank from my eyes until it was only a dark blot in the snow-covered undergrowth.

Uniforms were coming out of the cave, carrying crates and packages in their hands, stamping up to the truck that stood at the head of the valley, stowing and roping the load on board.

I felt as if I had seen it all before, only fiercer and louder, while my mother was stoning cherries. She would spit a cork on a hairpin, then put her hand in the enamel basin on her left, press the horseshoe-shaped wire into the fruit, hook it round the stone, pull it out so that it fell into a plate in her lap, and drop the empty cherry into the enamel basin on her right. I would be looking out of the kitchen window over the top of the garages at the bus terminal, over the roof of the engineering works past the overhead crane at the sawmill as far as the red-tiled walls of the yeast works. I used to practise focusing from the closest to the farthest roofs at increasing speed. My eyes sped back from the red walls over the wood shavings at the saw mill and the engineering shop to the tar-covered garages of the bus park, moved all the way back again, returned, moved back again, returned. After two or three minutes the roofs all disappeared, stacked themselves together and turned into a single roof reaching all the way from the kitchen window to the chimney stack of the yeast works, one steep slope reaching down to the level of my eyes. At the start of this game I always knew how it would finish: not with fainting, not with vomiting, but a sweet panic and shit and shaking.

I didn't have to urge them. No special magic was needed to hasten their arrival. They appeared on the dot like a bosun's whistle. At first they were crawling, then they got to their feet, but at the least danger they threw themselves down behind the nearest chimney-pot, with jerky, training-manual gestures, sometimes throwing their hands high in the air when they seemed to be hit. They all wore the same pot-helmet, rather like a British tin hat, but with a narrower brim and a higher dome. They rarely advanced alone. They would throw themselves down on the roof in pairs as if taking cover from enemy fire. In pairs they toppled from invisible ledges into impenetrable depths. Big black mouths opened under their helmets. They yelled but I didn't hear them. If I laid my head against the window-pane there was just the faint singing of the glass: far-off bugles and kettle-drums, horns and jingles. It was only when my mother's voice joined in the tune, or the hairpin scratched the enamel or a cherry stone hit the rim of the plate that I realised that it was myself who was humming the battle music against the window. My picture-book idea of war was all sergeant-trumpeters, lance-pennants, red tunics and blue tunics, snorting steeds, flashing eyes and maidens at the well, offering the victors salt and bread. As I looked through the window more men climbed on to the roof, crawled on their bellies, raised short carbines to their cheeks, fired without recoil, only the tiny twitch of their right shoulders revealing that they had pressed the trigger. Their faces did not show whether they had scored a hit. They looked straight ahead, though that did not mean that they were necessarily brave. When one left the formation and became separated from the next man, I could make out his uniform: black with silver buttons and facings and wearing top boots. He would always be in a hurry to get back to his mate in the line. Some flapped their arms above their helmets, dropped the short firearm and plunged down into depths I could not see. The further the carabiniers pushed forward, the more excited I became. I waited for the attack, could feel my pulse quickening, sweat on my palms, my guts emptying and pressure on the sphincter. I propped my arm on the back of the kitchen chair, licked my lips and breathed through my mouth. The helmets were close to the window, standing up now, already victorious, Siegfrieds in silver lace. This was my moment. I folded my arms on the window-sill, and all that anyone crossing the courtyard in front of our window would have seen was my round, blond face looking as if I were sleeping with my eyes open. But I was not asleep. I was shooting, soundlessly firing, mowing down the black soldiers in rows, bang bang bang, aiming with assurance at the heart and at the heart only, giving them the *coup de grâce*, putting out their light for good and all, rubbing them out so that not so much as a cur would remember them, sending them toppling forwards, pot-helmet first, down in front of the kitchen window, into the gap between the wide expanding eaves and the wall of the house, still clutching their firearms, nothing to be seen of their

59

faces except a shrieking mouth and then the silver facings on the black uniform and the matt silver buttons. They somersaulted through the air before my eyes, one after the other. Each one I saw I winded with my glance. He made a last leap, a final spring, and he was in range. As the last man jumped the roof disintegrated into the tar-covered garages of the bus terminal, the engineering works, the overhead crane at the saw mill, and the red-brick walls of the yeast works. Proud and assuaged, I turned away, chased the trembling out of the corners of my mouth with a smile, reached out to the right-hand basin, helped myself to a handful of stoned cherries, bent over and noisily relished the soft fruit. My mother did not look up. She stuck the hairpin into the next cherry, hooked the loop round the stone, pulled it out and dropped it into the plate that lay in her blue lap.

20

THE engine drowned the soldiers' voices. They were arguing. One with pips on his collar and shoulder straps was pointing to a small box, gleaming black, which he picked up twice, and twice replaced in the snow.

Standing small and green and much too solitary against the white snow, the officer fired in the air. He picked up the black box once more, carried it before him on extended hands, bearing it like a monstrance to the entrance of the cave, put it down immediately the motor revved up, left it there in front of the cave, drew his revolver again, without firing this time, and instead sprinted back, leapt onto the step of the moving truck, opened the door and disappeared.

I fell on my face. I groaned, rolled on my back, slid downhill. I crawled past the gleaming black box into the cave, felt the warmth coming out to meet me, staggered in a few yards, collapsed and wanted to go to sleep, but, shaking with curiosity, felt around me in the damp snow the soldiers had trampled into the cave on their boots, pulled myself up by the crannied wall and advanced towards the light down the passage. There was a wide open door with a notice on it: SHUT THE DOOR. A single pearl bulb hung from the ceiling of the room I was looking into, blurring the shadows of the crates, lockers, packets, canisters, tables, rifles, stacked ground sheets, central heating pipes and bunks, and giving at most thirty paces of visibility.

I stepped into the murky light and exclaimed: "Hey, hey, hey!"

I passed the cupboards and shelving, penetrated farther, a step at a time, kicked against bottles, lifted one, went on as far as the end of the cave, past two, three doors, saw finally that what had been a cave was now a depot, and apparently abandoned and surrendered to me by gentleman's agreement, the gift of the Wehrmacht, my share of the loot.

I counted seven rooms. The farthest contained the batteries for the electric heating and lighting, the water cistern and a ventilator system that provided a permanent supply of fresh air. I went back to the last room but one. A cupboard intersected the circle of light. I opened it. Blue, red and silver glowed within, and I saw the glittering black gloss of a cap-peak. Uniforms!

I threw my shoes into the corner, tore my jacket off, got out of my trousers, pants, vest, and stood there naked: I turned round and inspected myself in the mirror. My hair was already grey over my ears and bristly, though I had a good height of forehead over thin eyebrows and grey eyes which looked sometimes green, sometimes brown, according to how I felt; my nose broad with a tuberous end, and below, a large mouth and unenergetic chin. My shoulders were square and my chest deep; a bit of fat showed below my ribs, but my belly was flat and hairy down to the inside of my thighs. I farted and felt at home.

Next to the cupboard full of uniforms there was a shelf with underwear. I slid the cool soft cotton over my back, chest, legs and buttocks and wrapped myself up like a birthday present. The choice of uniform required some careful reflection. Infantry grey-green? Artillery blue-grey? Navy-white or Luftwaffe sky-blue? March, fire, swim or fly?

61

Footslogger, bombardier, fish or birdman? A triumph of common sense: the gunners. Blue-grey uniform, modest facings, a lightweight belt.

Here I stand, medium height, grey haired, I, Bonifaz, with and without a past.

A past, that was: fishing pike in mucky ponds where the fumes from the margarine works settle; being little, sitting on jam tins, lighting cigarettes with inflation banknotes; love in the park at the back of the Duke's pavilion, to the blaring of the frogs, and among the crickets, my nose touching the ear of a girl of twenty from the brickworks, for whom I had bought a silver ring with stolen money; friendships in hostels at Saarbrücken and Tilsit, where even the lice had T.B.; waiting in the harbour-board offices and customs houses and seamen's hostels, at the Kaiserdock at Bremerhaven, in the Untertrave at Lübeck, in the Upstalboomstrasse in Emden; by Levante line to Cadiz, Barcelona, Catania, Alexandria; four times across the pond in the *Robinson*, then Angola, and three years on the plantations: coffee, tobacco, sugarcane; one begins to soften up, but off Lobito lies H.M. cruiser: civilian internee. The Portuguese planter had three books, the Bible, *Don Quixote* and an overseas atlas; in the evening there was gin and the tom-tom and the Bantu girls and so I had never known clean barracks with their scent of boot-grease and sweat, the short hot breath of solidarity, far away as I was from crisis points, from the gravel paths and asphalt highways along which the left-right left-right tempo was being stamped out and the horse-columns rumbled, and all the chromium-plated petrol tins. I had a good deal to catch up with. I liked the look of myself in my general's rig with red tabs. I'm rising above myself, to where I ought to be. I'm a general. I'm surrounded by mountains of canned meat—manufactured, canned, sealed and labelled by other beings the same as I had been. I exalt myself above them, for I wear uniform now and I salute like a general, casually like a great general who touches the cap with only one finger, cabby-style. I am making up for what's missing from my past. Everything is here: canned food, water, Schnapps, heat, air. I shall make myself snug, I shall fill my belly with food and I shall make my fortune in the world.

I was standing in front of the mirror saluting when the wave of air pressure knocked me flat on the ground. I hit the concrete floor with my elbows, struck the cupboard with my head and was senseless for a while, and after that waited for the ceiling to descend on me. I got up, the splintered glass of the electric light bulb dropping off my face. I felt around for my cap, found it near the door to the last room and put it on. All doors were open, including the first one. But beyond the first one the entrance had disappeared: there was only soil, rocks, rubble; and now I knew what had been in the black box they had left standing at the entrance.

I found light bulbs in the outer room. I took six, screwed out the stumps which were all that remained in the sockets in the six rooms, and replaced the bulbs. Then I took stock.

First room—biscuits.

Second room—canned food.

Third room—arms and ammunition.

Fourth room—bunks, blankets and civilian clothing.

Fifth room—tobacco and liquor.

Sixth room—uniforms, shirts, underwear and shoes.

Seventh room—power installations, water cisterns, ventilators.

Article Fifty-Nine of the London declaration concerning the laws of naval war:

"In the absence of proof of the neutral character of goods found on board an enemy vessel, they are presumed to be enemy goods." No question about that. Enemy goods.

That night, lying in room four on a spring mattress that was so soft that it gave with each breath I took, I had a dream that I wondered about for the whole of the next morning and during the day, though for all I knew it could have been either night or day.

21

I was climbing up a red fire-escape with a woman whose face I never saw, up onto a roof and from that roof to another roof. Our shoes skated on the tiles. We seemed to be on top of a large public building, and below, right down below, a man was standing under a street lamp, smoking. I took the woman's shoes off, we dug out fingers into the joints between the bricks, and hauled ourselves higher up; when we had made it and looked over the top, we saw a flat roof in front of us. We lay side by side at the roof's edge, above the town. To the east we saw factory chimneys and aerials standing against the sky, and slowly the yellow light descended on to her arms and her bare shoulders, and I bent over her and didn't see her and kissed her. But it wasn't a kiss like a peck after lunch, it tasted good, wasn't wet, wasn't a come-along-and-give-us-a-kiss-dearie, it was the beginning and the end, it was night and dawn in one, and still tasted of Schnapps, and of falling asleep, and of being asleep, and at the same time of waking up. A kiss, a dream kiss with yellow heaven standing over it on a black, damp, thawing, tarred roof, one morning in a little town where you can see the river curve round the factory, where on Saturdays, as if at a command, whole streets suddenly expose their mattresses in the windows for the sun to get at, and where Sundays have a smell of soap and the scorched lining of bicycle brakes.

22

WHEN I woke up I was content enough with my lot, for if there's an ample supply of bacon and ham to console you for the loss of liberty, well, it's a different matter altogether. What do I care how the birch trees look in spring if I can get my teeth into a good chunk of ham? A cheese-plate sweetens the prospect. Beer soothes the heart, and tobacco the lungs.

In the uniform of an artillery general I stood in the outer door of my seven rooms and by the light of one pearl bulb contemplated the rubble that had been cast inwards by the blast. My tomb, my prison.

For three days and three nights I toped and gluttonised, and by the time I had killed all appetite I found myself staring at someone with three days' growth of stubble and holding a can-opener in his hand. Then I dragged myself off to the W.C., evacuated and started at the beginning again. I installed five bottles around the biscuit box on which I was sitting: Jamaica rum, Black and White, Anis, Danzig Stich-bimpuli-bockforcelorum, and Slibovitz. My beard was my calendar, and when I saw myself looking like another St. Jerome in his hermitage I knew that a lot of time must have passed and I started to consider the question, what is time? For this purpose I usually lay down on a camp bed in room four. I had measured the room and found it was six yards in each direction, a perfect cube. I shut the doors in order not to be disturbed, as I had the feeling that anyone may come in if you leave a door open. Then I floated for a while inside my two hundred and sixteen cubic yards and let them waft me away. It was like a quaking of the concrete floor; the cube began to revolve around me and I knew we were airborne. The greater the speed the more the walls closed in upon me; which isn't quite right, as my camp bed and I were getting smaller and smaller; we shrank together and if only I had a pair of nail scissors on me I could have cut the whole of my beard off in one go, so small had it become, but one never thinks of these things in time.

The fifth room was stocked with tobacco, and if it had not been for finding an India-paper edition of Hitler's *Mein Kampf*, I should have had to roll my cigarettes with lavatory paper or else take to chewing, which never did agree with me. It ruins the palate for Schnapps and then one might as well be drinking cold camomile tea.

It gave me a real delight to be able to send the Braunau boy up in blue smoke.

I discovered a door off the first room, hidden behind a cupboard, and it opened into a minute room containing a table and a map cabinet. Left on your own for long, with no one to cheer you up, you are likely to take such a dismal view of yourself that it becomes imperative to do something about enlarging your normal stature. Therefore, in the little closet off room one, with staff maps spread over the table, I promoted myself to honour and glory.

I pulled on calf-hugging riding boots before entering the map room and I never neglected to report to myself in the approved fashion, thus: Permission to speak, sir? Field Marshal von Mumps requests the Lance Corporal to conduct the council of war in person. Thank you. At ease, von Snobow. Well gentlemen, how are my dear Panzers getting along?

My reports, flashes, commands and directives were not altogether in accordance with military regulations, and I even went so far as to punctuate my map work with full knee-bends, splits, unseemly whistling and an occasional passing of water. But the war games enthralled me so completely that I was sometimes brought to a sharp halt, shaken by the view of some destroyed fortress, a ruin-world explored by my Panzers, and through which there now wove the strains of the Hohenfriedberger March I was whistling.

I selected as decisive theatres New South Wales and Luxembourg. Germany had no significance for me and I coined the phrase, as my forefinger traced the courses of the Elbe and the Rhine, that what you could count on finding there was Salvation, but never a Solution.

The hostilities between Luxembourg and New South Wales—provoked by a dispute which I myself had just unearthed, namely the Sardine Question—held a particular interest for me since they were conducted not only on land but principally at sea, as well as in the air.

In the course of the bombing of the New South Wales pilgrim shrine of Vrauquarrh, twelve deacons of the High Presbyterian Church had suffered injuries. As a result of reprisals, the major part of the artillery unfortunately fell into enemy hands, where it did not fall into the Alzette, the west bank of which, with the bridgehead of Mersch, had been disloyally evacuated by the Luxembourgers.

66

The crux of the Sardine Question lay in the fact that the question could not actually exist: as usually happens with two nations which have absolutely nothing in common except a distant ethnic cousinage from prehistoric times, and who get on very well together so long as they never have to meet, they had grown so fat and contented that pride induced in them the *folie des canons*. So the day came when the head of the Luxembourg government laid claim to the New South Welsh sardine fishing-grounds, in spite of the fact that Luxembourg possessed neither ships nor anybody who understood the first thing about deep-sea fishing, except of course for a couple of delicatessen owners.

Various efforts to drag other countries into the war having met with no success, it began to look, all things considered, as if the war had been started only in order to get me over my disappointment at discovering that practically all the cans in my stock of provisions contained sardines in olive oil.

I spent a lot of time lying in the various rooms staring at the concrete ceiling. Rolling on one side I could see the empty tins and count them, and as their trail grew longer I got the feeling that time was catching up with me. Weeks, months sank down over me, half a year had buried me. I was suffocating, the earth of my dreams went yellow, it was sand running out in an hour-glass. I sent out the last raven, through the crack still linking me to my past. I watched it clattering its wings, taking a few trial steps, stretching its feathers and taking off. After that I was left alone in my encirclement. I gripped the blankets with my finger-nails and pressed with my feet against the end of the bunk. But it didn't help. I suffocated. I would be dead within a month, or within a year. And yet I was still growing, more than most. Something was passing me by. A week, a month. The gap only opened when I ran into the empty cans, kicking them around, sending them bouncing off the walls. At that moment the glass dome would lift, birds swooped in, the earth was black and green and air returned. The stench, however, remained. I planted lime trees and jasmin in my concrete. I held Schnapps and shoe-polish under my nose, but the stench remained. I was running out of Hitler from smoking too much, I was bored with my offensives, breakthroughs, setbacks and tactical manoeuvres.

The Sardine Question had been settled, two million lives had been lost, and when the war was over canned sardines were unobtainable either in New South Wales or in Luxembourg. Worst of all: Lieutenant von Snobow had vanished! I had promoted him to lieutenant, captain, major, I ran through my rooms shouting for him, but he did not return. Ungrateful deserter von Snobow!

For a couple of days—or years?—I passed the time target shooting. Afterwards I aimed an army rifle at the mirror and shot my face to pieces. I kept firing until the last piece of glass had fallen out of the frame and then I swept myself up and threw myself away in the dustbin.

23

ONE night (at least, I was asleep) the ants came. They were running over me when I switched on the light. I leapt up and dusted them off with a brush. They had come from the entrance. There were not a great many—two or three thousand.

There was a jar of honey in the biscuit cupboard. I dipped a piece of rag in it and laid a trail to the map room. I drew a honey spiral by the big map table and sat down expectantly to wait. Two hours later the vanguard of the ant horde arrived. I erected an ant-hill out of sawdust, woodshavings, rags and matches. I soaked it with honey and salad oil and left the ants to get on with the job themselves. This was not a hotel. I sat on top of the table and watched them. They seemed to have brought a couple of queens along with them already, or some sort of Top Ant-esses. At any rate there was a terrific fuss the moment they appeared and any ant which happened to be carrying an egg or a piece of wood chucked it away and dashed to meet the ladies and show them the way. "In the multitude of people is the king's honour: but in the want of people is the destruction of the prince."

As soon as their majesties had been ushered through, the others went back to their drudgery. It seemed to me that it was no easy matter getting settled down in the land of milk and honey. Could there be such a thing as neutral ants?

I went to bed and said to myself, before falling asleep: you've got visitors. Things can't really be so bad. But I woke up suddenly in the middle of the night wondering how the ants had got in. I switched on the light and examined all the rooms. I tapped the walls. No, they had definitely come from the entrance. I opened the door that led out to the rubble-block and shone a light on the whole mass. One or two stragglers were still coming through. Otherwise the obstruction was complete. I went back to bed.

I was not particularly nice to the ants. After making a few attempts to introduce them to my staff maps and teach them the war game, for which they showed no enthusiasm, since they ran in all directions, penetrated into neutral territories, occupied strategically valueless mountain ranges and fouled their own capital cities, I took a bayonet and scraped a moat round their castle and filled it with water. It took some time before they noticed this. After trying to cross the moat at all points, as a few good swimmers succeeded in doing, they withdrew to confer.

I made a couple of little boats out of empty matchboxes, with which they ought to have been able to ferry themselves over, but the ants showed no interest. I lay down and couldn't be bothered with them any more.

When I woke up they had disappeared. They had used the materials of their ant-hill—rags, pebbles and pieces of wood—to construct a dyke and had retreated across it. At the entrance I could see them still leaving through a crevice, loaded with cocoons and honey. As this was already the rearguard, there was no point in trying to stop them.

24

I WAS alone again, and memories came. I was lying with Emma between two graves in a churchyard, eating liver sausage and dry rolls, while I spelled out and made anagrams from the gilded letters of the gravestone inscriptions. The result was the same every time—EMMA.

25

AT the gala day of the Shooting Company at Tesch, my father lifted me right up in the air and I could see the greenery and the flashing brass of the band. He carried me along astride his shoulders, but when we came to the refreshment tent where the beer was served he put me down again, and then all I could see were the dismal back views of men in Sunday suits and the women's colourful full skirts.

26

I WAS aboard a trawler. The man next to me drew his short gutting knife and stabbed out the eyes of the flailing cod which he had grasped behind the gills. He smashed off its head with the blunt side and felt inside for the columellas, which he washed with care and put away in a little box, as he was saving them up to make a necklace for his wife.

27

I WAS sharing a bed with a tight-rope walker in a hostel in Cologne. He wanted to get to the Black Forest, he told me in the evening, as the air was better there. He was brilliant at whistling through his teeth, but in the morning he was dead, and we had a lot of bother with him and the police.

28

DOM GOLVÃO in Angola was married to a former mental nurse. She lay on the verandah when I went to see him with my returns. She had taken to drink. She always had a bottle next to her. She would put the newspaper down when she heard me coming and each time she said: "I'm going completely mad here. Why on earth did I ever give up my career? I'm going back to Oporto." That was the place where the asylum had been. When Dom Golvão was away I had to spend the whole time in bed with her. In that sector she was completely normal.

29

WHEN we were crossing the Atlantic in the *Robinson* for the second time we were followed by so many seagulls that our ears began to buzz from their squawking. The second mate fixed a large piece of liver to the fo'c'sle with an explosive charge underneath it. Afterwards, when scrubbing down, we had to scrape blood and feathers from the white superstructure till our finger-tips split.

30

I HAD been sitting five sardine-cans long in front of the caved-in entrance before I remembered what I had come to do. I was holding the bayonet with which I had scratched the moat round the ant-hill, and now I used it to poke away at the crevice and enlarge it enough for me to get my foot in.

Why, I asked myself, shouldn't I get my whole leg in? I had time enough. Time was what I needed, and it was a very long time before I hit on the idea of assembling small blasting charges of small-arms ammunition and saving myself some of the heavier work. My right hand had already taken on a deformity from clutching the bayonet haft, but I could not risk fixing it to a rifle, where it might easily break off.

When I took time off to lie down on my bed and rest, I was able to persuade myself that I didn't really want to get out after all. Never again would I have it so good. But there was a smell of chestnuts and moss in the first rain to seep through the crevice, and I knew I must find out which year's spring it was that we were having. I had made four yards headway towards the exit: all the rubble had to be carried back into the innermost rooms. I had forgotten to leave myself a clear passage, which gave me twice as much work to do. I made roof props out of dismantled store cupboards, shoring up the tunnel over my head. Thirty sardine-cans ago I hadn't cared whether I survived or not, but now I was anxious and fussy, testing over and over again before I dared go on digging. I brought my bed out to the mouth of the tunnel so as to have less far to walk. I wanted to be on the spot, yet even so,

I slept through the great moment when it came. I woke up one day and there was a white spot on the green mattress. I tried to rub it off, but it stayed. I scratched at it with my nails, but couldn't make any impression. When I put my hand on top of it, it was still there. It was on my hand, and when I looked up I saw that it was the sun.

I spent the whole day lying on the bed and watching the spot, watching it travel, watching it approach my face, mount up a bit of the wall, grow pale and disappear. I was back knowing day and night: I chalked out a sundial on the floor and divided my work up into a forty-eight hour week with unpaid free time and Sundays off. Black Monday, grey Tuesday, white Wednesday, thou shalt keep the Thursday holy, for it is the day the Lord made, but for sailors only, followed by sweet Friday when the women of Germany gather for coffee together because their husbands are boozing up the wages, and then the short-winded Saturday. When I had got through to the end of the concrete rubble and came upon the first roots and tubers, I took on three full watches a day, extended the electric lighting down the tunnel and carried back earth by the bucketful. With a bayonet in either hand I hacked away at the face, my arms leading separate existences: I seemed to be watching them, right and left, tensing, bending, hewing, as if they had nothing to do with me, jointed pendulums, fore and aft carving me space and carving me time, in mutual extension. I crouched like the potato diggers in October and my loads dragged down my shoulders as I staggered through the room with sagging knees to tip the rocks out next to the provisions. I was already fearful I had mined too deep when one morning, at half past seven according to my sundial, I arrived at the site to find that the rock had collapsed and a face was looking in, a face with eyes, nose, a sharp chin and on top a cap tailored out of squirrel skins.

"Good morning!" I cried, but the face vanished immediately. It didn't even give me a chance to ask the time.

I felt better for the fresh air, a wood wren was whistling nearby and, to judge by the grass and leaves that had fallen in with the roof, it was getting on for autumn. I went and fetched enough boxes to stack on top of each other and climb up and out of the hole. When I pushed my head over the top, I saw four men standing about twenty yards away, all of them holding their noses.

"Come over! I shan't do anything!" I shouted, as I imagined that they must be scared to pieces, it not being an everyday occurrence for a person to emerge from the earth. I invited them with signals, but they all shook their heads without letting go of their noses. I recognised one of them as Squirrelcap, who had looked over the edge into my tunnel. I pulled myself right out and approached these faint-hearted fellows. I held my hands open in front of me with the fingers spread out, so that they should see I was concealing nothing. They stood where they were, only drawing closer together, their eyes popping with curiosity.

"My name is Bonifaz," I said. They nodded. "I'm a sailor by trade, so perhaps I ought to explain to you ... " I did not go on, as they started shaking their heads again.

Squirrelcap finally said to me, holding his nose: "It stinks."

I turned round and shrugged my shoulders. "Gentlemen—I can't smell anything. There's only a bit of mouldy wood and old leaves, but that's autumn for you."

The hypersensitive ones pointed at me and then at the hole I had climbed out of. "I see," I said, "perhaps you can smell a bit of fish."

"A very strong smell of fish," they replied as with one voice.

"Perhaps you wouldn't mind telling me what you're doing here?"

"We're poachers," said Squirrelcap.

"We're collecting wood to take into the towns," said the one next to him and pointed to four panniers standing at the edge of the wood.

"Rabbits go very well now before the winter."

"Would you have a cigarette on you?" I asked.

"No smoking in the woods," said Squirrelcap.

"Oh, come on—let me be a devil just for once."

"One cigarette, American make, costs seven marks. Do you have that by you?"

"May I suggest a can of sardines in olive oil in exchange?" I asked him.

"Oh, sure, two cigarettes for that," he said, and I could see the look he gave the others, as much as to say: here's a sucker.

74

I went back to my hole and climbed down. I felt sure that the stench would restrain them from following me for quite some time. I walked regretfully through my underground palace, reproaching myself now for having worked so well and so fast. I took leave of each of the rooms, not forgetting my staff headquarters where the war between Luxembourg and New South Wales had been fought to a finish. I called a last time for Lieutenant von Snobow, but again he failed to appear. I went to the uniform cupboard and took out a pair of grey trousers without piping. I put on a clean shirt and a dark blue nautical jacket. My own sailor's cap was still full of cement dust and I had to shake it out.

If one can of sardines raises an offer worth fourteen marks, I reflected, and the other fellow still thinks he has made a bargain, I might as well set myself up properly. I packed as many sardine cans as I could get into a fur-faced army knapsack, added a bottle of Kümmel, strapped the knapsack to my back and carried a single can of sardines in my hand. As a precaution I slung a rifle over my shoulder. As I climbed out I looked at my sundial for the last time. The time was nearly nine a.m.: off to work.

The four poachers had come a little closer, but were still keeping clear of the scent. When they saw my rifle they turned to run.

"Halt!" I shouted, "or I fire!"

I wasn't going to forgo that cigarette.

They gave in like tired Watusi cattle.

"Ten cigarettes," snivelled Squirrelcap when I had caught up with them.

"The whole box," I said.

They handed it over. There were only twelve left in it. I offered one to each of them, handed over the can of sardines and was about to go. But the shortest one stopped me.

"Pardon me, skipper, what's down that hole?"

"It's the place where they buried the German Reich," I replied. I shouldered my rifle and turned about.

"The town's over that way!" shouted Squirrelcap and pointed down in the direction where the trucks had driven long ago.

"Fine, fine," I said and took no further notice. I lifted the logs of firewood that covered the top of one of the panniers. Two rabbits lay in the bottom with the wire still round their necks, and big distended eyes and blood in their nostrils. I put the wood back and went up the hill into the forest from where I could see the four men still holding their noses, approaching the hole and encouraging each other with gestures of the hand. Soon they would be down in my stores, stuffing themselves with food and kicking the ant-hill to pieces. I hung the rifle on a fire tree and lit a cigarette.

I once knew a little girl called Babette, the daughter of my friend Maiko. She said to me one day when it was raining: the windows aren't happy, Bonifaz—look how they're crying.

But the sky promised fine weather today, and when I hopped over tree-roots the cans clattered in my knapsack.

31

IT's always a pleasure walking through a German forest. A German forest is reliable. In a German forest the trees are spaced exactly two yards apart and the branches are lopped up to a height of one and a half yards, and if it's a pine forest, tin cups are attached to the southward-facing side of every trunk to catch the gum. The birds in a German forest inhabit neat wooden boxes, as the foresters want to keep an eye on the laying for the current year. In winter the larger game in a German forest resort to a canteen, and there German deer and German stags may avail themselves of supplies of hay and chestnuts. In summer time German forest murmurs occur from four to six p.m., nobody being free to listen to them any earlier. In winter the German forest is photographed and, when printed on glossy paper, arouses that well-known nostalgia in the breasts of Germans abroad. No one can ever get lost in a German forest, since access to a German forest is forbidden.

This is the reason why the forest is a home for everything that won't obey *verboten* notices: witches, fortune-tellers, magicians, vaga-bonds, woodsprites, soothsayers, elves, dwarfs, dragons, Communists, Jews, hobgoblins, children and fairy tales.

A notice was hanging on the third tree of the fourth row to the left. It read: IMPORTANT NOTICE ON TREE 11 ROW 9. I had nothing to do, so I went to tree eleven, row nine. Another notice was hanging from the lowest branch reading: DID YOU KNOW THAT? TREE 6, ROW 14. I did not, but I wanted to, so I went on to tree six on row fourteen. On this tree I read: NEVER IN YOUR WILDEST DREAMS! TREE 2, ROW 19. I thought as much, and was beginning to have had enough. All the same, I went to tree two, row nineteen, but could not find a notice there. My knap-sack was weighing me down, but I nevertheless walked round the tree three times and still saw no notice anywhere. Once you start on non-sense like this, I said to myself, you might as well see it through to the end. Here I was—Important notice—Did you know that?—Never in your wildest dreams!—and I was bursting with curiosity by now.

There was another notice five or six trees away which I could make out from where I was standing: NOW HOW DO YOU FEEL? WHAT ELSE DID YOU EXPECT? I didn't trouble to go any closer, I'm not had as easily as that. Everything can go too far. Don't count too much on me, gentlemen!

As I left the forest I came upon another notice, one which really shook me:

CUP OF REAL COFFEE
ONLY 5 MARKS
10% SUPPLEMENT FOR ORCHESTRA

A woodland café? On the first tree in the thirty-fifth row an arrow pointed to a house standing on the highway. I walked across gravel and tar and knocked on the front door. Inside I could hear a scratching sound and then the blare of a brass band, quick and bright, which nearly knocked me backwards when the door was opened.

"Yes, please?" asked a stout lady with short crinkly hair, pulling off her ring at the sight of me and shoving it in her apron pocket.

"A cup of real coffee," I yelled through the pounding march. She nodded and preceded me into the parlour. She took off the record, as I had stuck my fingers in my ears as soon as I entered, and plugged in her electric percolator.

"How did you get down here?" she asked.

"You see, these notices . . ." I began.

"They're my husband's idea," she said and laid a cup on the table. "He's an interpreter with the Americans. He always knows best. I told him it would only be inviting all the riff-raff in from the forest."

I put my knapsack on the floor by the chair and sat down.

"Every other day there are these four brigands who come here and refuse to pay after filling themselves up with my hot coffee."

"They won't be along so soon," I said comfortingly.

"How do you know that?"

"I met them on my way here, and then I followed the notices."

"And you're still alive?"

"One does one's best," I said and laid my hand on her back as she poured out my coffee.

She was in her late thirties and had a lovely bottom, and if I had been Professor Wollgast I would have carved it in granite and bequeathed it to the nation.

"Ah well," she said and poured a little cup for herself as well. "To think you're still alive . . ."

"And how!" I exclaimed, as I took my first gulp.

"The thing is," she began, and I saw how pale she had gone.

"What's your name?" I asked.

"Are you going to report us?"

"On the contrary," I said going around to the other side of the table and putting my hand on her shoulder. "Quite the contrary."

"You smell so nice," she said. "My name's Elli."

"I've got canned sardines in olive oil. My name's Bonifaz."

She turned round and raised her hands toward me. I came closer to her and we put our tongues in each other's mouths. Her hair smelt of almond-oil soap and her nose was as cold as a dog's. When my back began to hurt I pinched her in the waist. She let go of my mouth. It was like spitting me out. "Willi won't be back till the evening," she said. I went and turned the key in the door.

"Supposing someone else reads the notices?" I said. But she just shook her head and pulled a handkerchief out of her blouse to mop her eyes with.

"Come!" she beckoned me, and took me into the next room where the conjugal beds were. She did not wait to be asked but undressed at once, pulled the black-out blind over the window and leapt into the bed and, notwithstanding the joyous ferocity she released in me, I still kept thinking of the tidy German forest where no one ever gets lost.

Elli had a round belly, and when she laughed I put my hand on it. I pushed my finger between her toes and tickled her, she pounded on my chest with her fists and laid the best cushion under her hips, and for lunch we had sardines and extra strong coffee.

"Did you really follow the notices?" she asked me after we had eaten.

"Yes," I said, "only they missed out one tree. Why do you keep asking?"

"Oh, you see," she whispered, "my Willi's so dreadfully jealous, specially about those four who come here for coffee. Yesterday evening he planted a land mine in the forest."

"And that for sure would be under the notice NOW HOW DO YOU FEEL? WHAT ELSE DID YOU EXPECT? That's the one I didn't go and look at."

"You're a clever little boyo," she said and annointed me with her tongue.

"Are you quite sure," I asked her, "that your husband hasn't fixed up a bomb under the bed as well?"

"It would have gone off by now," she said.

"You're right again," I admitted, stretching so that the bedstead creaked.

While the afternoon folded itself away and the forest was murmuring in complete disregard of regulations, I recounted to Elli everything that had happened to me, stroking her short hair and pressing my hot knee-hollows against the cool sheet.

Near evening we got up, dressed, and Elli smoothed the bedclothes. I went outside the front door and sat down, pulled at my bottle of Kümmel and waited for Willi, who would be coming home by bicycle.

79

Elli put another record on the gramophone and, while spreading sardines on slices of bread, she sang: *Hörst du mein heimliches Rufen? Öffne dein Herzkämmerlein.*

Far down the highway a bicycle came in sight: the interpreter cometh. He was very tall, wore tight trousers so that he needed no bicycle clips, and gave me an exceedingly dirty look, although I got up and offered him my seat.

He did not seem to listen to my explanations and did not even look at me as I spoke.

"You can't spend the night here," was the only thing he said when Elli pushed the plate of sardine sandwiches towards him.

"How far is it from here to the town?" I asked.

"If you're a good walker, two hours."

"But Mr. Bonifaz is tired," said Elli looking at me.

"Bonifaz?" asked Willi. "What the hell kind of a name is that? Don't you have any proper surname?"

"Sure," I said firmly, "but I don't give a damn for it."

"Well *I* do," said Willi and sat down rather straightly, showing me that all was not well with his glands.

"I hope you've got a proper identity card?"

"All I've got is a delivery certificate from the Royal Navy and a carbon copy of the document saying that I may not be further engaged in active military service as I am neutral."

"Piffle, the war's over. You should take your birth certificate along and apply for a proper identity card."

"But I don't want one."

Willi lay down on the ledge of the stove and pulled a newspaper out of his jacket pocket.

"You won't get very far like that," he said and flicked the first page over.

"If I'm going to have an identity card, then it's got to be an absolutely neutral one."

"Don't you think you could get him one?" asked Elli.

Willi squashed up his paper and snapped: "I've got other things to do."

80

"I think all that your wife meant was," I said sweetly, "that being with the Americans it probably isn't hard for you to get at all the forms and rubber stamps."

"You seem to have found out how to get her tongue waggling all right," he snarled at me.

I grinned at Elli and Herr Mummert screened himself behind his newspaper. I suddenly realised that I had left my shoes in the bedroom. They were under his bed. I always push my shoes under the bed as it gives me a good reason for getting annoyed at not finding them in the morning. I requested part of the newspaper from Herr Mummert, crossed my left leg over my right knee and kept the newspaper in front of my foot. I rolled my eyes, cleared my throat and blew my nose before Elli looked my way. I pointed to my unshod foot and nodded my head in the direction of the bedroom. But Elli got me wrong. She rolled up her eyeballs, shrugged her shoulders and tapped her forehead. I was about to try again and show her what I meant, but she looked put out, nodded towards her husband and went, "t, t, t".

"I see they're nationalising everything in the East," said Herr Mummert. "Have you read about it?"

"No," I said, "I'm just coming to it."

"Well, you read it. I'd be interested to hear your opinion."

So I had to hold the newspaper in front of me and read the article about nationalisation while Elli washed up at the sink and kept her eye on her husband.

"Well?" asked Herr Mummert when I was rash enough to rustle the paper in trying to attract Elli's attention to my bare feet. "What do you think of that?"

"Fine," I said, "they all ought to have their heads chopped off."

"Exactly what I think," said Herr Mummert.

Elli had at last grasped that I did not want to go to bed with her but simply to get my shoes back.

"But wait a minute," said Herr Mummert. "Who ought to have their heads chopped off?"

I had lost the thread, and was busy tucking my feet out of sight under the chair. "What do you mean?" I asked.

"Whose heads ought to be chopped off? Who were you thinking of?"

"Oh, the factory-owners and the profiteers and all that gang."

At this moment Elli was about to close the bedroom door behind her but Herr Mummert leapt to his feet and stopped her.

"Elli, stay here."

"I'm not getting involved in politics," squawked Elli.

"You're a witness that this man, who declines to give his proper name, demands that factory-owners should have their heads chopped off. Did you hear that or didn't you?"

He was shaking all over and fanned his newspaper up and down at me, as if dipping ensigns, coiled his other arm on Elli's round shoulders and waited for my reply.

"Herr Mummert," I said, "Don't get worked up. None of this affects me, anyway. I'm neutral."

"I really don't think," said Elli, "that he's quite right in the head. Just imagine, Willichen, he followed your notices through the wood without anything happening to him."

"I see," he said and let go of Elli, who immediately popped behind the door. "You came through the forest. And what did you see there?"

"There were these four notices. One said IMPORTANT NOTICE, and then the next one said DID YOU KNOW THAT? and as I obviously did, I went on to the third one. That said NEVER IN YOUR WILDEST DREAMS. And then finally I found the one which said NOW HOW DO YOU FEEL?"

"Yes, and—?"

"I felt fine, only as I was thirsty I came along to get a cup of coffee from your wife."

"I see," said Herr Mummert and sat down opposite me at the table. "You can consider yourself lucky."

Elli came back into the room carrying something under her apron. She sat down beside me and spread her legs wide. Herr Mummert gave her a reproachful look and I must say she was pretty clumsy in the way she bent forward over the table to stroke the hair back from his brow while letting something fall with a thump to the ground, instead of quietly and unobtrusively handing it over to me. As it was, Herr Mummert gave a jump and asked what that was.

82

"My shoes, Herr Mummert," I said.

I bent down but could only find one shoe, the left one. Herr Mummert was looking underneath the other side of the table.

"Have you got your shoes?"

"Yes," I said.

"And where's the right one?" he persisted.

"I," I stammered, "I was only wearing one shoe when I arrived."

"I wonder whether you lost the other one in the forest?" asked Elli cheekily.

"I'm afraid that could easily have happened, Frau Mummert," I agreed, "in present-day conditions . . ."

"I'm going back into the forest," said Herr Mummert.

"It's already getting dark, little man," said Elli.

"I said, I'm going back into the forest," he repeated, and, to show us he was serious, got up and put on his overcoat.

"You could have a look and see if Herr Bonifaz's other shoe is anywhere about," suggested Elli, but that was not what he had in mind.

"If I find you still here when I get back," he said to me, "I'm going to blow a hole through you."

He tapped his overcoat pocket, which might easily have contained a revolver. His adam's apple was vaulting up and down. So he was scared. Most heroes are shit-bags at heart.

"I'll go," I promised.

Before leaving he took his toolkit out of the cupboard and slung it over his shoulder. The pliers and screwdrivers clattered together and he hissed at me: "Clear out of here!"

"Yes, sir," I said.

"Why do you let yourself be bullied by him?" asked Elli when she saw that Herr Mummert was across the highway.

"If I'm going to defend myself I prefer to have both my shoes on," I answered, "including the right one, which happens to be under the bed."

She went to fetch it.

"It oughtn't to have happened like this, Elli," I said, "Your husband's got a revolver and all I've got is a paper saying I'm neutral."

"Will you be leaving me with a can of sardines?"

"Two cans, Elli."

I eased my feet into the shoes, as with two hours' walking ahead of me I wanted them to fit comfortably.

"Or you could take the bike," said Elli. "All you'd have to do is hand it in at the Kommandantur in the Knesebeckstrasse. I'll just tell him you took it by force."

"Ah, Elli," I said, "if only I could take you by force just once more."

"Supposing we did it quickly?"

"Oh, what the hell, it's no fun like that."

She heaved my knapsack onto the table so that I could get my arms comfortably under the straps. When I had fixed both buckles and was about to step to the door, the window-pane dropped into the sink and we both heard a shattering explosion.

I put my knapsack back on the table and said: "I think you're a widow now, Elli."

32

THERE was really nothing left of Herr Mummert apart from a couple of buttons and a small hammer which I found near tree eight in the twenty-first row, not far from the place where I had seen the notice NEVER IN YOUR WILDEST DREAMS.

"He was a good sort, really," said Elli, as I took her by the hand to lead her back to the highway.

"Definitely," I said, "only don't let's go on running around the forest in the dark—it wouldn't surprise me if your husband, I mean, if your late husband had laid a couple more mines to be on the safe side."

"Yes," said Elli, "he was always so thorough."

84

I must confess that Herr Mummert's death did not particularly affect me, and even Elli seemed to be getting used to it quite quickly. She made coffee for us and sat on my knee.

"I shall have to go into town tomorrow."

"Yes," I added, "and tell them he isn't coming. I hope they've got a replacement for him, because otherwise they'll go talking American to everybody and who'll know what to make of that?"

"I'll be going to see the lawyer, too," said Elli. "I know he made a will."

"Is anyone else likely to inherit anything?"

"No," she said, "but he was always so thorough."

At last the tears began to come. She threw her arms round my neck and howled away as loud as a street hawker. But that was all right by me, because women who know how to howl properly are always the best.

I reached for my knapsack and took out the bottle of Kümmel. "Come along Elli, take a nip."

Her face disappeared behind the bottle.

"Hey, it wasn't me who's been blown up," I said reprovingly.

She detached herself from the bottle and put it on the table.

"I don't give a damn for him. We were married in '44. He didn't get called up because of his T.B. He was getting extra rations and learning English at the same time."

"What about you?"

"I was a home-front conscript. Cooking for eastern deportees. Take a look at that," she said pointing to a wooden platter, "they gave me that."

"What, as a going-away present?"

"No, for the fried potatoes. I always did them a bit extra."

She laid her head on my shoulder again.

"Now *you're* there," she said.

"Yes," I said.

"Are you staying?"

"For the time being, sure."

"Always," said Elli. "Promise you'll stay here always."

"You see, really I'm a sailor," I tried to explain, but she put her hand across my mouth and then she took my shoes off and back we went into the next room.

Lying awake beside her at night I painted myself a picture of life with her in the country: keeping chickens, seven hens and a cock, radishes and lettuce in the garden, white gravel on the path, a kennel in the yard and two cats in the house, we'd add a verandah at the back so as to avoid the mosquitoes in the summer. Elli was snoring, but I'd try to get used to that. Anyhow, I usually fell asleep first. Perhaps a little auxiliary generator would help, rattling the foundations a bit at night and giving me at least the illusion of being at sea. I might even lay on a goitre and gradually go batty. One foot was already in dreamland when there was a knocking on the window. I gave Elli a shove and she sat up with a rustle.

"What's happening?" she asked.

"Someone's out there," I whispered.

"Willi's ghost," she whimpered.

The knocking had gone round to the front door and was a good deal louder than one would expect from Herr Mummert's ghost.

"Shall we open?" asked Elli, accidentally putting her cold hand on my face. We could hear the sound of a door being smashed in.

"The door," said Elli and took her hand off my mouth.

"It doesn't sound like your husband," I whispered, "there's several of them."

We could hear the chairs being thrown about in the front room quite clearly now.

"Where's that bastard?" asked a voice.

"Police," whispered Elli.

"No," I said comfortingly, "we're not back to all that yet."

The bedroom door was flung open and the light dazzled us. The four intruders took some moments to get over their surprise before bawling at us. "Our old sardine skipper!" they yelled.

"Where's Willi?"

I pointed upwards.

"On the roof?"

86

"Higher still," I said.

"Is that so," said Squirrelcap, "and so you've stepped in straight away. Been comforting the widow?"

"You'd better ask Frau Mummert herself," I said and had a closer look at the four of them. They had rigged themselves out like musical comedy princes: red stripes to their trousers, blue and white jackets with bars, orders and medals I had never seen before, officer's caps on their heads, and revolvers in their hands.

"How did you do him in?" one of them asked me.

"Who?"

"Mummert, of course."

"We fed him with veronal," I said, "a tablet at a time."

They thought this was very funny and had already drunk enough to go weak at the knees with laughing.

"Get dressed, Elli," said Squirrelcap.

"What for?" asked Elli, pulling her sheet up to her chin.

"You're coming with us."

"Listen," I protested, "we're as good as engaged!"

The four had to clutch each other so as not to fall down laughing. Then they became serious and switched the light on. They all pointed their pistols at us and the small one said: "If you don't lie down and keep quiet you can go and keep your predecessor company. Elli, get dressed."

Elli moaned and got up, but what else could she do? She got dressed while I clenched my fists under the bedclothes, but kept quiet.

"Pack a few more things," said the little one, "we're going to be away for a few weeks."

"The depot is fine," said one of the others to me, "but it's not much of a place without women."

"I had to do without," I growled.

"The world's full of pretty girls," said Squirrelcap soothingly.

"Why did you have to pick on us? We were going to get married, weren't we, Elli?"

Elli nodded and snapped down the lid of her suitcase.

"Are you a little bit sorry, at least?" I asked.

"Yes, Bonifaz," she assured me, "only I've had too many surprises today."

"Come along now," said the little one, "we couldn't very well have made an appointment."

"Do you think I ought to wear a hat?" Elli asked me, looking at herself in the mirror.

I did not reply—I had doubts about her love and turned over on my side. Squirrelcap picked up the suitcase. They all raised their hands to their caps, and the little one said: "We trust that you will enjoy a good night's rest."

"You can all take a running jump," I said and stuck my tongue out.

"There you are, Elli," said the little one, "you see the fellow's got no manners at all. How could you have thought of matrimony with him!"

Elli looked at me with big round eyes and smiled. "Goodbye, Bonifaz. You see, I can't help it. If you like, you can go into town tomorrow on the bicycle. But you must hand it in at the Kommandantur in the Knesebeckstrasse. I really am sorry about this. Or will you wait for me to come back?"

"Clear out!" I said.

I heard Elli's footsteps on the highway for a bit, and then nothing. I wished them all a nice round anti-personnel mine in their path.

In the lips of him that hath understanding wisdom is found,
But a rod is for the back of him that is void of understanding.

The Bible is right. I am an idiot.

33

THIRTY-FIVE thousand marks were offered for a dove of Basle, only twenty-two thousand marks for Geneva pairs, and fifteen thousand marks for a Vineta provisional. I wondered how many cans of sardines I should have to provide in exchange for three rare stamps and so start to be a celebrated collector: my whole knapsack-full would not have gone very far.

I looked in the window of a shoe mart. Glittering top-boots polished like glass to be exchanged by their owner for three pairs of children's shoes: a fecund man. The shoes were all paraded for inspection and it was easy to picture the people who had stood in them: the anti-aircraft gunneress, yearning for cork sandals; the fixed-income man whose canvas shoes didn't keep out the cold; the fourteen-year-old war veteran, decorated with the Iron Cross, who had grown out of size sixes.

On the trees in front of the station were pinned little barter, seeking, and wanted notices:

Business Lady
seeks Husband age up to 50.
Ex-Concentr. Camp or Jewish preferred.

———

Scientific Graphology
for
Business and Private Life

———

Lady's Panther Stole
Wednesdays 4 p.m.
Apply Frau Oberleutnant (retired) Winkelmann

———

Esperanto for World Reconciliation

———

Seeking Relatives?
Apply to the
REFUGEE INFORMATION CENTRE
(Service also available to needy persons)

Schwabeldingen was not going to hold me. I crossed the station forecourt, past the trucks with their wood-gas generators, went into the hall and joined the queue in front of the ticket office. We crept slowly, the knapsack patrol, bearing our offerings on our backs, tea-sets and silver spoons, lace counterpanes, electric bulbs—it's worth sitting in the dark if it will get you a full belly—speaking spivvish hoarder-German ("two cans of monkey grease for one old balalaika? I'd sooner go straight out and steal the stuff"), under-dressed women who for the sake of a sack of potatoes or six eggs were ready to put their backs to the nearest haystack, as if the farmers noticed any shortage of *that*.

I pressed my nose against the glass window and said: "A single to far away."

The girl whiffled through the German Reichsbahn directory, a comforting thought that there still was a Reich, and asked me: "First or second?"

"That depends on the price," I said.

"Faraway isn't listed," she said and shut the volume with a slam. "Where's it supposed to be?"

The people behind me were getting restless.

"Eggs or potatoes?" asked the booking clerk.

"Neither nor," I said, "I just want to go far, far away."

"This is the limit," protested someone behind me.

"How so?" I asked back. "I'm only just starting."

"But you must know where you want to go?" insisted the girl, tapping her long nails on the counter. I unhitched my knapsack, opened it up and placed a can of sardines in the window.

"Bribery and corruption," said a fat man.

"How far do I get on that?" I asked.

The Reichsbahn girl picked up the tin and read the label.

"Portuguese?"

"Yes."

"That'll be Danneburg."

"And for two?"

"In which direction?"

"North-west by north. Fifteen degrees."

"Berlin."

I nodded, and she handed me a third-class piece of cardboard for

Berlin. I added another can of sardines and then it was the fat man's turn.

The train came in in a cloud of steam, that means rain, I thought, the potato bags hurried through the white clouds, a tactical smoke screen against enemy observation was what it looked like, thronging past the barrier, the children between their legs, sleepless and exhausted, all their relatives in the station forecourt, fishboxes under their arms, every grease spot guarded and cherished, you can boil up two or three lots of soup from a fishmonger's apron, the necessary vegetables grow by themselves if you find them room in the kitchen garden underneath the subsidised tobacco plants.

34

SITTING next to me on the wooden bench under the life insurance advertisement and the smashed mirror, three bonnets, a hybrid head-gear, part Salvation Army and part beret, three bi-focals: reading below, seeing above, a look at the book, a look at life, three black overcoats, six gloves clasped together, an obvious case: a family bereavement.

"Excuse me, where is the dining-car?" I asked one of the ladies. She looked at me and shook her head. I see, deaf-mute. I wrote DINING-CAR? on a box of matches and held it up for her to see. She had a look at it, but only tapped her forehead with a black-gloved finger.

Bad, I thought, deaf-mute and can't read either. How on earth did they manage to make her understand that one of the family had bitten the dust? Perhaps by mime: one of them must have taken the part of Uncle Jacob, the other one playing Old Father Time with scythe and egg-timer, just as he appeared on Dom Galvão's *ex libris* in Angola. Sister Gertrude must have put on a man's hat and fallen to the ground, while Sister Helene pointed to the sand running out in the glass.

"Neuendorf!" bellowed someone on the other side of the polyvinyl corridor window, obviously a drill-sergeant who had missed his calling, but times are changing, don't lose heart, little station master, your chance will come again when you shall roar, " 'Shun!" The sisters were whispering among themselves. The deaf mute murmured in bass and the wart on her upper lip rose and fell. They took council together and then one of them said to me: "You aren't from around here, are you?"

"No," I said.

"That's it," they all said together.

"Are you on your way to Berlin, too?" the middle one asked, placing her hands together as if she were about to pray.

"Yes," I said.

"You're such a fine, sturdy fellow," said the third one, sitting by the window.

"You are," said the other two.

"All I really wanted to know was the way to the dining-car, fore or aft?"

"This train has a baggage-car, and that's all, sir," said the sister with the wart. "You can't have travelled by train for a long time."

"About five years," I calculated.

"That's it," they all said together again.

"Have you been to Berlin before?" asked the one with the wart.

"Yes," I said.

"That's fine," said the three, and the one sitting at the window unpacked two slices of bread from a napkin and offered them to me.

"But my dear lady," I said, "what have I done to earn that?"

"You are *going* to earn it," she said, "we would like you to regard this as something on account." I opened up the sandwich: fat and onions, more onions, then more fat.

"Wouldn't you prefer me to eat it outside?" I asked.

"No!" they all protested together. "Stay here!"

"He was a big white Vienna rabbit," said the pious one as I bit into the sandwich.

"A real Vienna with red eyes. His name was Zucki," she said looking at her sisters, "but we had to kill him, if was terrible. Ernst wasn't there to do it any more."

"Who wasn't?"

"Ernst," they all said, and got out their handkerchiefs.

"Forgive me," I said with my mouth full, swallowing and choking, "my condolences. If I had a wreath—you know, I feel this personally. Perhaps you could tell me where the funeral is taking place?"

"In Berlin, at the cemetery of the Jerusalem church."

"And where's the body, I mean Ernst, the deceased, the departed?"

"In the baggage-car," they all said together, and blew their noses.

"Now don't let us bother you any more," said the one at the window. "You must eat up. You must get up your strength."

"And what about the killing?" I asked.

"Poor Zucki," they sighed.

"You stun them first, don't you?" said the pious one. "We got a rolling pin, and Irene, we're all sisters as a matter of fact, Dietz is our name, well, Irene aimed the blow. We looked the other way for a moment, and when we turned back, Zucki was sitting by the grating over the drain and staring at us."

"Oh, that look!" said Irene.

"Elephants have the same look before dying," said Gerlind (the one with the wart). "Sven Hedin killed one thousand elephants without turning a hair."

"That was Schomburgk," interjected Dora, "and Schomburgk was excommunicated."

"Hannibal's elephants died on him, too, when he was trying to cross the Alps," I said.

"I see that you're an educated man," said Dora.

"My name is Bonifaz."

"That means Doer of good," sighed Irene. "In the state she was in Dora had missed the aorta, and we had to operate again."

"Was he dead after that?" I asked.

"Certainly," said Gerlind, "you've just been eating him."

35

AFTER Danneburg I must have gone to sleep and I don't know whether we crossed a border, the Dietz sisters merely laughed when I asked them and shook their heads. When I woke up I was lying face downwards across the black-clad sisters' laps, my head on Irene, my stomach on Gerlind, my feet on Dora. My arms were round Irene's waist, my nose stuck in the coarse fabric of her coat. Gerlind was resting her hands on me, and Dora was tickling my stockinged feet and saying: "We'll be there in ten minutes. Now up you get, young man."

They had let down their veils and sat there like friendly frogs looking through nets at the sun. For two pins I'd have rolled over on the three rabbit aunties' firm thighs and gone on sleeping, carrying the three poor souls off with me in my lewd dreams, but suddenly I felt cold, for Irene had dropped my head, stood up and opened the window to look out and make sure that the baggage-car was still on the train. I sat upright, lingering for a few moments in Gerlind's gigantic lap, and then tied my shoes, a bit wobbly and stumbling.

Before finally coming to a halt, the train stopped half a dozen times, we were thrown together, grasping nets, veils, brooches and buttons, and there was some cursing at the Reichsbahn, people saying that if *they* were engine drivers things would look very different, but as far as I was concerned I kept my mouth shut.

I helped Gerlind, Irene and Dora down the carriage steps, shouldered my knapsack and went on ahead to the baggage-car at the end of the platform.

"The bicycle?" asked the guard.

"I don't mind," I said, but the Dietz sisters, panting along behind me, insisted on their coffin.

"I hope it's got handles at least?" I asked. Gerlind nodded. The guard helped me to put the coffin on the platform, and then slid the van door to again, and no doubt slipped out by the other side.

"And now where?" I asked.

"To the Hermannplatz," said Irene.

"How do you think we're going to get the coffin onto the tram? In the rush hour of all times?"

The stationmaster came up, tapped the coffin with his signal stick and enquired: "Express delivery?"

"I think the gentleman has been on his way for some time," I said.

"All right then, hand baggage," said the stationmaster, "no concern of mine." He turned round and stumped away, his right leg a piece of wood, his green and white paddle clamped under his arm like a swagger stick.

"We shall find a way," said Dora prayerfully.

"Isn't anyone meeting you?" I asked.

"It was meant to be a surprise," said Gerlind.

I took my knapsack off again and stood it on the coffin.

"Have you all gone off your heads?" I said. "You can't just turn up with your dead uncle ..."

"Ernst is our cousin," Irene corrected me.

"Well, all right, your cousin, then ... you can't just sail into Berlin with a corpse. The people here have got enough worries of their own."

"It was his wish. His last wish," said Dora.

The sombre trio stood at the narrow end of the coffin, throwing their slanting shadows on the platform and waiting to see what I would do. What I should have liked to do most of all was simply to disappear, although I had no idea where. Where, where ...

"Our relations live at the Hermannplatz," announced Irene.

I looked around the platform, clambered over turnpikes, rubbish dumps and stacked bricks until I found what I needed. I took three straight lengths of gas piping and returned to the sisters who were standing with their handbags on their bellies, exactly as I had left them. I pressed a length of gas piping into the hand of each and explained how we were going to get the coffin moving as far as the ticket barrier for a start.

"We put the pipes under the coffin and roll it along, savvy?"

They wagged their heads. I raised the head of the coffin and Irene shoved her pipe underneath. I pushed the coffin forwards until the pipe was under the centre of gravity and Gerlind slid the second pipe underneath. I went on pushing, and by the time the first pipe was at the foot and the second was under the centre of gravity, Dora introduced the third pipe. We were making reasonably smooth progress. Each time a roller emerged at my feet one of the sisters picked it up and hurried down to the other end with it. They began to sweat a bit, bending down, drawing out the pipes, dragging them to the end and letting them clang down on the platform in front of cousin Ernst. We gave up our tickets at the barrier, and that brought us to the end of our cunning: a staircase fell away before us.

I could feel the stationmaster's eyes drilling in my back, and the Dietz sisters had thrown up their veils and were mopping the sweat from their brows. I unfastened my knapsack straps and tied them round the handles of the coffin. There were about thirty steps down to the booking hall and, if we held on tight and uncle Ernst didn't drag too hard, we could manage to slide him down to the bottom. I put the sisters onto the left-hand strap and wound the other around my forearm.

"Beloved Captain Bommalaria," I prayed, "we are all of us passing guests on this earth of ours. Help this corpse to make a respectable exit!"

Dora was also praying, but in somewhat different terms, I imagined.

I gave the coffin a slight prod over the edge with my foot to tip it downwards. The leather straps quivered. The Dietz sisters threw their bodies back like shot-putters, Gerlind had her handbag between her teeth and Irene was treading on her feet. We let the coffin down three steps, but it felt as if someone had been greasing them, the straps were cutting off my circulation and turning my hand blue, and the sisters' faces went tomato-colour under their embroidered brims. A couple of louts hung onto the banisters and grinned. Germany, oh my Germany, you'd think they might at least lend a hand, but they preferred to clutch themselves in their own trouser pockets, many's the one for hanging onto boyhood vigour even after the Easter Eggs have come his way seventy times already, and then it was like a landslide, in fact it was more like the descent of the fallen angels, for the sisters had let go of their cousin, for a moment he clung to me like damned souls to the avenging angel's hem, almost pulling me into the abyss with him, but his corpse wasn't so precious to me that I'd give up my life for it, so I flung off the straps and he hurtled downwards, head first, feet last, a good guest goes at the height of his welcome, and on the tiled floor of the booking hall the coffin split asunder. Gerlind snatched her handbag from her teeth, glanced at her sisters with a short shudder, and in a flash the trio was rattling down the steps in front of me, three fluttering black veils, three furies, self-flagellant, hopping, precise, as if descending a scale, mustn't miss a single step, mustn't fall, at last . . .

"Ernst!" I heard Irene shriek. "I hope you aren't hurt!"

"Oh, my God!" said Dora, kneeling beside her cousin, who was floundering in the padded interior. I picked up my knapsack and went down the steps. A short man in glasses lay among the posh cushions, stroking his hair back from his temples, and the sisters grew completely calm now that his eyes were on them, you could hear them clicking back into place as he said: "You really are a lot of complete idiots." He looked at me from his mouse-grey suit and said: "The pipes were a very bright idea." He drew a gold watch from his breast pocket, snapped open the cover with the aid of his thumbnail, and compared it with the big station clock. "Forty-five minutes late," he said. "The German railways started running in 1834, and in more than a century they still haven't learned to be on time."

"Don't get excited straight away, Ernst." said Irene.

"I'm not getting excited." He snapped down the lid of the watch. "I'm quite satisfied with establishing that I'm right."

He pulled a leg out from under the coffin lid, raised himself up with his hands on the lower part and stood up. I heard the wooden step of the stationmaster pushing his way through the crowd and shouting: "What's the meaning of this?"

"My name is Dietz," said the grey-clad cousin by way of introduction.

"I didn't ask for your name," said the stationmaster. "I want to see your ticket."

"We've got the baggage receipt," said Gerlind.

"I know that," said the stationmaster. "The receipt is made out for a corpse from Ratzenstedt via Schwabeldingen and Danneburg. Show me the corpse."

"Here I am!" said Herr Dietz.

"You won't take me in that easily," threatened the stationmaster, waving his paddle in front of Herr Dietz's nose. "You're avoiding paying the full fare, travelling as a corpse, indeed! We'd soon be in a fine state if everyone tried that on."

"Not everyone hits on a good idea like that," I said.

"I'm not discussing anything with you," the stationmaster bellowed at me. "As far as I'm concerned, you don't exist!"

"Well, if I don't exist . . ."

"Silence!" he shouted.

"I am naturally prepared to pay the difference between the fares," said Herr Dietz.

"The difference? The difference between a corpse and the ticket for a live adult? You're going to have to pay extra for a full ticket from Ratzenstedt to Berlin, with express supplement!"

"Excuse me," said Herr Dietz, "but what would be the cause for the forty-five minute delay? Who is paying for that?"

"Not the Reichsbahn's responsibility."

"I see," said Herr Dietz, taking off his glasses and polishing them on his broad lapels, "and let us assume that I was on urgent business, where the minutes counted?"

"In that case, you wouldn't have travelled as a corpse," said the stationmaster.

"That is my own affair," observed Herr Dietz and put his glasses on again.

"That's right," said a few people round us, "it's freedom we want!"

"Political demonstrations are not permitted on premises of the German Reichsbahn!" admonished the stationmaster. "You can now pay for a supplementary ticket and the matter will be closed. I shall turn a blind eye."

"Listen to him!" cried the onlookers.

"Instead of being glad the man has come to life again," said someone who had just arrived and had seen nothing, and whose view of the situation was consequently quickly taken up by the others.

"Doesn't happen every day," remarked a young man with prominent ears.

"If anyone chucks himself out of a train, they make a fine to-do," said someone else, "but when someone rises from the dead, all they can think of is fining him."

"It never used to be like this," said an old woman, backing him up.

"I'll call the police," warned the stationmaster.

"Go ahead, please! I should have thought we'd still be allowed to believe in God!"

"You go and look after your filthy platform and sweep up the potato peels, bigmouth!" shouted someone.

"No insolence!" said the stationmaster, but he was already being jostled aside, the people thrusting ahead and driving Herr Dietz and the three sisters in front of them towards the exit.

I swung my knapsack on my shoulder and looked at the shattered stationmaster. "I wouldn't lose any sleep over all this," I said to him. "When the lion's dead, the rabbits nibble his mane."

"Look, sir," said the stationmaster, "I'm human, too, but it's going too far—when it goes too far."

I pressed a can of sardines into his hand. "I put the pipes down by the ticket barrier," I said, "in case you're looking for them."

36

THE station forecourt was empty and almost dark by the time I got there. There was no sign of Ernst, Gerlind, Dora, Irene Dietz—a pity, I should have liked to know what happened next, why old pince-nez came to Berlin by coffin when he had the money for the full fare. Over and done with; I belched up the taste of Zucki and would have given half my life's span for a Schnapps, but the only life moving among the dry bones of the houses around the station was a couple of flitting whores in wooden-soled shoes, clop, clop, the best of life's pleasures, I tell you indeed, are tasted astride the back of a steed, gallop, gallop, little hussar, and there was I having to walk, down the narrow path between the ruins, the U-Bahn flashing away over my head, a glimmering caterpillar, the canal water stank as high as the railings, and a tug lay by the bank without lights. Ahead of me walked Kreti with a long pole, lighting the lamps for me. We made the same zigzag together, backwards and forwards across the broad street bearing away to the right, and at the Otto-Platz he said: "Are you following me?"

"Yes," I said.

We were standing in the blue shine of the gaslight. He was not more than twenty-five, but with three times that number of hairs on his head, and wore a short American army coat.

"What are you acting the sailor for?" he asked. "Is it a good line?"

"I *am* a sailor," I said.

"That's funny," he said leaning his long hook against the street lamp, "what are you doing ashore?"

I shrugged my shoulders as well as one can with a knapsack on.

Kreti's eyebrows were brushed smooth and his lips seemed over-red by this light.

"Do you dye your hair as well?" I asked.

"Go to hell," he said, spitting on the road, "you don't think I'm a real queer?"

"I just thought you might actually be a blond," I said.

"I am, too," he said, "but black's more in demand."

"Do you do it every night?" I asked.

"What?"

I pointed to the street lamp.

"Yes," he said, "you get paid for it, and it doesn't attract attention. Really, I'm a commercial artist, but what's commercial about being an artist nowadays?"

"Did you make that up?" I asked.

100

"No," he said, "my sister did."
"My name is Bonifaz," I said.
"Kreti, the pleasure's mine."

37

THE following morning the newspaper headlines ran:

"MIRACLE" ESCAPE OF HITLER'S BARBER
PICK UP THY COFFIN AND WALK!
THE UNLAMENTED "DEAD" COME BACK
DO WE WANT HIM HERE AGAIN?

Ernst Dietz, with his sisters around him, polished his glasses in all the pictures and smiled. No one remembered me.

38

To me a chair's a chair, and it's nothing to me how old it is. I don't care if it's Chippendale, Louis Quatorze or Biedermeier. I sit on it: that's what a chair is for.

When I smell soup, I don't ask for the cook's name. What do I care for Waldorf-Astoria, Solyanka, Hotel Paris? So I sit down on the nearest chair and eat my soup.

When I fall for a woman, the stars don't apply. I'm not bound to black, I'm not bound to blonde, I'm not bound to brunette. Oh, a breast and a thigh, and trust the Most High! So once I've eaten I reach across the table and help myself to a girl-friend.

39

PULLE was Kreti's sister. She was nearly sixteen. She looked out of the window in the mornings and laughed at us lying around in the courtyard playing games with the children since we had no jobs to go to. For lunch she boiled two litres of water, one old belt and a lot of marjoram and called it Wurstsuppe. In the evening she got into a blue dress with white spots and stood in the street door. Pulle was such a virgin that she even blushed at the thought of it.

The street that Kreti and his sister lived on led from the Jerusalem church to the Otto-Platz. There was a cigarette shop by the Jerusalem church and a dairy at the Otto-Platz. Between the two of them, on either side of the road, stood forty houses and eleven or twelve ruins. Three hundred men, four hundred and fifty children and two thousand women lived on this street. Any man willing to live here needed to be worth three.

The cigarette shop by the Jerusalem church belonged to Kläre Enke, known as The Rump.

The dairy at the Otto-Platz belonged to Yvonne Dreissig, known as The Gorge.

Kläre, a woman of thirty-five married to a pale-faced printer of forms, ration cards and school reports, sat behind a wooden crate covered with brown oil-cloth from six in the morning until seven in the evening. She had very long narrow fingers, yellow with nicotine; she had a haggard face and big T.B. eyes. Over the lunch hour she locked the door leading to her basement shop, pulled back the curtain in front of her kitchen-bedroom alcove and put the soup pan on the electric cooker. Then there would be a knock.

"Just soup, nothing else," she said as I came down the steps.

"Don't worry, Kläre," I said every time. I sat down on the little bed she slept in with the printer at night and watched her stirring he soup. She would leave it for a moment to go to her box and fetch out a packet of cigarettes, which she gave me. That was my day's ration. For that I stroked her bottom. Kläre Enke had a rump, all right.

I lit myself a cigarette, lay back on the bed and observed the photographs that Kläre had fastened to the wall with drawing-pins. They were all of the same young man in Luftwaffe uniform. He had small neurotic eyes and his head looked as if it was attached directly to his shoulders with no neck between.

"Never had any news?" I asked.

"No," said Kläre, serving the soup in a plate. She shook her shoes from her feet, sat down beside me on the bed and tucked her legs under her skirt. The man on the wall had been her fiancé.

"Harry was an airman," said Kläre Enke.

"I can see," I said.

"Harry was in the bombers," said Kläre Enke.

"Yes," I said, "he went in for the big stuff."

Kläre took the empty plate from my hand, stacked it on top of her own, and put them both down beside the cooker.

"Harry," she whispered.

Making room for her put me directly underneath the photos of the airman. Kläre Enke drew off her green silk waist-slip and dropped onto the bed beside me.

Regularly at about two o'clock, Kläre Enke, known as The Rump, would fall asleep. I waited for a little, stared at the ceiling, winked at the airman or tried to press my thumbnail between my front teeth. Then I got up, helped myself to some more soup from the pan, but not over-doing it, so that enough should be left for the hungry printer, and crept away. The door to the street only had a catch and it clicked into place with a little rattle from the panes of frosted glass where the putty had fallen out.

During the lunch hour I crossed the road from the Jerusalem church side and went down to the Otto-Platz, where Yvonne Dreissig, known as The Gorge, had her dairy. A distance of forty houses at a medium pace lasted one cigarette-long. In the past few days I had become rather careful not to be noticed by Pulle when I passed her front door. Rather than risk it, I almost hurt my neck with craning it up to stare over the top of the houses at the sky.

Yvonne Dreissig lived on the first floor above her shop. Long—short—long—short.

"Who's that?" shouted The Gorge.

"Your honey," I answered: in the doorway stood Yvonne, forty years of age, white skin, brown hair, her nose half a size too small.

"What weather," she said.

"This isn't weather, Yvonne, it's a meteorological metaphor for describing happiness," I said.

"Kiss me," she demanded. I kissed her.

"What was that like?" she enquired.

"After you the deluge," I replied.

For that I got a cottage-cheese sandwich and was permitted to sit on Yvonne's leather-covered sofa while she watched me.

"I'm still hungry," I said.

"But I'm not letting you take any away with you," said The Gorge as she spread me another slice of bread and butter with well-peppered cottage cheese.

"Just one," I pleaded, thinking of Kreti and Pulle.

"Promise me you're going to eat them all by yourself."

I promised.

"Tonight! In bed!"

"Yes."

"And thinking of me at the same time!"

"I'm always thinking of you."

"You and your greed," said Yvonne.

"Yvonne," I protested, "I love you."

She undid the hooks of her blouse. "You get me down with all your fancy talk." She was in a hurry, for her dairy had to be open again at three o'clock punctually. When she was quite naked she took her slip and blindfolded me with it. She led me, chewing away at the last piece of my cheese sandwich, into the middle of the room, placed my right hand on her body and asked: "Will you remember it?"

40

PULLE cut the cottage-cheese sandwich into three, as I seldom kept pace with my hunger on afternoons like these, and I usually gave in by the time I reached the staircase. Kreti never asked where the cheese came from. Pulle had a belief in kindness and charity: who'd want to disillusion her? We sat in the window, all three, relishing the clotted curds and counting the cracks in the wall. Kreti was waiting for his boy-friend to call, my eyelids were dropping, and Pulle crossed and re-crossed her overheated legs. Jacques cooed in the courtyard, Kreti pinched his trouser creases, murmured something about "piano lessons" and "evening classes", smoothed his hair with spit and vanished. I put my feet up on his empty chair and snored, Pulle couldn't bear it, ran down the stairs and stood in the front door. She could see the whole street from the Jerusalem church to the Otto-Platz. If she felt really bold she would prop her hands on the cornice above the basement flat, press her heels against the pavement and bounce up and down.

One Saturday I couldn't sleep for the heat. I went down the cool staircase, stopped in the open doorway, and looked at Pulle from the side. She had not heard me. She was leaning against the wall, her eyes shut, her mouth open a bit, her right foot propped on her left one. Down below, Wendelin Zygan, the builder's labourer, was telling his sons the tale of Hajji Halef Omar Ibn Hajji Abul Abbas Ibn Hajji Dawud al Ghossarah, who had smuggled himself into the sheikh's seraglio: "All of a sudden he sees all these girls sitting behind the straw matting and picking the bugs out of their hair. Rosi, get the nappies! Ludmilla needs changing. Hold on, says Hajji, all I need is to sock the chief eunuch one in the kisser and I can scoot back to my noble Effendi with the one in the pigtails he's so gone on. In the bucket, Rosi, not in the jug. For her eyes were like almonds and her silky eyelashes were as long as matchsticks. Her body was the colour of alabaster.

You've fair filled your pants, Ludmilla. Her toes were small and as if made of ivory."

I took Pulle's hand, folded my fingers between hers and went with her down the street towards the Jerusalem church. At the corner Pulle opened her eyes and asked: "What's his name?"

"Hajji Halef Omar Ibn Hajji Abul Abbas Ibn Hajji Dawud al Ghossarah."

I took her arm. Women and girls were standing in all the doorways. They were smoking or spitting cherry stones into the street. We could feel the cherry stones through the soles of our shoes. A cherry consignment had arrived in town. Pulle was my cherry stone princess. Pulle was my cherry blossom princess. The cherry stones rolling across the road sprouted into cherry trees. From the Jerusalem church, whose tower had come off in the war, there came a peal of bells. Out of the ruins emerged tradesmen who had had their heads cut off in the war, shoving out brown stands laden with bananas and grapefruit. Executed butchers stood in the entries to office buildings, offering us liver paste and ham. The all-plastic harness-maker put the snaffle on his dapple grey. Waiters in black dinner-jackets, two by two, served gateaux and coffee, propping trays on their crutches. They came and went beneath the white cherry trees, too busy to worry about tips. Children were standing on the burnt-out balconies with rusted, broken railings and threw balls in our path. They bounced around us, flew up, burst in the air, soap bubbles rising against the grey clouds and turning into stars.

We clambered over red-and-white-banded poles, bumped into rough brickwork corners, slithered over rubbish and rubble, clutched outside drainpipes, lay down on the rain-washed air-raid shelter bunk. The wool substitute smelt of old potatoes, Christmas and mice.

"Do I have to get completely undressed?" asked Pulle.

"Yes," I said.

She unbuttoned her dress from top to bottom. I took it off her. She lay half-way back, propped herself on her elbows and said: "Put your cigarette out."

Near the bunk I could feel a curved piece of flaking, rusty metal. I stubbed out my cigarette on it and kissed Pulle on the belly.

106

"Hajji Halef Omar," she said.
"Ibn Hajji Abul Abbas Ibn Hajji Dawud al Ghossarah."

41

THINGS I shall never forget:
Doorknobs, when you're going into other people's houses, Brasso-polished ones with period-moulded keyhole guards, wooden ones with clumsy tin caps and notches down the side, like big green paws shaking handies and leaving their print on you; the smooth summer hair of dogs following me; the aim of a gutting knife and the gills of the pale river perch; the wet jute of a rope ladder and the oil-soaked sailcloth we sewed our bosun into in the Sargasso Sea; the fibrous, ribby tobacco leaves on Dom Galvão's plantation in Angola; and Pulle's thin knees which fitted into my hand as if there was only one hand to suit them in the whole world: mine.

42

"LOVE'S nice," said Pulle, "but why does it mean such a lot of touching?"
"That's the best thing about it," I said, tapping the rusty metal with my knuckles.
"Have you had a lot of women before?" she asked.
"Not as many as Solomon."
"How many did he have?"
"Eighty thousand."

"Oh."

She shifted towards me and laid her head on my chest.

"You're an old show-off," she said, "but Manuela said the same: the first time's better with someone who's already done it a lot."

"That's right," I said.

"She's still going to school, you know. She's been left back in class twice running."

"What about you?"

"I'm going to work in an office in the winter."

"And Kreti?"

"You can take him with you."

"But I don't want to go."

Pulle propped herself up on me and brought her face close to mine.

"You're real sweet," she said, "but you aren't the sort, Bonifaz. Anyone can see in two minutes you wouldn't stay for long. Right?"

I didn't say anything, but I felt sure she wasn't quite right. Perhaps I really didn't want to run away any more.

"A white four-master with a broad red hull-line and a full wind astern," she said.

"Where did you get that from?"

"From you. You say it to yourself sometimes."

"Perhaps I do . . ."

I covered up Pulle with my jacket and we went to sleep. I dreamed I walked through the empty city with Pulle. All the house keys and flat keys of the whole city lay side by side in a line down the centre of the street, precisely at right-angles to the kerb, and they jingled as we walked over them. Somebody was coming towards us from the end of the street: a fellow made out of boards and slats, clattering and scraping, and his face was a piece of old sackcloth.

It was, however, a fireman who woke us up. We stared into his face, red from shaving, trying to understand the words it uttered with difficulty as the chinstrap was clamping his teeth together.

"Boiled eggs?" I thought I heard him say. "Thanks, two or three for me, please," I said, "with coffee and sugar and not too much milk.

Oh, barn dance, did you say? No, no thank you, no barn dance for me right now!"

He pushed the strap up off his chin so as to be heard better. "*Bomb squad!* You're lying over an unexploded bomb."

I sat upright and put my feet on the rusty metal shaped like a small torpedo.

"Careful! That's a landmine!" bellowed the fireman. "We've evacuated the whole block and you have to go and lie down on it."

Pulle got into her dress and buttoned it up. "Fancy that," she said.

Firemen in blue uniforms and highly varnished helmets were standing behind the barriers staring at Pulle. Civilian heads popped up between their shoulders, wagged and were thrust back.

"What are you doing here anyway?" I asked the fireman.

"I'm the superintendent. I'm going to de-fuse the bomb," he said, switching his chinstrap down again. "I hope you haven't interfered with the excavation. That's all I'm concerned with."

"No," I assured him. "I only stubbed out my cigarettes on the bomb."

"You can thank your lucky stars you aren't in heaven already," said the superintendent.

"But we are," said Pulle.

"That's no concern of mine," said the superintendent. "All I'm interested in is the bomb. Now scram!"

Pulle went first. It was still fairly cold and it chilled us even more, running the gauntlet of all the faces. I put my arm round Pulle, and the firemen laughed.

"Must've been a tight squeeze," said one of them.

"You do up your flies for a start," I said, and he actually felt for them.

From the Otto-Platz we went towards the Jerusalem church. Yvonne was just opening her shop and looking like three days in hell.

Kreti was still in bed asleep. He had his arm round a pillow and was dreaming restlessly.

"I'll make some coffee," said Pulle and put on the water.

I went to the window, looked into the empty courtyard and counted the chalked faces on the asphalt.

Kreti woke up and said: "A telegram came for you last evening. Your Uncle's died. You're to go to the funeral."

"Who from?"

"It says Emma at the bottom. From Tesch."

Pulle looked at me over the saucepan of water.

"Emma's my wife," I said.

"How did she know your address?" asked Kreti.

"I sent her a picture-postcard once," I said.

"I suppose you haven't cleaned your teeth yet, either of you?" asked Kreti.

"What for?" said Pulle.

"Pulle, my golden angel," sang Kreti, "we shall have to leave you now."

"I know," she said.

We all sat on the bed and drank corn coffee. Kreti balanced his cup on his right knee and was trying to drink from it without touching.

"Stop it, silly!" said Pulle. "I put on clean sheets."

"I hope you'll permit me to accompany you?" said Kreti.

"How are we going to pay for the tickets?"

"They'll be ready this afternoon," he said. "Two first-class to Osterode."

"First's too conspicuous," I said. "And what shall we do at the border? I haven't got an identity card."

"Look, I can't make an identity card as well," said Kreti.

"Two cans of sardines in oil."

"We could go and ask Herr Huth, he always seems to be hungry," said Pulle.

"Herr Huth's at least seventy-two," said Kreti.

"Nobody'd notice," giggled Pulle, looking at me. "Bonifaz has got grey hairs already."

"You can send the identity card back from Osterode. All we have to do is put a different picture in. You go to the photographer's and I'll talk to Herr Huth."

110

We stacked the cups, and Pulle put them in the sink.

"A passport photo," I said to the photographer at the Jerusalem church.

"A passport photo? What are you going to do with *one?* The police keep one of them."

"Well, then, two."

The photographer wrote down my address and said: "You can come and collect the prints in a fortnight."

"Is that when you take my picture?"

"No, I'm going to do that now."

"I see," I said, "but I need the photos in half an hour."

"That's impossible!"

"Listen," I said, "supposing I order another ten portraits besides the passport photographs, and you send me them in two weeks or a month, if you like, would the passport photos be ready in half an hour?"

"That's another matter," he said.

He took me into his studio and asked me if I had any particular preferences as to the poses.

"In all positions," I requested.

I lay on a polar bear skin, put my arm round an elephant, crammed a green shooting hat on my head, pulled on a front half of evening dress, pressed a laurel wreath around my brow, held a cigarette between my lips, had a picture taken of the back of my head, clasped a dagger between my teeth, tried on the photographer's own glasses, and last of all faced the shutter just as I really was.

"If you will permit me to use some of the prints for publicity," said the photographer, "I can let you have the passport photos free of charge."

I permitted him. Twenty minutes later they were ready and I could easily have been taken for seventy-two in them, if not more. I shook the photographer's hand, promised to collect the other prints in a fortnight, and closed the door myself.

When I entered Kläre Enke's cigarette shop she stood up and asked: "What can I do for you?"

"A packet of Texas," I said.

Kläre reached into the box and placed the packet in front of me.

"You can have them with my love," she said.

I put the cigarettes in my pocket and went up the steps again to street level. I felt like a half-empty balloon, like a tired old umbrella with the ribs sticking through. I tottered back to Kreti, who was sitting at the table, drawing railway tickets with a fine-pointed pen on brown cardboard.

"We'd better put our own punch-holes in. We can't afford to take any risks. We'll get on to the train with platform tickets."

With a small screwdriver I prised up the flanges of the rivets through the seventy-two-year-old Herr Huth's passport photograph, one above his right temple and the other at his left shoulder. I did not want to hurt Herr Huth, but he had, after all, sold himself for two cans of sardines and ought to be able to stand a scratch or two. I stabbed my own photograph with a pen-knife, pressed it on to the dotted rectangle and hammered the rivets down again. Kreti snipped a few pieces out of an old rubber bottling ring, dabbed them on an ink pad and laid their mark across my passport features, with the result that the police would not only take me to be seventy-two but also assume me to be in an advanced stage of leprosy.

Pulle came back, cut us each a slice of bread, ran her duster over our shoes and stood beside the door as if we were in a hotel. Had she put out her hand we would have given her a tip. But she went out with us, right up to the Jerusalem church.

"Have you at least said goodbye to Jackie?" she asked Kreti.

"Yes," he said.

"And you'll send back the identity card?" she asked me.

"Yes," I said.

She hugged Kreti.

"I'm not coming to the station."

"Why not?" asked Kreti, "We're quite grown up."

"I'm seventy-two," I said to Pulle.

She kissed me, there in the street by the Jerusalem church, where you can change from the twenty-two bus to number eight, and said: "Good luck, Herr Huth, I love you."

43

CHANGING trains. Waiting. The coin drops. The arm swings round and dips into the row of records, seizes, grips, raises, turns, retreats, swings, releases.

A man in a checked shirt is sitting in front of the juke-box, nodding. He jerks his foot and claps, but we don't know why. Suddenly: a voice. A wail, then a woman who might be chanting a lullaby to an ox. The checked man jerks and claps. He calls the waiter and gets change.

The coin drops. We hear a humming that swells and rises like a plane taking off, lasts for some moments and then breaks off with the starting operation again and we seem to be in a vacuum, aware only of a faint gonging sound.

"Bass guitar," says the man in front of the juke box.

All we can see are the legs of the man in the checked shirt and his blue trousers and yellow shoes rising and falling to the burbles and falsettos of the voice. He drops a butt on the floor and stamps it out to the beat: reveille, last post, signals for deserters and lost dogs. Funfare for brass, swings on the half-tones; your stomach turns, monotony on a Ferris wheel, come to my bower on an empty stomach. Don't leave me alone tonight. We're gliding over Lake Constance, over Switzerland, Venice, the campanile, the New York skyline, the Reeperbahn, child's play, a piece of cake. All the time unendingly with the same throaty tone: Oh yes. *I can't give you anything but love, baby.* Oh yes. *When the saints come marching in.* Oh yes. *Jenny Towler ward gefunden.* Oh yes. The fleshy ferns meet over our heads. Hold your hand in the water and the crocodiles won't bite. Don't be scared. Get him between the shoulder-blades. Can you feel the little key there? Wind him up and he'll go on swimming. I can bite no more.

I'm watching his feet. His shoes leave the ground. To the beat. One, Two. One, Two. I clutch the edge of the table. I order myself to keep still. Unless I take my eyes off his legs, I can't do it. Now the chair falls over behind me. I reel to my feet, my elbows turned outwards, my shoulders hunched forwards, my feet jiggle, I pull them inwards, I lose control over them. Dancing, I shove my way through the people in the waiting room. The waiter gives me a wide berth. Suddenly the music stops. The man at the juke-box has had enough. He stands up. I run up to him and point to the juke-box. For a moment we face each other. My eyes are staring. The man pulls a coin out of his pocket, drops it into the juke-box and presses on a key. Then he goes away.

I take the chair he has left. The wailing comes close. Cats on the roof, hurricane noises off-stage, rescue in the fog, tear the joint to pieces, a car the size of an express, fast as a rocket, dazzling as a mosquito, girls . . . my shoulders are still jerking, then I slow down, my feet feel heavier, sweat comes off my hands onto my pale trousers, my lower lip is sticking out, my stomach is knotted up.

I get up. I collide with the table, a glass falls over, beer pours onto the planking. I run into the door. I am outside in the air as the juke-box gives its last shriek. I lean against the wall. The wail is still in my ear. I spit and choke and then bring everything up, wipe my mouth on my jacket sleeve and start walking. I stumble over stones and laths. Splinters and nails tear my trouser leg. I keep going, on and on, until Kreti catches up with me and takes my arm and says: "Pull yourself together. We're on our way to a funeral."

44

OSTERODE, Osterode, give my love to Osterode, greeted us with its red brick station, yellow mail truck and blue stationmaster. There were poplars round the station that would have met with Napoleon's approval, tireless nurseryman that he was.

Kreti and I stalked across the cobblestoned platform, gave up our phoney tickets very casually, and walked to Aunt Pasemann.

"Good morning," we said with one voice.

"Bonifaz!" she exclaimed, "you've come a day too soon!"

"Really? Isn't Uncle Otto properly dead yet?"

"But of course," she chanted. "But of course."

"My very sincere condolences," Kreti assured her.

"Herr Greifenhagen," I said, to introduce him. "How did it happen?"

"He ran into a motor-cycle. Is Emma coming?"

"God knows," I said.

"You've put on weight," said Aunt Elke.

"I hope it suits me," I replied, "we haven't seen one another for twenty-one years."

"I trust that you will at least receive the insurance money?" enquired Kreti sympathetically.

"The League of African War Veterans and the Queen Luise Association have promised to help," said Aunt Elke, "but please come inside."

We sat at the kitchen table and drank warm milk. Aunt Elke spread slices of bread and butter for us, dashed out to the henhouse but was back again in a moment, changed and wearing a black dress, doing up the bodice with twinkling fingers.

"You know, I told him to be careful, I said to him, 'Look out when you go down to the Green Man, and don't get tight,' but then he went and ran up a bill for seventeen marks, and now I've got to pay it."

"Did he die at once?" I asked.

"Immediately," said Aunt Elke, "the man on the moped said that he suddenly ran into something solid and he flew out of the saddle and travelled a long way through the air."

"How far would that have been?" I asked.

"At least twenty yards, he said, but if you'd seen Uncle Otto afterwards you might easily have said it was thirty or forty."

"Where is he now?"

"Lying in the chapel. We put him into his khaki uniform and his sun helmet and he's taking his old shotgun to the grave with him as well. The German community at Windhoek cabled Bulling's for a wreath with a silk ribbon and an inscription in Gothic letters—it says, 'To the memory of Kaffir-Killer Otto Pasemann'."

"I think that's very considerate of them," said Kreti.

"I hope they're going to pay for it too," remarked Aunt Elke. "Until lunchtime, you can wander around the village, as far as I'm concerned."

The Osteroders kept indoors, behind their bottle-glass window panes, spying between the sunflowers, and even the children ran away from us: people don't change their skin so easily. The farmers and tenants still arranged their houses as if the spring tide was about to break, kennels in front of the door with savage yelpers inside to set up a din at night, howling at the moon or at glow-worms, it doesn't matter which as long as there's plenty of noise, enough to give the tellers of fairy-tales fresh material so they can go on with Yorinda, Yoringle and Henry-True-in-Grief. Sheep and ducks shat upon the road, oblivious of tourists and hikers. In front of the house each man grows his private coppice of lilac and elder but with branches and twigs all cut short on the neighbour's side, that'll teach him who owns what, but the neighbour is just the same, lying in wait inside the window with his shotgun and sandwiches, knocking off the chicks as they pop through the rabbit wire into his onion rows. They are all down at the Green Man in the evening, not one table acknowledging another, solitary in the fog of Bruns's cigar smoke, mug handle in hand, and when it's lifted one of them might just go so far as to suck his moustache between his teeth and remark "Yeah".

At the post office we bought a stamp, I put Herr Huth's identity card in an envelope and addressed it to Pulle. We enclosed a dove's feather, shoved the letter through the slit and got the bewildered clerk to book an urgent overseas call, personal, to Mr. Modjokertensis in Surabaya, Java, who a million years ago had bequeathed his lower jaw to the palaeontologists.

"You'll have to wait a few minutes," he said, slamming the local directories together and, in spite of the open window, taking off his jacket, for Asia was dawning within him, setting his heart pounding as he drew aside the curtains to a thousand and one harems, laid his inky middle finger on Yessufa's white breast and dialled the local exchange, asking for Java and fanning his brow with his meagre telephone book while we were already running down the street, digging each other in the ribs, dancing on our way back to Aunt Pasemann's.

45

A BLUE and white checked cloth lay on the table; silver cutlery with the monogram O.P. beside the plates, a basket full of fresh black bread, crisp and aromatic, porky dill soup poured from Aunt Elke's ladle, dumplings gently bobbed to their stations, and a transparent bubble-flecked tide of fat advanced up the side of the plates, hovering for a moment at the floral band until scooped away with the spoon and lifted out or stirred back into the greenish-white broth.

Baked sauerkraut lay beside notched crackling you could squeeze up with your fork, golden onions plopped onto floury white potatoes, there were sips of beer to go with it, and afterwards mutton chops, firm on the bone where one's knife crunched into the marrow with a pale little thread of blood gushing into the glazed, stringless beans.

A leg of chicken jutted from the top of a mountain of peas, the brown crispy skin split with the first slice, the grey meat fell apart, in the yard outside the cock crowed, and we spat our plum stones into the empty plates.

The flypaper in Aunt Elke's white attic room swung its starving guests on a line south-east-north-west. Kreti lay beside me on the double bed, snoring, the roots of his hair showing fair. I reached with my toes for the counterpane and sheet, tucked them in, stretched, and watched the flypaper oscillating south-east-north-west. A bluebottle put a foot on it, got stuck, dragged the paper off its arc, spinning with its aerial prison like a merry-go-round until it got itself unstuck and crashed against the window. What did bluebottle-freedom mean to me? I went to sleep.

Next morning, *adagio con brio*, I sucked the autumn air into my bronchia at the open window and beat time to the music the Ohio boys were making beneath the Wesphalian lime. They worked out two blues, by which time their lips were swollen and they were thirsty.

"Blackamoor cakes and turks-head salad for breakfast," called Aunt Elke, from the kitchen. The Negroes laughed. They hadn't understood and thought the whole thing was a joke anyway. Having left Frankfurt at four a.m., they had been blowing on the journey to keep in form and were as a matter of fact rather tired by now.

"Bonifaz! Bonifa—haz," shouted my aunt. "Come down!"

I looked out of the window. Aunt Elke was standing in the front garden.

"Being on show always makes me sweat so," I shouted back.

"No excuses," she chanted from the garden, "you're just trying to get out of it."

By the time I appeared downstairs, everyone had formed up. At the head was my aunt in her black dress pulled tightly over her bosom and hips. Next to her were Aunt Emily and Uncle Gerhard, who owned a local motor repair shop. I looked round for Kreti, but he was presumably still asleep.

The church approached gravely. The men dropped their hats, the women their hymn books.

"I haven't had a bite to eat yet, Frau Pasemann," said the pastor.

Uncle Gerhard drew himself up. "I thought we were going to bury him before breakfast?"

The pastor displayed indignation. "What an idea! To appear before one's Maker on an empty stomach?"

So we went back into the dining-room where the breakfast had been prepared, only that Aunt Elke had not imagined that she was going to entertain the mourners at luncheon as well.

The pastor and I were quite the most diligent guests. We despised neither the underdone roast nor the hard-boiled eggs, neither the sausage nor the ham, and we applied ourselves to the brandy in agreeable quantities.

"Was there now, in fact, a will, Frau Pasemann?" asked the pastor.

Aunt Elke shook her head.

"But wasn't it the intention of the deceased to remember our little parish?"

"No, no, pastor, you must have mixed that up with somebody else."

"Indeed, I must have erred," said the pastor reaching for the plate of sliced sausage.

I was surprised, for I had reckoned on money.

"I wonder whether the dark-skinned gentlemen couldn't manage to perform something rather more suitable?" asked the pastor and poured himself out his fourteenth brandy.

"They'll get round to it," I said.

Eventually Kreti appeared, half blond, half black, like a mourning band around his head. He didn't spend much time on formalities, just said "Blessed be Jesus Christ" when he saw the pastor and poured out a cup of coffee.

The Negroes had to sit in the kitchen, but did not seem to mind it themselves any more than the others minded the fact that the Negroes had to sit in the kitchen.

Uncle Gerhard, the owner of the motor repair shop, said: "This evening Dr. Hilpert is coming to read the will!"

Aunt Elke's hands trembled. "The will? What will?"

"Otto made a will a fortnight ago, I know that for a fact," said Uncle Gerhard, counting off the links on his watch chain.

The pastor smiled and poured himself out a final Schnapps. "Ah, well then, our own little parish will not go empty away," he prophesied.

46

It was noon when we finally formed up, the soldiers in front with their flashing helmets and trumpets, then the pastor and Aunt Elke holding each other up, followed by the relatives with their visages as if hewn out of plaster, and last of all Kreti and myself and a few village oafs.

At the chapel four mourners fetched the coffin from the vestibule, placed it on a cart and, with solemn mien, tugged and pushed Uncle Pasemann along the gravel path. I noticed the pastor reaching under his cape for a half-bottle which he put to his lips and took a swig from.

The wind drove the brass band's music before us, set the hedges rustling and the mourners' coats flapping, and the tapes on the coffin were lifted into the air: black, white and red, Uncle Otto's favourite colours. But burying is a business with inexhaustible custom, and who's to foretell the idols of a year from now? White sand had been strewn round the hole Uncle Otto was going into, and across the gap the black-clad undertaker's men laid some hard-worn, crumbling boards, to be pulled away when they let the coffin down on ropes.

The band took up position at the head of the deceased, their faces dark and grave.

The tear-moist pastor released himself from Aunt Elke's arms and whispered: "My dearly beloved fellow mourners." But he did not sustain this gentle note and instead his sentences rocketed full blast to a period, reverberating against the weeds of the aunts and the top hats of the uncles. He said: "Otto Pasemann was a *human being*," and any-one standing in the open within a radius of five kilometres heard the words "human being!" bellowed from the cemetery at Osterode.

"Gut-merchant!" yelled the pastor. Quite so, Uncle Otto had been a gut merchant.

As he couldn't get any further, we all cast sand and flowers on the coffin, some sand and some flowers, whatever was closest at hand, and the pastor threw his notes into the grave saying: "Thou departed soul, there, read it for yourself!"

Yes, sir, that's my baby, played the soldiers, and the wind blew the music back in our faces, and Aunt Elke would gladly have shaken us all off immediately we halted in front of her bereaved gut-merchant's cottage, but the pastor, who during the walk had threatened to turn himself into a caterpillar, die and rise again as a butterfly, staggered through the door and shouted back from the table:

120

"Dearly beloved black-skinned brothers, come ye and regale your-selves with our rotten Schnappses, ye sweet and artful North American moths! I want to kiss you all!"

47

DR. HILPERT, Osterode's lawyer, nursed his popularity in the district by still driving to court in his landau, whip in one hand, reins in the other, and his right elbow clasping a pigskin briefcase to his hip. He sat next to the pastor at the end of the table, and rubbed his cheeks so that his duelling scars glowed, out of embarrassment at having to break the news to the relatives. "Frau Elke Pasemann," he said, "is sole heir and beneficiary."

"Aha!" cried Uncle Gerhard, the deceased's brother. "At least we now know why you married him."

"But all that happened thirty years ago!" sobbed Aunt Elke.

"Exactly," shouted Uncle Gerhard. "And for thirty years you've been waiting for him to die. All you've done for thirty years is wait for him to die. But that's not the end of the story. You can count on that, you hypocritical widow, you!"

"To Gerhard Pasemann," Dr. Hilpert recommenced, "my only brother, I bequeath the entire collection of mementoes of my military career in German South-West Africa . . ."

"You know where you can put that!" laughed Uncle Gerhard.

" . . . to wit: one khaki uniform with zip fastener . . ."

"Such a good pair of trousers," sighed Aunt Elke.

" . . . two pairs of tropical boots with dropped arch supports, Sala-mander brand, one sun helmet . . ."

"We buried him in that," laughed the pastor.

"I demand an exhumation!" bellowed Uncle Gerhard. "I won't be cheated! I insist on the helmet!"

"Perhaps the widow will consent to purchasing a new helmet for you."

"And what about the church?" asked the pastor and spilled his beer by trying to drink from the glass without holding it.

"To the parish of St. John I bequeath the small black idol which is kept in the linen chest underneath the kitchen towels."

"Sacrilege!" howled the pastor. "Blasphemy!"

"I like your uncle's sense of humour," said Kreti to me, laughing and pushing a glass of Schnapps towards me.

"To my nephew, the seaman Bonifaz, I bequeath all my real estate lying between latitude seven degrees four minutes seventeen seconds east and fifty-two degrees eight minutes nineteen seconds north, in perpetuity."

"Aha!" cried Uncle Gerhard again.

"What does 'aha' mean?" I asked back, half rising from my chair.

"Aha," said Uncle Gerhard, "the cap fits."

The soldiers were looking from face to face, Aunt Elke carried the tureen into the kitchen and Aunt Emily said: "Stop it, Gerhard! That's what you get for not licking his boots. Ingratitude is the way of the world."

"So we're landowners," said Kreti to me.

"Well, well," was all I replied. Aunt Elke came round the table and sat down beside me. Since becoming sole beneficiary she looked twenty years younger.

"Bonifaz," she said.

"Yes?" I asked and looked at her. But she blushed right back to the ears and dropped her eyes.

"Tell me something, auntie," I began, "how was it you got the Negroes here?"

She raised her eyes again and was grateful for the distraction. "Well, you see," she said, blowing her nose on a black handkerchief, "it was quite easy, really. As soon as Otto was dead I sent a telegram straight off to Frankfurt, to his old mate from Africa, the one who afterwards went to America. Now, you see, he's working in Frankfurt as one of the occupiers."

"And he sent the soldiers over?"

"Yes. He meant to come himself, but he thought it would be better if he came a fortnight later, because . . ."

"Because?"

"Oh dear, Bonifaz," gasped Aunt Elke, reaching underneath her for her handkerchief again, "you do properly embarrass one."

She straightened the black dress on her knees, cleared her throat with a sudden explosion so that I jumped, and said: "Come along with me."

She took me into the bedroom. Uncle Gerhard boomed after us: "The rats are quitting the sinking ship."

Aunt Elke switched on the light and sank into the red ticking cover of Uncle Otto's feather bed. She pulled the peasant boots from her feet, opened the big wardrobe, took out a pair of lightweight brown deerskin shoes with heels and laced them up on her big round foot-bones.

"Well?" she asked.

"Nice," I said.

"So," she said, "you see what I'm going to do?"

"Yes," I replied, "get married."

"To the Frankfurt American. He's coming here in a fortnight, we'll stay on for a couple of weeks, and then we'll go across the big pond."

I trod on the bedside rug in some embarrassment. Aunt Elke went back to the wardrobe and pulled the doors wide open.

"I've been shopping," she said and pointed to an array of dresses and coats. "I've turned everything into material: hen's eggs, pig's guts, goat's cheese. Now I'm set up."

"How long have you known that he was going to marry you?" I asked, closing the wardrobe doors.

"For twenty years. He came on a visit once and that's when we agreed. He wanted to go to America and make a life for himself. Then there was the war. Now he's got a little canning factory in the Middle West. Boneless chickens in tins, you know."

"I see."

"But that isn't the reason. You need to get out and see something of the world, too. I've spent my whole life in Osterode. At least Otto had been to Africa, but the likes of us . . . anyhow, now you know and, if I suddenly go away, you needn't be afraid I've thrown myself into the river. By then I shall be far away in Texas or Kentucky or whatever it's called, riding over the prairie with my Billy."

"And what would you have done if Uncle Otto hadn't died?"

"I would have thought of something," she said as she took off her deerskin shoes. "Don't you imagine it's any such marvellous good fortune being married to a gut-merchant for thirty years. He'd have popped off soon enough, but as it was the Lord in his lovingkindness placed a moped in his path."

"If that's the way it is," I said, "won't you give me your address? Perhaps I'll be going to America some day and then we could talk the whole thing over at our leisure."

"The matter is closed," said Aunt Elke, folding her face up.

"I shall go and see my estate tomorrow," I said.

"The best of luck," said Aunt Elke, laying the key on top of the wardrobe.

48

THE morning sun was shining through the heart-shaped hole in the door. I rubbed the sleep out of my eyes. I must have got myself pissed last night, I told myself. My uncle had died. We had buried him and then we had all got drunk.

Kreti's face blocked out the sun and said: "Seven degrees four minutes seventeen seconds east, fifty-two degrees eight minutes nineteen seconds north."

"What's that drivel?" I asked.

"Your uncle was run over by a moped, and in his will he's bequeathed you a piece of land. Whereupon you get drunk. You're now sitting on your aunt's privy. Approximately six degrees three minutes forty-five seconds east."

"It's a long haul we've got in front of us," I said.

"I've been up already and got hold of a surveyor," announced Kreti, his face disappearing, and being replaced by a long and bespectacled one that in turn opened its mouth.

"I am Overbeck, chartered surveyor. I am manager of and acting for the Untraceable Lands Survey Association. Would you oblige me by handing me the will of your late uncle so that I can verify the topographical particulars?"

"How long's that going to take?"

"Two years."

"Thanks for letting me know," I said, and handed him a sheet of paper.

"Look here," stormed the surveyor, "this is a piece of old newspaper, not a will! Unmistakable shit-house paper."

I pushed the wooden door open and stepped out beside the two of them.

"How long," I enquired of the surveyor, arranging my eyebrows at an angle of forty-five degrees, "did it take you to distinguish a piece of bumph from a will?"

As the surveyor did not reply I went on: "Ten seconds. So how long would you need in order to verify the topographical particulars in my uncle's will?"

The surveyor adjusted his glasses and said: "We could deal with it on our way."

I winked to Kreti, and we set out towards the north-east. The pastor was lying in front of the house, arm in arm with one of the Negroes. The lower branches of the lime tree were festooned with tubas, trombones, trumpets and horns. Cold roast beef and potato salad was standing on the front doorstep.

"Sodom and Gomorrah," said the surveyor.

We left the village behind and reached a large meadow which the surveyor considered suitable for taking his first bearings.

"You haven't any rough idea what it is that your uncle has left you?" he asked.

"No," I replied.

He unfastened the tripod from his back, spiked it into the meadow and adjusted it with the help of a water-level and a plumb-line. He screwed on the theodolite and looked through it.

"What can you see?" I asked.

"Nothing," answered the surveyor.

"Naughty uncle," commented Kreti.

Horned cattle were standing in groups in the oak-grown hollows or lying on folded legs, belching up grass.

About noon the surveyor unpacked a loaf and some sausage from his rucksack and set to. Kreti and I watched him.

"What would you say, Herr Overbeck," I asked, "to sparing us a piece of bread?"

"Haven't you got supplies for the journey?" he asked, astonished. "How do you expect to survive the return trip?"

"We don't know," I said. "Perhaps we're inheriting a house with a full pantry and smoked hams and chickens in the yard. We would repay your kindness, Herr Overbeck."

"Can I really count on that?" asked Herr Overbeck. "Times are bad. Why should people be any better? The Untraceable Lands Survey Association has had unfortunate experiences with legacies."

The surveyor unscrewed the cap of a bottle and held it to his lips. My tongue went dry. Kreti looked the other way.

"A tenth of the legacy, Herr Overbeck," I offered.

"A third," demanded the surveyor. I shook hands on it.

Herr Overbeck took a pen, ink, a rubber stamp and an ink pad out of the pocket of his rucksack, and drew up a short contract.

The Undersigned hereby undertakes
to make over surrender and disburse
One third of his entire legacy
to the Chartered Surveyor Overbeck
as and how and in such manner

I put my signature to it and we both received a slice of bread and a mouthful of corn coffee from Herr Overbeck.

That evening I assigned a further third to the surveyor.

By nightfall the manager of the Untraceable Lands Survey Association had become owner of the entire estate, with the sole proviso that I might be permitted to reside on it for the next fortnight.

Next morning—none of us had slept more than a couple of hours—the surveyor turned his spectacles to the sun and said without further explanation: "we are not far off."

He set up his tripod and fixed his theodolite more quickly than the day before and forced me to adjust the water-level and Kreti to hang the plumb-line. He peered through the eyepiece for a long time.

I could smell the river, thought pleasurably about an early swim, and had almost forgotten the legacy. Kreti was crouching by one of the tripod legs and was swearing at my uncle, my aunt, the surveyor and me. The surveyor's glasses were steamed over with excitement. With the tail of my shirt I wiped the perspiration from his forehead and glasses.

"We shall have to go two hundred yards upstream," said the surveyor.

"Have you got anything left to eat?" I asked.

"How can you think of food at a moment like this?" he said, shouldering the tripod and turning northwards.

"Easily," I said. "What's the hurry?"

"The impatience of a discoverer," panted the surveyor.

We approached the waterlogged banks. In the river pike were snapping at perch, perch were snapping at flies, and flies were settling on the backs of lizards and riding away. Kreti and I took off our shoes, rolled up our trouser legs and paddled in the lukewarm, brackish water. The surveyor set up his tripod and peered through the theodolite.

We could hear him shouting. We dragged our feet out of the mud, beat the mosquitoes off our calves and made our way up the little mound on which he was standing. When we had rejoined him, I felt the hairs on my legs prickling as the swampy water dried.

"Solved it?" I asked, to show a bit of interest.

"I'm not absolutely certain yet," said the surveyor.

He looked through a few more times, jotted down some figures, checked them against a table in *The Surveyor's Manual*, clapped his hand to his head and then from his head to his chest, went white and sank to the ground with blank, uncomprehending eyes.

"He's got it," remarked Kreti. "He's got it. We're idiots! Why the hell didn't we hold out a little longer without refreshments? Now he's got it."

"What's he got?" I asked.

"Why . . . the golden treasure your uncle brought back from Africa . . . diamonds big enough to cram up your nose. Hell's bells! Now it's all his!"

This shattered me. Only the surveyor seemed unaffected, lying there without moving.

"He's fainted," I said.

"Sure. For joy," said Kreti. "I would have, too."

"We'd better splash water on his face."

"What for?"

"Perhaps he's had a heart attack. If we don't put something cool on his nose, he might pop off."

"So what?" asked Kreti and tried to look mean.

I shook my head, and took off the surveyor's hat. "Stay with him," I said and went to fetch some water in it.

I dipped my fingers, and carefully cast five drops into his face. However, Herr Overbeck did not move.

"A tough customer," said Kreti.

Finally I tipped the hat up and the water poured into the surveyor's nose and ears. His face twitched, he stood up and spat. He scraped his maps and papers together, unscrewed the theodolite, snapped the tripod legs together, wound the string round the plumb weight and was about to go without saying a word. That, however, was not part of our contract.

"Excuse me," I said, "you gave me your assurance that I could reside for the next fourteen days on your estate. You told me yourself that the Untraceable Lands Survey Association always gives a fair deal. You can't just back out as if . . ."

"Come with me," said the surveyor. "I'll show it to you."

Herr Overbeck marched ahead of us in the direction of the river. Without hesitating, he led us straight out onto a spit of the bank that projected two or three yards into the water. We stood beside him.

"Here it is," said the surveyor.

With his right hand he pointed over the water, where the perch were still eating the flies and the pike were still eating the perch. "One hundred square yards—all yours!" And with that the chartered surveyor Overbeck took the three contracts out of the side pocket of his rucksack, each one relating to a third of my legacy, tore them up and dropped the pieces into the water.

"The Untraceable Lands Survey Association regards its invesitgations in this case as having been completed. The costs will be charged to the executors. Gentlemen, allow me to congratulate you on your piece of water. The very best of luck."

Pale and offended, the chartered surveyor Overbeck stalked into the woods while we stood staring at one hundred square yards of water which were now my property.

49

THERE wasn't much wind—force three or four—and quite frankly, the river got smaller and smaller as the afternoon wore on. We could have drained it into an empty can. All you would have needed was to tilt the river bed. But we preferred lying in the sun, leaving the flies to fly and the frogs to hop.

"Fishing," said Kreti drowsily once or twice.

"Hm," I murmured, turning over on the other side.

"Pike-perch *meunière*," said Kreti, "or a couple of pounds of trout *bleue*, onions, parsley, capers, butter *meunière*, new potatoes, but not too new, and not too pale, leave the fish steaming for not more than ten minutes, curled nicely round with the tail in its mouth, drain on a white napkin, a slice of lemon and then ever so gently lift the first pinkish layer off the bones."

"Yes," I said, "but there are supposed to be people who throw away carp's blood . . ."

"Never!" grunted Kreti. "Stir it with vinegar and add to the sauce after half an hour. That's the Polish way."

"You've forgotten the raisins," I reminded him.

"That's right," he said, "you must have raisins . . ."

"Cuckoo-flower, bay and dill would not a hungry gnat's gut fill."

"Eh?"

"Just that." I went on chewing tansy and coltsfoot. Across on the opposite bank the curtains were coming down on the Indian summer, but from behind the woods came a pop-popping sound and round the bend of the stream shot—or rather, sneaked—Dr. Richard Hilpert, lawyer and notary, of Twenty-Two, Thirtieth of January Street, Osterode, rigged out in white, his dazzling cap at a saucy angle, red hair on his chest and arms, a mission African's idea of hell's demons to the T; an air of the hunter about him, not really butterflies, definitely safari-style. As I could see, he was accompanied by a girl resting her hands on top of the out-sized launch's windshield, making it easier to kid herself it was Palma de Mallorca or Hawaii.

"Here comes Dr. Hilpert," I said to Kreti.

"An empty belly has no ears," he replied.

"He's got a woman with him."

"Women and horses want beating," he said raising himself on his elbows, "that's a fact."

We watched the boat. Dr. Hilpert had caught sight of us and waved as if to shake his hand right off. He said something to the girl. She too began flinging her arms about in the air. Dr. Hilpert steered not at all unskilfully to the sheltered side of the breakwater, drew in with the boat hook and deposited mademoiselle on land. For my taste she was rather broad. She left Kreti utterly cold. Dr. Hilpert moored his boat and landed.

"Well, and how are we?" he enquired.

Kreti lay back and spat nine feet into the air. He only barely missed hitting himself.

"This is Herr Bonifaz and Herr Greifenhagen," he said to Broadbeam, "and this is Fräulein Severin of the Regional Theatre."

"Must have been a hell of a show for you to be taking the cashier out already," said Kreti.

Dr. Hilpert drew a white handkerchief from his trouser pocket and wiped the sweat off his collar. "Fraulein Severin is in the chorus, Herr Greifenhagen."

"We'd be glad to be left in peace," said Kreti.

Dr. Hilpert cleared his throat.

"Come along, Rikki," said Fräulein Severin, "let's get back to the river."

"And remember me to Herr Pasemann, the lousy old colonial!" said Kreti.

"Whosoever insults the memory of a deceased person in that contrary to his own knowledge he states or propagates a falsehood such as would in the lifetime of the deceased tend to slander his person and bring him into public disrepute shall be sentenced to a maximum of six months imprisonment."

"Lovely," laughed Kreti, "That'll at least get us away from here. Quick, Bonifaz, say something rotten about your uncle!"

I shook my head.

"Can't you think of anything? Let me try!" He sat straight up, took a deep breath and said, "What a ..."

"Excuse me, Dr. Hilpert," I interrupted, turning with as friendly a look as possible to the lawyer, "do you happen to have anything to eat with you? I'm afraid my friend Greifenhagen—commercial artist by profession—is going slightly nuts, and I must confess that if I could just get a buttered roll or any old piece of black bread ..."

"But of course, my dear friend, I'll take a look in the boat at once," said Dr. Hilpert and was about to step out onto the breakwater.

"Please don't trouble yourself," I said, "I'm a sailor and I don't mind fetching for myself. Just tell me where it is."

"Under the back seat," said Fräulein Severin. "You could bring the bottle and a couple of blankets at the same time."

"With pleasure, madam," I said.

"Hey, you," I shouted at Kreti, "get up! Can't you hear what the lady said? Blankets! D'you want me to do it all?"

"Let her go herself."

I gave Kreti a long, hard look in the eyes. I must have got through to the optic nerve by the time he caught on, got up and followed me. The boat had a mahogany hull and was called *Baby*. A pretty name. I let Kreti get on board first, unwound the mooring rope from the post and jumped in after him. Dr. Hilpert had not noticed anything, and when I started up the motor all we heard was a wordless roar. I pushed the helm down to the left, got caught in the eddies in the open water, and tried to change into second gear, but the motor died on me. Kreti stretched back as if all this was no concern of his and rested his elbows on the gunwale. By this time Dr. Hilpert in his white linen suit had got down as far as the bank.

"What are you doing?" he shouted.

"You can see!" I shouted back.

"I shall report you!" he shouted.

"Please yourself," I said and started up the motor again.

"Section 243 Clause Four," he shouted, "whosoever shall in a public way street square waterway or railway . . ."

"This isn't a public square," bellowed Kreti, "this is the private estate of my friend Bonifaz, kindly note! Sections 123 and 124! Call yourself a lawyer and don't know that? Trespassing, get me?"

By now I was in second gear and we were moving away.

"Chuck the two blankets out for them," I said to Kreti, "so they won't catch cold."

Kreti felt for the camels' hair rugs under the back seat, I steered to the bank and the blankets flew over. I scraped a few stones, bore back to the left into the channel. We could still see Baby and Rikki dashing to snatch the blankets, jumping in the air, waving their fists at us, shrinking in size, and then we looked ahead, screwing up our eyes a little, Kreti drumming on the windshield, and I said: "The creature I like best of all is roach. Monkshood is our name for it. It's as big as a briefcase, greyish-green, and has a long, gristly tail. When they've been freshly caught they make wavy ripples round the edge and flap their eyes. Underneath they've got a tiny, neat little mouth."

"It's getting dark early," said Kreti. "How far are we going?"

"As far as the fuel lasts."

"And then what?"

"We'll get out."

"Is it true, Bonifaz, that sailors are so brutal?"

"It depends," I said, shifting to low gear again, as it really was getting dark and you couldn't see the breakwaters clearly any more.

"It may have something to do with our always being like visitors in our own houses. You wake up at night ready to go on watch and can't get to sleep again. Then you start rummaging in your seabag and wondering whether you ought to take your long underpants with you, and as soon as your wife begins to grumble, your hand's on the door-knob: 'I'll drop in and see you again next year some time'."

"And supposing she goes with someone else?"

"I know one guy who spent two years in the jug. Came home too soon and his wife was in bed with a stunt bicyclist from Lübeck and they were spinning on the wheel together. He chucked the fellow out, went and got a rolling pin from the kitchen, and . . ."

"D'you think that's right?"

I took my shoes off. "The great revolution must come in love, the same as in everything else. Otherwise all we're doing is piecework, whether it's for ourselves or for society."

"I've come to the same conclusion."

"And it turned you queer for a start, I know." I spread my toes and dangled my feet over the side into the milky water, first the right and then the left. The big toe cut quite a wash at the speed we were making. The boat was heading against the current for a spell. I took

133

a bite of the chocolate that we had found on board and handed it to Kreti. He gobbled it up and aimed a silver-paper ball at my toes. I hauled my legs in and leaped up so that the boat wobbled.

"Kreti, I'm going to get a wife for you."

"But Bonifaz, what's the point? You're making fun of me. If it wasn't you, I might be hurt by that remark."

Kreti picked up the yachting cap which lay on the after seat and clasped it to his breast as if on church parade. He knew just how pitiful he looked when he crossed his feet and scratched his left shoulder with his unshaven chin. But I had seen the act before.

"My dear friend, I want to make a man of you. But man is a social animal, and society includes women. Grub, booze and a Christian democracy can give fullness of life, but only the love of the sexes, I say to you, will raise you above your neighbour."

"Does one have to be raised?"

"Of course. Be an example in your life, stand for something, commit a crime, only don't let it be a small one, fornicate, preach with the patience of an atheist, put matrimonial ads in the papers, and feed the three hundred before checking out; if anyone asks your name, tell them you were found in a hat-box on Mont Blanc. The ultimate object's the same for everyone, that's to say, serve as a warning for others."

"Shouldn't we try and get an hour's sleep, Bonifaz? I'm tired, and I'm getting mad at you."

We moored the boat to the riverbank, Kerti stayed on board, I slept under a willow. I could hear Kreti mumbling for a bit, then clatter as he lay down, and then his soft, singsong snoring. I pulled a silver twig from the willow and cleaned my pipe, reached for my pouch, filled it and lit up. As I drifted off to sleep I wondered how I could make a man of Kreti. But nothing occurred to me.

50

IN the morning we pulled the big tarpaulin over the boat and tied it down, and went into the town. Our fuel was finished. After walking for a few hundred yards we heard an empty truck behind us driving the same way, but it did not stop.

We slogged on until a huge private car stopped, in which everything short of actually breathing was automatic. I sat next to a tweed suit, and Kreti next to an Alsatian. Tweeds had a nice American leanness and when, as we followed a long bend, he asked me: "Have you come from the river?" I said: "Yes," and felt I owed the man with the automatic car a kindness merely for having asked the question, as if he had been really concerned about our well-being.

"We're on a long trip, you know. It's hard getting along. It was very good of you to give us a lift," said Kreti.

Tweeds did not understand, so he asked me: "What does your friend mean?"

"He wants to know what your job is."

"I see. Well, you know, it's quite phenomenal . . ."

This time Kreti had not understood.

"What does he mean by that, Bonifaz?"

I turned round a little and said: "What he means is that he's an exploiter, Kreti."

Tweeds smiled and said happily: "Quite right. That razor-blade factory over there belongs to me. Only you needn't imagine I don't have worries."

We were already driving across the bridge over the river into the town when Kreti said: "I wonder, sir, whether we could be of any assistance to you?"

"That depends."

"I'm the man you need," breathed Kreti.

Tweeds nodded but drew up outside a grey shed in the suburbs, pointed to the notice board reading "Hostel" and said: "I don't do business in my car. Here are ten marks. If you have an idea for marketing a hundred thousand packets of razor-blades you can come and see me. I'm not a monster. Goodbye."

I was glad to be out of the car. I had been mightily shocked when Kreti offered himself to the razor-blades tycoon. However, we both had ten marks in our pockets now and the world looked a kinder place than it had done before.

"We can last out until the afternoon, Bonifaz," said Kreti, "we've no one at home waiting for us, so we can go and eat."

We walked down the path from the hostel back to the road and on into the town, myself in my uncle's patched-up khaki trousers, worndown Wehrmacht boots and the frayed jersey that Pulle had given me, and Kreti in his black corduroy jacket. Walking revived us after the sleepy warmth of the car. I demonstrated some knee bends and Kreti practised a new-style shimmy as we passed the windows of the dismal jewellery shops. The savoury wind from the grill shops and bakeries blew the scowl out of our faces, polished our cheeks and foreheads, reddened our ears and put a foretaste of boiling and roasting on our tongues.

We went into the cafeteria next to the filling station, changed our money, ate a half-pound cutlet each, drank beer, wiped the froth from our lips and stood, satisfied but melancholy, outside the fitfully revolving doors.

It was noon, and the maples in the streets were yellow against the black, charred walls of the ruins, the empty children's swings in the front gardens and playgrounds looked like guillotines, and the sadness of them hurt worse than toothache.

"What do you think one would have to paint on a poster to make people buy razor-blades?" asked Kreti.

"A boy scraping his first growth of down—Dauntless Siegfried slaying the dragon, razor-blade in hand—An out-of-work, middleaged man cutting his arteries—A girl with big breasts shaving her armpits—"

"O.K., Bonifaz, the last idea'll do."

136

Kreti lay back in the autumn sunshine again, slept until the first children came out again, belched loudly, and allowed me to drag him back towards the hostel. As we crossed the fairground he stopped in front of a tent with the placard "Musical Magic", scratched his left calf with his right foot, nodded and pulled me to the ticket booth, where each of us had to part with fifty pfennigs.

We sat on a splintery bench. In front of us a few children were holding hands and talking in whispers, for the stuffy tent was closed against the sunlight and the satin curtains shed a bluish light into the front room, a pale and not very cosy glow.

The curtains opened, and on the minute stage there stood a slender, waxy-skinned girl of perhaps seventeen, holding a young brown bear on a lead. She bowed to the children and to me and Kreti, ran her hand from her face to her bosom and back to her face, and then immediately grabbed the bear, which was on the point of clambering off the margarine-box stage into the auditorium.

The girl released her silk sari, showed her round, sun-tanned belly, and picked a tambourine off a wobbly stand and manipulated it most unskilfully with her right hand while singing. Or perhaps she was only speaking, for she had a singsong tongue anyhow. She came from Leipzig and she sang her story.

"I am the daughter of the widowed master-baker Händle from Stemmzig, who gave up Communism because he owed taxes and hated it from the bottom of his heart. Thanks to credit and the Party open brackets Christian Democrat Union close brackets he felt solid ground beneath his feet again, though in time this proved to be comparatively unsteady, in addition to which came the establishment of a machine bakery in the town. As a result of his regrettably early death he left me just enough to buy a brown bear, with which I have now been travelling for two years through the free world doing a comedy turn. Offers have been made to me from the East but I turn down anything of theirs. A poet who knows the story of my life has written this song for me:

> *Jimmy, Jean-Pierre and Volodya*
> *discovered a girl in a forest chase,*

her breasts were white and soft as down,
She offered them peace and a resting place.

Jimmy, Jean-Pierre and Volodya
three hearts at once she did gain—
they brought her whisky, vin rouge and vodka
to drive away hunger and wipe away pain.

Then came her lover-man home from the war,
a big-fisted German of good six foot three,
he kicked out the strangers, the heathenish lot,
as he fancied to live in his own house free.

Now she sits with her giant, his helmets and swords,
combing her hair by the banks of the Rhine
and he greases his gun as she sings her sad song
When not swilling whisky with gallons of wine:

Haul away, haul away, slim sailor boy—
let 'em all keep the jam on their bread,
don't give a damn for their wealth!
You in your blue are my love and my joy
For ever and ever
and ever and ever
You're my gold-headed love. Olé!

We were shattered.

The girl, whose name really was Händle, seemed to be freezing, for she pulled the material round her hips again and snuggled up to the bear. "Encore!" I shouted, but Fräulein Händle shook her head. Leading the bear, she twice walked round the stand the tambourine had come from, with her toes pointing at a wide angle and her eyelids lowered. The second time round the bear bumped into the little table and knocked it over and just as Fräulein Händle looked up the curtains closed.

Kreti was beside himself. "I must see her, Bonifaz!"

"Ay, ay," I said and laughed, "you're on the brink of a derailment."

"I must see her, Bonifaz," he said again.

"All right then, let's pay a visit."

"Oughtn't we to get some flowers or something first . . . ?"

"Flowers, for God's sake! A bunch of beetroot for the bear. *Flowers!*"

We went round the outside of the tent and approached a shed next to the bear's cage. The bear had stretched itself out on the floor to sleep. A laundry line was strung in front of the shed and from it hung a green pullover with a Finnish design. I knocked.

"Come in," chanted Fräulein Händle.

"Please excuse us, Dolly," I said, "but my friend has taken a liking to you."

"Oh," said Fräulein Händle.

"You know, Kreti," I said, turning to him, "I should think that's as much as you'll ever get out of her. She does the rest by body."

"Bonifaz! How can you say such a thing! Please excuse him, Fräulein Händle," snapped Kreti.

"Ah," said Fräulein Händle.

"Why don't you ask her if you can draw her?"

"Bonifaz—a goddess like that!"

"Look here, little bear-tamer, can my friend paint you?"

We made an appointment for the following morning and to many "ahs" Kreti and I left Fräulein Händle's dressing-room.

"The little goose," I said when we were in the street.

"Oh," said Kreti.

"Don't you start! We weren't given speech just to grunt with. Anyhow her ears are too big. You'll have to mask them a bit when you do her portrait."

"They never struck me, Bonifaz."

"She combs her hair over them. You could get the whole Old Testament on to them in shorthand, with a bit of practice of course."

"You're horrible!"

"I'm only opening your eyes."

51

WE took the bus to the razor-blade factory. The fruit shops and café awnings beckoned with stripes and dots and pale-skinned girls walked hatless in flimsy dresses under the solar bombardment, leading huge dogs in summer coats. Briefcases full of statistics on stomach tumours, the hop content of ale and the presence of strontium in last month's rainfall were being carried through the town, past dogs and girls, past sunny-hearted sun-drenched policemen presiding dreamily over the intersections, come red, come green.

Hands touched hot car bodies, were wiped dry on trouser legs. How do you do? I hope the swine lets go before long. Imagine offering that sticky mit. Kreti is sweating round his stubbly chin. He sticks a handkerchief inside his collar. Kreti has wool on his chest. I've got none over my eyes. I can look after myself. I'm as sharp as mustard. I know how to take my corners. No, thank you—you must be mixing me up with someone else. I'm not a Grand Prix driver. No, not an amateur either. Do you really? Well, it's the practice that does it. Mille Miglia? We'll see. Have an orange. Stop at the pits! The tires are smoking. A mild cigar. An orange, Mr. Moss? Yes please. And a quick coffee. Brakes off. My God, what a guy. A bank is saluting. The little bank at the big roundabout. How I love you, little bank. Commercial Bank. Deutsche Bank. How I love you. Berliner Bank.

The asphalt is clean. In Italy there's rubbish all over the road. The cyclists here even fix little brushes to their rear mudguards. In the schools they make artificial puddles for the infants' classes. Instead of mire and mud, slops and slush, they use porridge or tapioca pudding. The kids in the public kindergarten ate up all the shovels one day. They'd been made of licorice and chewing-gum. For dessert, sir, I would recommend trying the cutlery. Crime is abolished. Knife-blades crumple on their victims' skin. Night watchmen plant crowbars in the strawberry bed. St. Joseph-buds sprout on blackjacks and budgerigars peck barley-corn from knuckledusters. The bus stopped in an avenue of pear trees.

And from there to the gate of the razor-blade factory was a matter of a few weary steps over the badly worn pavement. One razor-blade was over the gate and another was revolving above the main building. We tried to walk straight past the gatekeeper but were obliged to state our names, birthdays, birthplaces, addresses, skin colours, and the direction of our whisker-grain. The gatekeeper then spoke into a small microphone and nodded. "You may," he said.

Herr Rumpus, the owner of the razor-blade factory, was a large and apparently completely hair-free man, the white skin of whose face showed a little colour only on the point of his chin and on his jawbone. His upper lip had the soft form of a duck's bottom, his lashless eyes stared coldly at Kreti and me. He walked up and down the room as he spoke, with his arms swinging wide. When he reached the end of the long black runner he swirled his arms round in a semi-circle and for precisely one second rested on tilted heels. Judging from his movements during the conversation, he must have spent the best years of his life behind iron-studded doors.

"Before I show you my plant," he said, "I would like to give you the picture as to our position. As a business man I frankly confess that I made a bad mistake. I backed the wrong horse at the time Mechelke went bankrupt and Gellert took over his holdings; I was sure electric shavers were old hat. Since then, however, half the world's population has taken to shaving on 220 volts and I am sitting on two million packs of razor-blades at a mark apiece. I can't go cheaper than that. My sales line is RELY ON A RUMPUS. My sales people have made various suggestions, all of which strike me as completely idiotic, but you may perhaps be able to do something with them . . ."

The razor-blade manufacturer went to his desk, pressed on the intercom. button and said: "The tapes with the sales talk."

Herr Rumpus started tramping again. From the loudspeaker over the door we heard: "Rumpus and Rumpus, manufacturers of razor-blades, are opening their own branches in all P.O.W. reception camps. We can expect the repatriated German ex-prisoner of war to be in a receptive mood. The P.O.W. of yesterday is the citizen of tomorrow. His appetite for enjoyment means that our publicity must be easy and attractive, while our well-tried motto RELY ON A RUMPUS immediately evokes an atmosphere of security and familiarity which will help homecomers to respond all the more easily to our publicity. The slogan we suggest for this is: DON'T RETURN HOME BEFORE SHAVING!"

"Cost a fortune," said Herr Rumpus, "branches in all the camps! Just think what's involved: timber, paper, posters, cash registers, staff, night watchmen—we've no idea what sort of fellows they'll be sending back to us . . . Next, please!" he called out.

"Experience in selling Rumpus and Rumpus in world markets has shown that best sales results are achieved if the buyer can be contacted and disarmed at the psychologically decisive moment. Our suggestion is as follows: engage immediately one thousand unemployed men, each of whom will have two thousand packets to sell in the course of a fourteen-days' engagement. As the morale of the workless stands in a natural relationship to the scale of the assistance they receive, we should anticipate an expenditure of two hundred thousand marks, plus the cost of firearms. The salesmen will then be assigned to posts in metropolitan urinals and brothels, that is to say, in surroundings where modern man's individualistic isolation is demonstrably at its bleakest; in these, our armed salesmen will be instructed to act on the slogan: SHAVE—OR BE SHOT!"

"Six months ago that man was in the union," stormed Herr Rumpus. "A thousand revolvers! Just try and imagine, gentlemen, what would happen if I gave a thousand unemployed a thousand revolvers at this moment. There'd be nothing short of a revolution."

"Then at least you'd be sure of getting rid of your razor-blades," I said.

"Would you like to hear the third plan?" asked the razor-blade manufacturer. "It's from my American special adviser. He wrote a book at Princeton about the filthy things Americans do to their girls or the other way round. Got made a professor for that. Monstrous when you think of it, the way they'll make the rest of us sweat before

142

they'll hand out an honorary Ph.D. Number three!" he called out.

"America's ad-men are noted for their world-topping know-how in public relations. Basing my program on the principle of subliminal perception already tested in cinema and television (a frame reading BUY FARMPRIDE held for one-fifth of a second produced a five hundred per cent sales boost) I have succeded in developing an entirely novel process to which I have given the name 'Interruption Command'. In view of the extreme vulnerability of the German public to political battle-cries, my program can be expected to be particularly effective. By a *pro capita* investment of two hundred Deutschmarks (government party) and one hundred Deutschmarks (opposition) respectively, four hundred members of parliament were persuaded during our recent market survey to insert before their peroration slogans AND-DEFEND-FREEDOM for the government party, alternatively AND-DEFEND-FREEDOM for the opposition, the following interruption command: SHAVE-WITH-RUMPUS. The outcome was the easily intelligible and compelling slogan SHAVE-WITH-RUMPUS-AND-DEFEND-FREEDOM. Over a period of ten days, two hundred government personalities and two hundred opposition speakers, with an average attendance of one thousand per meeting, of whom fifty per cent are men, would promote the sale of two million packs of Rumpus blades against an expenditure of only sixty thousand marks."

"Well, what do you think of that one?" asked Herr Rumpus.

"Very American," I said.

"Do you know the States?" asked Herr Rumpus.

"I once brought a magazine back from America, that's all there was time for. There was a picture in it of a character who had hanged himself with his suspenders, but it said the suspenders came from Woolworth's. As we don't have any suspenders good enough for the job over here, we have to have wars instead. But just imagine if they'd started out in 1914 with their belt-buckles saying WITH-GOD-FOR-KING-AND-PORK-CHOPS instead of FATHERLAND. There's a big difference for us Germans between shouting 'freedom' and shouting 'razor-blades'. It seems easier to die for freedom, though it comes to exactly the same thing if you die for razor-blades. Nowadays, you'd get much further if you didn't assume either any positively good intentions or any positively bad intentions on the part of your customers."

"Yes, so what's left?" asked the manufacturer.

"Let's say: average intentions," I replied. "Advertising is much the same as the law. Both, if they're going to be effective, have to assume that all men are equal, whether before God or before his deputy on the bench, it doesn't matter which. The person you're addressing may be a criminal or a policeman, a murderer or a welfare worker. If you're going to succeed in advertising, you must give the public the illusion that they're getting the better of you. Unfortunately most rich people are much too clumsy about it, and prospective buyers are put off by bluffing."

"What about competition?" asked Herr Rumpus.

"I'm glad you mentioned it," I said, "I should have started with that point. It forms an essential part of my theory of average intentions and fits in with what I have been saying about the law. Just as we can't any longer leave our protection from criminals to a simple appeal to their consciences, so likewise it's stupid to see a good Samaritan in every prospective buyer. If your competitors held to that line they'd soon be on the rocks. PLEASEBUYFROMMESOICANSTAYRICH sticks out a mile."

"Would you mind coming to the point, Herr Bonifaz?" said the manufacturer, agitatedly rubbing his nose between two fingers.

"Let's suppose," I said, "that you were the owner of a dairy and had a surplus of cheese."

"I've got razor-blades, not cheese!" roared Herr Rumpus.

"Cheese won't rust, razors don't smell, I take your point. But I can see already. You aren't with me. It's very easy, really. FORODOUR-FREEDOMEATROMADOUR! You'll see: the cheese'll go like hot cakes!"

"This is a razor-blade factory, not a dairy!"

"But during a war, for example, a dairy means you can . . ."

"All right then," confessed the manufacturer, "I do have a dairy."

"The slogan FOR-ODOUR-FREEDOM-EAT-ROMADOUR is, like all good advertising, based on an illogicality. The clever thing about advertising is to be superfluous. The smell won't hurt anybody before they actually

144

get the Romadour in the house. Yet the slogan FOR-ODOUR-FREEDOM-EAT-ROMADOUR boosts sales and the reason is that it is supplementing American techniques—remember Woolworth's suspenders—with German techniques. I am referring not to cheese, but to metaphysics. This slogan . . ."

"Not again," implored the manufacturer.

"You see," I said, "it's working on you already. It's no good just saying: eat cheese. It's got to be: eat cheese or else . . . you won't have any children, you'll get ill, you'll put on weight, you'll waste away, flying saucers will land . . . he'll be twisting and jerking all night. It'll pursue him into his dreams: I must have the new collar stiffeners for the new shirts with the fly-button fronts. If you'll let me tell you a story, I knew a women in Tesch once who used to get epileptic fits all because her husband wouldn't buy her a pendant watch—you remember the jingle, LIFE-WILL-TAKE-AN-EASIER-TURN-WHEN-YOU-WIND-YOUR-WATCH-FROM-SCHOEN?"

"Now I'm throwing you out," said the manufacturer, and advanced from the end of the runner to his desk.

"I wouldn't do that if I were you," I said, "because I can tell you how to get rid of your two million razor-blades."

"Make it snappy, then," said Herr Rumpus.

"The latent death-wish," I said, "since we live under a Christian government, needs to be dressed up in religious style. My friend Kreti will provide the artwork. I will provide the text."

"Well?" asked Herr Rumpus.

I got up and approached Herr Rumpus, who had sat down behind his desk.

"FACE YOUR MAKER PROPERLY SHAVED: WITH A RUMPUS"

"LOOKING SCRUFFY ON JUDGEMENT DAY?"

"SUICIDE? NO!—BUT IF YOU MUST, THE BLADE FOR YOU IS RUMPUS"

The razor-blade manufacturer clutched his throat, I leaned with both fists on his desk and watched him.

"Right," said the razor-blade manufacturer, baring his teeth. "Here's a cheque. Now I'll show you over my works so that you can see how I run things."

Herr Rumpus pressed black and white buttons, spoke a few numbers into the microphone and strode out to meet the secretary who was already bringing his hat.

"Fräulein Übrig," he said, "these gentlemen and I will be lunching in the private room."

"And a world tour to follow?" enquired Fräulein Übrig.

"As usual," said Herr Rumpus.

Fräulein Übrig looked at us carefully from the side, gasped at Kreti's growth of blond bristle and enquired finally: "Will the two gentlemen be going too?"

"I told you before," grumbled Herr Rumpus.

"Actually, we aren't either of us properly set up for that," I said.

"We'd have to say goodbye to one or two people at least," said Kreti, thinking of the one and only Fräulein Händle.

"Don't worry," said Herr Rumpus, "come as you are. We'll be back again within two hours."

"It must be a completely new type of machine," I whispered to Kreti, as we followed Herr Rumpus out of the room, "for flying against the earth's rotation. I hope the weather stays clear. I'll be really mad if it's raining over Africa."

"It's just that I'm hungry," said Kreti and the razor-blade manufacturer must have heard him, for he turned round at the next door and said to us: "Now we'll have lunch in our private dining-room."

Herr Rumpus pranced ahead of us on rubber soles, tapped a cigarette against the concrete wall in passing, struck a match and let us trot behind him in an aroma of tobacco smoke. The stone floor sloped noticeably downward, doors were few and far between. We came to an iron-sheathed door which Herr Rumpus opened with a key. We stumbled over the threshold and found ourselves in a greenish obscurity in which we gradually discerned the outlines of a low table and several armchairs.

"I fitted the place up like this for people to adjust their eyes to the lighting in the private room," said Herr Rumpus. "Please sit down."

I pulled up a wing chair, Herr Rumpus and Kreti sat down on a sofa. It slowly grew lighter. The green that had been glazing faces and

146

furniture gave way to a pale grey that was almost white. The end wall of the small room had a three-part sash window in it, next to a tiny door, and white light was shining in through it. Our eyes had adjusted themselves during the transition from green to white and I went and looked through the window. On the other side of the glass I saw a square hall lined with mirrors throwing back the white light which revealed a crowd of people who had just sat down at a horse-shoe table and were evidently awaiting their lunch. Behind each chair stood a bunk. I was just in time to see a stout elderly lady roll herself off her bunk, shake out the eiderdown, straighten the pillow and go straight to the table without bothering to tidy her hair or her clothes. The gentlemen on either side of her kissed her hand, stroked their beards, bent forward over their empty plates and shook their heads.

"They'll start serving now," I heard Herr Rumpus saying. "We'll have to hurry, although nobody apart from the servants is going to notice we're late, as some of them have been here for fifty years."

"Who are these people?" I asked.

"People who were dangerous or stupid enough to get in my father's or my way," said Herr Rumpus and unlocked the door. He carefully bolted it again behind us. "We asked them here, but didn't let them go again—a sort of party *in perpetuo*."

Everyone had stood up when we entered. There were about thirty of them, mostly aged about sixty, though I also noticed some even older, shaky ones who were finding it difficult to shove back their oak chairs and make a polite bow as we passed them on our way to the top end of the table.

The razor-blade manufacturer spoke to some of them: "Your Excellency—Professor—Madam—Mr. Speaker!"

I found myself sitting next to a grey-haired woman. "Councillor Hellbohm," Herr Rumpus introduced her. "How do you do," I said.

"Why are you so late today?" asked the lady councillor.

"Am I usually more punctual?" I asked.

"But surely, my dear!" she breathed, "the most punctual of them all!"

The lady councillor took a sip of the consommé which a grey-faced waiter had served her, and pushed the plate away. "I've now been here for thirty-five years," she said. She counted off on her fingers: "precisely."

I picked up a soup spoon and drummed my head with it.

"That's perfectly correct," said Herr Rumpus who was sitting on my right and boning a trout. I looked left to where Kreti was and he seemed to be feeling the same as I did. With his lips stuck out he was staring at his plate as if trying to count the grease spots afloat in his soup. I took a mouthful of wine, replaced my glass carefully, as my hand was shaking, and said, when I felt I had got over the shock: "Well, you haven't missed much, Frau Hellbohm."

"Who is it, actually, who gets into my bed at night?" she asked.

"Perhaps it's the general," said Herr Rumpus. "Why don't you ask him?"

"Pooh, the old field-marshal!" shrieked the lady councillor and tugged at her stays. "Somebody's run off with my laces. Give me back my laces!"

"Excuse me, madam, but I don't even have any shoe laces," I protested. "Anyhow, I've had enough of this." I picked up my glass, the carafe, my plate, knife and fork and hurled them down on the parquet floor. In the silence that followed I saw the faces as they slowly rose from their plates. White, chalky, sunken, ash-grey; jutting noses, cheekbones, jawbones; bushy white eyebrows, hair in the ears, crooked black teeth; dirt-spattered dinner jackets with medals askew; twisted misshapen ties; stumpy, slimy, grimy fingers holding silver knives; slobbering, dribbling lips; watery, gummy eyes; brown worn-out cuffs holding gold links; baggy, glandular, unwashed throats; spiky, shivering, jerking shoulders under the padding; wide flickering nostrils —watchful, cautious, cringing, gutless, all crouched there on one perch: the razor-blade manufacturer's guests.

"Lay his place again, please." said Herr Rumpus, breaking the silence. "Go on eating, Herr Bonifaz."

He poured out another glass for me, leaned back and said with a smile: "The *élite* of the nation, but alas *perdu*. Who shall we begin with?"

"Him over there," I said, and pointed with a liqueur glass at a white-bearded man at the end of the table who was pressing a steaming potato into his mouth with his fingers.

"That's a minister of finance," said Herr Rumpus. "My father invited him forty years ago. It was something to do with a tax reform, as far as I can remember. The Reich government had given him the job of raising income tax on the processing industries. As usual, he set up a commission of which he made himself chairman, and produced some really astonishing findings: tax evasions, allowable expenses exceeding annual income, declarations of dividends on fraudulent balance sheets, minority stockholders squeezed out, and then naturally, speculation in a falling market and assured options for the majority holders—need I say more? My father got wind of this and invited him to our *soirée*. And there he is."

"But doesn't ever occur to him . . ."

"To want to go home! But I ask you, he's a very well-mannered old gentleman and he receives every consideration. Besides, for the first few years he had his wife with him as well. She's dead now. Since then all he's cared for is potatoes, but they keep him young. Between our-selves: he's the one who pounces on Councillor Hellbohm at night."

"How do you know that?"

"Perfectly simple. We switch our concealed lighting over from white to green every twelve hours. That makes it night time for our guests. It would be barbarous to let them out again. They would be like the blind in sunlight. Which is also the reason why we mustn't stay here too long. Would you like to meet him?"

"No, thank you," I said, "but tell me, who's the one in uniform?"

"That's the general."

"Could you bring him over here?"

"Of course," said Herr Rumpus, "but we'll need music to do it."

He signalled to one of the waiters, whispered in his ear and asked me to wait a minute. "We have a moment before the music starts. In the old days he liked to hang around the imperial observation mound and one day he had the fantastic luck to be in a position to bring His Majesty a handwritten message from the Tsar in which the Tsar recommended to His Majesty a prescription for haemorrhoids which proved to be efficacious. He was promoted to colonel, became general by seniority and, on the death of the old chief-of-staff, colonel-general. The Republic took him over on account of his experience—he had lost two battles which cost about forty thousand lives—and reappointed him to his old post. Later on he mistook the general strike for a monarchist demonstration. Somebody or other—he had relations among the Junkers of Pomerania—must have put it into his head that he ought to take over the government. When he tried to turn on the light in the presidential palace and start directing affairs there wasn't any electric current. He couldn't even wash his hands. They weren't able to lock him up on account of his splendid record; so he was invited. He's sitting there. Now he's getting up!"

A kettledrum pounded, bugles sounded, there was a drum roll, the Hohenfriedberger march. The colonel-general flung back his shoulders, stamped with his left foot, then with his right. He hauled himself upright by the edge of the table, the chair fell backwards, a waiter took it away. He tugged the Pour-le-Mérite straight at his throat, made a sharp left turn, a waiter handed him his spiked *Pickelhaube*, into which his shrivelled head disappeared, it was a scream, but so solemn. With a jerk he shook his helmet back so that he could see straight ahead, his extensors jingled in two-quarter time, moustaches shedding last drops of gravy. The old wreck on the march! One-two-one-two. Old Fritz, Old Wilhelm, Old Guard! Up and at 'em! Keep at 'em! Up your muskets and inna' those Masurian marshes! Right turn! We made it, what an angle, just by eye! Last four yards: goose step! Knees up! God, get that leg straight, General! Audience with the Kaiser! Hohenfriedberger's ceased. 'Shun!

"Take a quiet look at him. Perhaps we can still use him again. Tradition, you know. The new army needs men of experience."

"Quite right," said a man behind my chair. He was taller than me, wearing brown storm-trooper uniform and a Sam Browne as wide as a razor strop. Brown hair grew out of his ears and nostrils. Over his trousers he wore stiff brown boots gone dry and hard with time.

"Party member?" he enquired.

"Not yet," I said cautiously.

"I am Obersturmbannführer Richter."

"How do you do. I am Bonifaz, part-time waiter."

"It's going to be the turn of the big joints next," announced Obersturmbannführer Richter, and raised the arm with the swastika on it.

"Just what I think," I said. "First we'll booze out the little ones and after that the big ones."

My answer did not satisfy Obersturmbannführer Richter.

"Storm troopers only booze on January thirtieth," he said sharply.

"I really don't mind about the day," I said and tried to turn away, but the Obersturmbannführer reached out his hand and caught me by the shirt collar and pressed me against the back of the chair.

"And how is the Führer?" he asked.

"Well."

"How so?"

"Adolf is in heaven. The Lord has reserved a nice little corner for him, and he's sitting there with Eva feeding his Alsatians."

"Is that true?"

"I give you my word."

He clambered onto a chair, propped his hands on my shoulders and shouted: "The Führer is dead! the Führer is dead! Long live the storm troops!"

He got down again and said to me: "I hereby appoint you pack leader."

"Thank you very much, sir," I said. "And what are your immediate plans?"

"To begin with we shall expropriate heavy industry, basic industry, big landowners, and later on all the big joints."

"But from what I heard from a certain Herr Mummert, a good deal of that's already been done," I said.

"By my storm troops?"

"No. It couldn't be done everywhere, only in Thuringia, Saxony, Mecklenburg and so on."

"But there isn't any industry there," declared Obersturmbannführer Richter.

"Well, they took what there was," I replied.

"We shall start with the Ruhr," ordered the Obersturmbannführer.

"That's just what I think," I said. "But it'll be hard going."

"Why? Who is Hitler's successor?"

"An elderly gentleman, getting on towards eighty."

"Party member?"

"Certainly not."

"Then everything isn't lost yet."

He raised his arm again, let it fall rather unwillingly and lay down on the nearest bunk. The general also trotted back to his place.

Opposite me at the table was a man of fifty in a brown, post-war, two-piece suit which did not go with the tails, uniforms, dinner jackets, damask dresses, puffed sleeves and pearls of the others.

He introduced himself morosely as Herr Feldafing, levered up the flank of the trout with his fish-knife and then squeezed out its eyes with his fork. "Always trout," he said. "Why not flounder for once, or carp, or pickled herrings? During the war we were jolly pleased to get pickled herrings."

"Which war, Herr Feldafing?" I asked.

He pushed his trout plate aside and looked at me suspiciously. "Which war? What makes you ask that? Do you think I can remember what the food was like in the first world war?"

"You haven't been here for long?"

"About half an hour," said Herr Feldafing, "and I'm already eating trout for the fourth time."

"I should go home if you don't like trout."

Herr Feldafing shook his head. "I quite *like* it, but it doesn't agree with me."

"Well then go home, if trout doesn't agree with you."

Herr Feldafing shook his head again. "I'm a Social Democrat and I can't flout the basic rules of hospitality . . . Herr Rumpus would be very upset."

"Do you know Herr Rumpus?" I asked.

"But my dear friend," said Herr Feldafing, "he's sitting next to you."

"Does Herr Rumpus always lunch with you?"

Herr Feldafing looked at me in consternation. "What do you mean by always? What d'you mean, does he lunch with us? We've only been here for half an hour. I was somewhat delayed. I had had a meeting with the chancellor. They were all here already when I arrived. His Excellency Eberhard Prince von Eichwalden, our ambassador in Málaga; his Magnificence Professor Dr. Kiepenbruch, the former Rector of Homburg University; his Excellency Herr Ballhaus, Minister of Finance; his Excellency Colonel-General Struck; Landtag-president Müller; Obersturmbannführer Richter; Messrs Kaczmarec and Finke from the Foreign Ministry (Finke is the tall one with the 1923 Medal); Pastor Schnurr from Berlin and a few other people whom I don't know . . ." Herr Feldafing pulled the trout towards him again and sucked the fish off the bones.

"What's the date today, Herr Feldafing?" I asked.

There was suddenly complete silence.

"What?" asked Herr Feldafing. I repeated myself. Everyone was listening to me. Councillor Hellbohn stuck her hands on her hips and crowed: "Here's someone who wants to know what date it is!"

They all shouted together: "December the nineteenth!"—"April the second!"—"January the twenty-eighth!"

Herr Rumpus tried to stop me, but I yelled: "Today is September the twenty-second, September the twenty-second, September the twenty-second!"

The general and the lady councillor laughed with all their black teeth and they infected the whole company with gaping mouths. The excellencies crowed over their baked pork, the Landtag-speaker held his belly, Herr Kaczmarec from the Foreign Ministry rolled among his potatoes, Obersturmbannführer Richter hooted till the glasses jangled, the ladies squeaked and tittered: "September the twenty-second!" Professor Kiepenbruch fell off his chair and Pastor Schnurr grinned. Only Kreti kept sitting quietly on his chair in the corner and Herr Rumpus smiled. I watched him carefully. He leaned backwards and reached with both hands under the table cloth. Suddenly there was darkness. Only after a pause did the same green glow appear in the big hall of mirrors as it had done before in the ante-room. The guests were still sitting with their mouths wide open in distorted faces; gradually their muscles relaxed, their lips closed, heads, hands and shoulders returned to normal positions. Herr Feldafing seemed to be taking a particularly long time subsiding, and I was tempted to give him a shove. The place became insanely silent, and I could hear Kreti's scraping and sucking as he fell to on his food. Everyone apart from Herr Rumpus, Kreti and myself rose as if by a secret command, shoved back the high-backed chairs with the force of their thighs, stepped away from the table and went to the bunks behind the chairs, turned down the eiderdowns, lay down fully dressed, pulled the bedclothes over them and turned their heads to one side.

"I'm worried about Herr Feldafing," said Herr Rumpus. "He hasn't been here long. There are moments when he remembers. You shouldn't have asked him the date. He's unsettled."

We finished the green meat course with green potatoes and Herr Rumpus and I returned to the door. I turned round for a last look and was just in time to see Kreti preparing to lie down on an empty bunk.

"Kreti!" I shouted, but he was already unable to hear me. I ran back to him, turned him towards me and slapped his face for his own good.

"All we needed was for you to get stuck in this dump. Get going, forward march! What's the date today?"

"September the twenty-second," answered Kreti. "I'm sorry, but I'm so tired."

He went ahead of me into the anteroom and Herr Rumpus locked the door.

52

WE left the main building and were taken to a circular courtyard with a giant-sized car standing in it. From radiator to tail-lights it measured sixty-six feet, and was about twelve feet wide.

"My holiday model," explained Herr Rumpus. "Got it specially made and I really only use it when I have time off."

He went ahead of us and opened the front off-side door with his little master key.

"You can stand up inside—come in."

We stepped into a sort of corridor with several doors leading off it. The walls were painted in black eggshell. The doors had white handles.

"We won't waste time with the other rooms—I've got two bed, one sitting, one dressing, two toilets, bath, kitchen and a small storeroom— so let's go straight through to the driver's seat."

"If you don't mind my saying so," I said, "my friend Kreti has an appointment at about six o'clock with a certain Fräulein Händle . . ."

"That doesn't matter," said Herr Rumpus. "You'll soon realise why."

We sat down on the sofa at the back, Herr Rumpus took his place at the wheel and we had a very good view of the whole courtyard.

"Before we start," smiled Herr Rumpus, "I would like to give you— as in the case of my private room—a short explanation. People are always talking about exploiters and capitalists. In my razor-blade firm, however, I have established a climate of industrial relations, thanks to the use of my private room and the construction of this car, which can hardly be equalled by any other business anywhere in the world today. You have seen the private room. It is a refuge for the temporarily redundant. I need not dwell further on that. Now my car," said Herr Rumpus thumping with his hand on the wheel, "is the first step in achieving the welfare state for which we are all striving. The people who work for me ought to realise that I've read my Marx. They produce me my surplus value, don't they? And what do I do with it? Squander it? Do I live in luxury? Do I keep race horses, women, painters? No—I travel, and how I travel you will now see for yourselves."

Herr Rumpus pressed the horn. The factory gates opened, a couple of men in blue overalls came out and hooked back the gates, went away again and returned with huge screens. These were canvasses, each carried by two men. Landscapes had been painted on them in glowing colours. They were carried round immediately in front of the windshield through which we were looking. We recognised Vesuvius on the first screen.

"See Naples and die," said Herr Rumpus.

After that came the Pyramids. The workmen walked slowly past us, turned back to the gate and fetched the next screen, while their mates were already passing in front of us like a procession marching with banners.

"Really extremely progressive," I said, goggling at Sugar Loaf Mountain. A completely plain white canvas was carried past.

"The Arctic," explained Herr Rumpus. "We decided the simplest thing would be to leave the priming the way it was."

A picture of palm trees and naked girls wobbled towards us.

"Hawaii," said Herr Rumpus, "flower of the sea. Would you like to have music?"

"We'd rather not," I said and watched Hawaii going.

The next canvas had been brushed over with glue and then strewn with sand and gravel.

"The Sahara," said Herr Rumpus. "Its mystery revealed."

The next picture needed four men to carry it.

"This must be something new," said Herr Rumpus. "My workmen sometimes give me a surprise with an original idea of their own."

We saw a long, light-coloured wall on the canvas, with spires and onion-domes appearing behind it, and on the top of one of them a red five-pointed star. There was water in the foreground, and in between the cumulus clouds there were masses of hammers and sickles overlapping each other. This picture did not march on, but stopped in front of the windshield and came closer until it was only just far enough away to keep out of the car's shadow.

Herr Rumpus hooted, but it did not move away from our eyes, reminding me of Yevgeniy Yurievich Sapunov and of raisins and pork.

"Take it away," shouted Herr Rumpus. He wound down the window and yelled: "Get that picture out of the way! And get a move on, if you don't mind!"

Nobody seemed to be listening, for the picture stayed where it was.

"Aren't we going on?" asked Kreti.

"You can see for yourself," said Herr Rumpus.

"Nice kind of world tour."

"What can I do about it?" he spluttered.

"I don't know what you're so upset about," I said. "That's quite a pretty place."

"Do you realise what it represents?" shrieked Herr Rumpus.

"I know," I said. "And you'd prefer a razor-blade to the sickle. If you like, my friend could even manage that for you. Only we'd have to change the wording."

"Workers of the world, get shaved, eh?" asked Herr Rumpus. "No, no, we'll stick to the old one. I'm sorry, gentlemen, I have got to see to the climate of industrial relations. Contact me again when you have something for me. Goodbye."

He got out, and we stayed in the car until we had had enough of Moscow; then we too clambered down and walked past the gatekeeper and out into the town.

53

We spent a few days in a small hotel and Fräulein Händle with her double-bed physique crept down beside Kreti.

"Wouldn't you like to be next?" she asked while Kreti was having his tub.

"I'm a married man," was my standard answer, turning on my other side. She was too dumb for me.

As soon as Kreti realised that he had landed himself a dose of clap he chucked her out and started moaning to me. They gave him an injection and that was the end of the razor-blade manufacturer's money.

Finally he did the rough for the poster, and naturally it was Fräulein Händle who was to be seen shaving her armpits with a Rumpus blade.

We took the design to the post office and sent it off to the factory. We did not have much hope, but a week later we got another cheque. I went out and bought a litre of grain spirits and finished it on my own, as Kreti was not allowed any liquor.

We still had four hundred marks left when the first posters appeared announcing: FACE-YOUR-MAKER-PROPERLY-SHAVED·   ITH A RUMPUS!

We spent hours walking around the town, stopping in front of every hoarding to eye Fräulein Händle's breasts rising as she shaved herself.

One evening Kreti asked me whether it might not be better if he cut off his beard. All I said was: "If you must—the blade for you is Rumpus!"

I quickly discovered what I had started. With some scissors Fräulein Händle had left behind he cut off his beard and threw it down the w.c. He bought razor-blades and scraped at his skin until it bled. I advised a milder brand, at eight or six pfennigs. He tried them all out and in the end we had a table covered with rusted razor-blades, caked along its rim with dried lather and chips of his golden bristles. Everywhere we went in the streets we were faced with our poster, and Kreti was so carried away that he was always dragging me into chemists and toilet shops to buy Rumpus blades. He was like a farmer gorging to death on his fruit rather than share it with anyone. Kreti not only shaved his face, but his legs, his chest and his arms as well. Our money gave out, and when we were thrown out of the hotel each of us stepped into the open with a grip of Rumpus razor-blades in our hands.

"I'm trying to imagine," I said to Kreti, "what would have happened if we had met a pill-maker instead."

But all the way out of town Kreti saw nothing, heard nothing, strode past his own posters in new-found masculinity, cast lecherous glances at the girls as he used to do at the boys, and smiled when I asked him where we were going and how. All we needed was for him to enlist as a soldier, as had indeed become possible again. The reason for his wanting to get to Schiebach at all costs, a walk of twenty kilometres, became clear to me as soon as I saw the posters announcing the Olympia circus there, including the appearance of Fräulein Händle with her brown bear. Kreti accompanied me as far as the big top, stretched out his hand and said: "Love, Bonifaz, is the strongest thing on earth. I

158

know you don't care about it and I must admit that I've had my disappointments as well. But I can't help it. Farewell, and give Pulle my love, if you see her again."

He slapped me on the shoulder with unexpected force, took the bag of razor-blades from my hand and left me standing. He walked round the big top in the direction of the caravans and that, for the time being, was the last I saw of him.

54

IT was not far to Christmas, where all the fir forests are chopped down, children's eyes are polished until they sparkle back from the silver balls, and tears are shed over new pyjamas and wrist-watches.

I wanted to avoid the whole business and it was a good thing I did, for otherwise I might have missed meeting Vieth and Dierk, a remarkable pair whom I met on the road to Gundelfingen. None of us actually wanted to go to Gundelfingen, and two of us, namely Vieth and Dierk, were never to find out exactly where Gundelfingen was.

Vieth, the elder of the two, was a person whom it was hard to imagine as having any relatives. Furthermore, he was easily excitable, which caused him to lose charts and log. tables. Dierk, the younger one, was very fair and small, an ex-jockey with the urge to fly. They told me all about themselves as we walked along.

"We are space travellers," began Vieth.

"I," said Dierk, "I am the only space traveller."

"That's right, Dierk," continued Vieth, who was used to the objection, "get behind and push, while I explain our project to this gentleman."

Dierk, in riding breeches and muddy boots and with a silken neckerchief, trudged to the rear end of a handcart, on which lay a gleaming fish-shape in metal, while I grasped the shaft with Vieth. The B-class road sign pointed to Gundelfingen and indicated a distance of sixty kilometres. The sun was low in the sky and with a Tessar lens and a number eighteen filter you could easily have photographed it without melting a hole in the film.

"We are space travellers," repeated Vieth.

"And you can make a living from that?" I asked.

"So-so. Judging by tangible successes, I should have to confess we were going down rather than up."

"It's the saints who scale heaven."

"Did you hear that, Dierk," shouted Vieth over his shoulder, "he's one of us."

Dierk banged his assent on the fish's fuselage.

"I should tell you that until not long ago I was still a pharmacist. At a place in town. More or less senior pharmacist. I had developed a completely new type of explosive which caused the destruction of a third of the town. It's understandable that I lost my job."

"You've got this explosive with you?"

"Naturally. But it detonates only in combination with water."

I looked at the sky, but there was no sign of rain.

"But I mustn't only talk about myself," Vieth lit a pipe. He took a match, evidently another of his inventions, struck it on the rocket-whale and held the flame to his nose. Guessing my thoughts, he remarked reassuringly: "I have already told you: only in combination with water."

"Exactly why is that?"

"Well, actually hydrogen. You see, I have discovered the means of controlling helium diffusion, my good friend."

I was astounded. "But that's . . ."

"Isn't it?" said Vieth. "But let's leave it at that. And please don't start asking me why I'm not at the moment thinking of industrial exploitation."

"But excuse me," I insisted, in spite of his warning, "you could have everything you wanted. I mean, for example, a multi-axle car with furnished rooms. I'm thinking of a razor-blade manufacturer whom I met the other day. You wouldn't even have to travel, you could have panoramas of the most beautiful places in the world carried past the windows. And so on."

Vieth laughed at me. "Who are you trying to kid? Furnished rooms! Panoramas!" Vieth was helpless with laughter. He leant against the fish and drummed on it with both fists. There were faint bangs and the log. tables fell in the mud. It was only gradually that the pharmacist recovered himself.

"Oh well," he said at last, managing with difficulty to assume a more or less serious expression, but still chuckling, "I suppose everybody has one little bee in his bonnet, my dear Bonifaz. But as you see, one can't help laughing over it. You must realise, after all, that in our case you're dealing with serious people. You shouldn't come and try to spin us yarns like that."

"I'm sorry, Herr Vieth," I said, justifying myself, "I must confess I did regard his form of self-indulgence as rather enviable, since it combines a certain eccentricity with fantastic luxury in such a conspicuous manner."

"I'll say it was conspicuous!"

"I do have a weakness for idiots," I said. "But you're the sort of person I have downright respect for. There's something so well-bred about you."

Vieth thanked me deprecatingly and picked up the thread again. "Dierk was a gentleman rider. But, as you can imagine, the sky-flying impulse seizes one in the saddle, too."

"Has Herr Dierk had many falls?"

"He has not. He was a master jockey. He held the blue ribbon with white sash."

"That must have suited him very well, with his fair hair."

"Of course it did. But that isn't all. He rode a winner at Epsom."

"I can't believe it."

"But I tell you he did."

"Then it must be true."

"His trouble was winning too often. And do you know why that was?"

"Probably on account of his being so good at it, if I can put it like that," I answered rather indecisively.

"He was too light."

"Aha?"

"He was much too light," added the pharmacist, beaming all over his face.

"What you mean is that he was too light for the mounts, and that the other gentlemen-riders complained that he was always winning because he was so light? And so they told him: either you eat yourself full to bursting or else . . . How much did he weigh?"

"Fifty-eight pounds, and now he's fifty-six—dead weight."

"There was a man in Tesch once, who was under fifty-six pounds, and they put him on show when we had the church dedication, though in his case it didn't come from riding. His trouble was the children eating him out of house and home."

"Where does he live?" asked Vieth.

"In Tesch."

"Can we go that way?"

"I don't think so, Herr Vieth, what do we want to do there?"

Vieth drooped his head. "I might eventually need a second man, you know. Unfortunately you wouldn't do, as you weigh about three times too much."

"What do you need a second man for, Herr Vieth?"

"Not so loud, Bonifaz. Dierk needn't hear this."

Cosmonaut Vieth bent towards me as he walked. His nose touched my temple. "Today or tomorrow the rocket will be launched."

"What rocket?"

"The one on the cart."

"That fish?"

"The rocket has been given the aerodynamic lines of a fish to increase its speed. We've got to fire it today or tomorrow."

"Why?"

"Because the Russians have a space rocket ready for next week."

"Oh I see, and so you want to . . ."

"And so we want to—in other words: I want to beat them to it. Germany is going to have the glory."

"But what has the second man got to do with it?"

Vieth looked sad. "He might lose his life."

"Dierk?"

"Science demands her sacrifices."

"And so does Germany."

"Exactly."

For a while we went on in silence, Vieth and I in front, bent forwards with our hands on the shaft, and at the tail of the cart, bent like ourselves and splashing the mud on his breeches, gentleman-rider Dierk.

"So you see, I might possibly need a stand-in. He'll get through the atmosphere all right. He'll even probably orbit the earth for a time. In an ellipse, obviously. I calculate that the apogee of his orbit lies in the constellation of Virgo. If, however, he escapes from the earth's gravitational field and proceeds outwards into the universe, he might orbit the sun or land on the moon."

"It's pretty hard going on the moon."

"No, I want him to come back! Only, if he does come back . . ."

"How will he come back?"

"You've got the point. I need a real lightweight. Dierk is by far the most suitable person imaginable. But if he comes back at too high a velocity—assuming that he does in fact reapproach the earth—he is bound to burn up in the atmosphere."

"Which could be the day after tomorrow."

"Today or tomorrow it's bound to be go."

I looked up at the sun, if you can call it looking up, as it was setting at the moment.

"Don't you think that it's a bit late to start now?"

"Perhaps you're right," said Vieth.

"And besides tomorrow would be the best day for it. Tomorrow is Christmas day. You'll be giving us a magic Christmas candle."

I let go of the shaft, whereupon the cart stopped immediately. I went aft and waved to Dierk. "Go forward, feather weight! I'm pushing."

And so we crept ahead with our rocket-whale on the highroad to Gundelfingen.

163

55

IF we had navigated by the stars and the moon we should have been in bed long ago. But we were navigating by our lights within, and so it was not until about midnight that we reached an inn at a country cross-roads.

"I shall reconnoitre," said Vieth, "and find out whether we can spend the night here. Wait for me."

After Vieth had gone I had a question for the gentleman-rider. "Show me the constellation of Virgo."

"What's that got to do with you?" he said, swaying his fifty-six pounds.

"When I'm looking at the sky tomorrow evening I shall be thinking of you. As the maximum radius from the centre of your orbit will lie in Virgo, I shall have the pleasure of actually witnessing the apex of your career. At this moment you're still only a bum and a nut. The day after tomorrow your name will be on the lips of the whole human race. A mausoleum will be erected over your grave. You're the man who is about to pluck humanity's chestnuts out of the fire."

"I'm flying exactly nowhere."

I was not able to go on for Vieth came back. Behind him was the landlord, who was nice and fat.

"What's that?" he asked and shone his pocket flashlight at the rocket.

"A fish," I said.

"Dead fish stinks."

"This fish isn't a *fish*," said Vieth, "it is a space ship."

"A space fish," said the landlord.

"A flying fish, so to speak," I added.

"Of course," said the landlord. "You can put it in the stable. It is no good trying to pull my leg," he said to me.

"Can you let us have something to eat?" asked Dierk.

"Are you out of your mind?" shouted Vieth. "Are you trying to make me a laughing stock in the whole scientific world? Do you want all my experiments to end in a noose round our necks? Pull yourself together!"

"Well then, just for two, landlord," said Dierk humbly.

But I noticed that his adam's apple was going up and down, which is a poor sign in a hungry man who's waiting to be launched into space.

While Dierk took the fish round to the stable, we sat down to an aromatic lentil soup, seasoned it with vinegar and sugar and emptied our plates. The landlord sat with us, following each spoonful with his eyes.

"You're staying over Christmas?" he enquired.

"Yes," said Vieth, "probably just for Christmas day. And then we're off to the observatory at Gundelfingen."

"If you'd care to join us for the solemnity of present-giving in the evening, please let me know. Then I'll set places for three more."

"How long does the lark go on for?" asked Vieth.

"We're very attached to our traditional ways hereabouts. An hour or so."

"It's a deal, then. And now to bed. Would you give my assistant a small dish of buttermilk?" Vieth left the parlour and I heard him going up the stairs.

"Don't you want to go to bed?" asked the landlord, tapping eight dirty fingernails on the wooden table. I pushed my plate up against them, listened to the ticking of the clock on the wall, counted the cats around the stove and said quietly: "No, I'm waiting for the assistant."

"I'll leave you, then," said the landlord, "only mind you don't drop off down here. I like the air to be fresh in the mornings."

After a little while Dierk came in, light as a feather and hungry. He gulped down the buttermilk.

"Is he asleep?" he asked.

"He's no Newton," I said.

"You have to be born with brains."

"And as twins," I said.

"I suppose you're one?" asked Dierk.

"There's two of me when I'm dreaming," I replied.

"I never dream," said Dierk, "and anyhow I weigh too little for a man of my age. You need to put on weight to get things off your mind. Children are fat and they can dream about the seven dwarfs. Fat men dream of food. I can't even do that."

"Don't you dream about your great flight?"

"I'm not making any flight, Herr Bonifaz. Vieth should go and fry his own skin. He's the inventor of the miracle-weapon. Just too bad that the war was over when his final experiment came off. He'd have been something bigger by now: deputy leader or Führer or president or something. The capitulation beat him to it by eight weeks. I know he doesn't give a damn if I'm killed."

I rubbed my knees; I was cold. "And have you always been a gentleman rider?"

"No! Wherever did you get that idea from? But can I be frank with you?"

"If it helps you."

"Do you have any children?"

"I don't know of any."

"That's just as well. I was a child extermination expert. Horrible, isn't it? I had to get used to it. If there's a thousand people fewer in the world today, it's my fault." Dierk laughed and twisted the empty bowl the buttermilk had been in between his hands. "You may think me a bit naïve to start talking about my past. Usually people do it when they're drunk. All I need is a sip of buttermilk and an honest face. Like yours."

I put one fist on top of the other and laid my forehead on them. "Go on," I said.

"In the last year of the war, when they were pulling out from everywhere, we were short of ammunition for decimating the civilian population. We had to work under very different conditions from those fine white overalls in the camps. No gas chambers. No injections. No rat poison. Our task was in some ways an extremely manly one. We were the quintessence of leadership. I had a brigade under me and unrestricted powers. My weight was then a good hundred and fourteen pounds. I was bursting at the seams. In the villages along the line of withdrawal I used to drum together the six to ten year-olds: boys and girls alike. Those whitewashed walls in the Balkans make an atrocious light for shooting. Aiming against them around noon burns your eyes. Five kids would line up in a file, noses to back of head. The nose and the back of the head—racial characteristics, Herr Bonifaz!"

"Yes," I said.

"My men took up position beside the kids, well spaced out. The kids'd be laughing until they heard me take the catch off my tommy-gun and switch over from bursts to single shots. Then they'd stand like a deck of aces. Nobody ever tried to run away when the moment came. Of course it depends on getting them the same height if you're going to hit the top vertebrae all the way through. It's advisable to keep them together in age groups. You can't leave them lying around half dead. The penetration you can get from a tommy-gun always surprises me. The front fellow's already down while number four's still alive. Number four frequently did survive and number five always did. I imagine they'll remember that! Like the first time one really falls in love, I expect; one simply can't forget it."

Dierk stood up and walked across the room. One of the cats jumped over his boots. "After the war I became a jockey. For my father-in-law's stables. My name's different now. Shall I tell you my real name?"

I did not reply.

"I owe him a lot, eh?"

I lay with my face on the table.

"My God, here I am pouring out my heart, and you can sit there dozing!" Dierk turned around in the middle of the room and went to the door. Gingerly he lifted the latch. A cat ran out between his legs, light and hungry. I turned my head to one side on the table and gouged short, deep grooves in the wood with my fingernail.

56

THE following noon Vieth and Dierk, with my assistance, heaved the rocket onto the tarred roof of a shed outside the inn. It was snowing and we had to cover the rocket with a blanket to keep it from blowing off in the wind. It had two seats, one behind the other. We placed a log under its nose and pointed this towards the area of sky indicated by Vieth's calculations. Dierk tested the circuits, and tried on the helmet and the thick quilted gloves.

"Don't you think you should make a test flight first?" I suggested, but Vieth only shook his head and smiled.

Dierk clambered out again and, while Vieth made his way down the ladder to go and take a grog with the landlord, he said to me: "You might do me a favour, Herr Bonifaz."

"With pleasure," I said.

"What do you say to our launching Herr Vieth into the air on his own?"

"Aha," I said.

"I don't feel like sacrificing myself for him," he said.

"I can understand that," I said, "but how are you going to set about it?"

"We're both getting into the rocket this evening, Vieth and I. He says he wants to be at my side for the countdown. I'll ask him to stay in his seat for a moment, then I'll get out, jump off the roof and you'll pour the bucket over it."

"Over what?"

"There's a scaffold beside the rocket with a bucket of heavy water hanging from it. If the water hits the fuselage he's launched."

"Well, yes, I could manage that," I said. "But why don't you want to pull the string yourself?"

The inn door opened and Vieth called out: "Come along in! Time for presents!"

The landlord had put a few chairs round the Christmas tree and his four children were sitting there and singing *Silent Night, Holy Night* in the gloom. I sat down beside Vieth, who reeked of rum.

The landlord handed out the presents. The two girls got dolls, the boys got soldiers, the landlord's wife got an apron and the landlord himself, to his great delight, got over-sized underpants. Then he went behind the bar and came back with six kippers, which he tied to the Christmas tree in between the candles. He asked his wife to open the kitchen door and let the cats in. Dierk leaned forward and enjoyed it as much as the children, watching the famished cats jumping for the red herrings, burning their fur or scuffling with each other when one of them managed to get on target and seize the smoked titbit. The landlord watched impassively, only once remarking to Vieth: "After all, we've got to let the children have some fun at Christmas. We couldn't afford an electric train."

"Of course not," said Vieth.

"Your elder boy is very thin," said Dierk.

"That's true," said the landlord, "he ought to eat better. We sent a birthday message for him to the children's programme." He turned to the boy, "what was it they told you on the radio, Helge?"

The little boy came up, holding a tank in his left hand and two soldiers in his right, and said: "Helge is seven today and our message for Helge is—eat better, Helge."

"Good," said the landlord, "now, back to your games—But he just won't eat."

"I hope he doesn't starve some day," said Dierk.

"My wife's keeping an eye on that."

"Tsk," said Vieth. "Well then, shall we?"

"What are your plans for today?" enquired the landlord.

"This gentleman," I said aloud and pointing to Dierk, "is going to fly to the moon."

"What?" said the landlord.

The children dropped their toys and came closer.

"Who's flying to the moon?" they asked.

"I am," said Dierk, as Vieth slapped him on the shoulder.

169

"Are you really?" asked Helge.

"And when will you come back?" asked the four-year-old girl.

"Next week," said Dierk.

"Will you bring us something nice with you?"

"What would you like to have?" asked Dierk.

"A pistol," begged Helge.

"A star," said the little girl.

"A sausage," said Ulrike.

"No, a pistol," insisted Helge.

"But you're much too small to have a pistol," said Dierk.

"But I want to go shooting," said Helge.

"What do you want to shoot at?" asked Dierk.

"At daddy," said Helge, "then I won't have to eat any more."

The landlord laughed and drew clever little Helge onto his knee.

"Now, I mean, really," he said, "are you really flying to the moon?"

"Yes," nodded Vieth, "immediately."

"Why didn't you tell me sooner? I'd have invited the press and done myself some good. Reporters are great drinkers."

"It's a complete secret," I said, "that's why."

The landlord behaved as if I did not exist. It was now dark outside. The moon, still untrodden by Dierk's boots, was shining through the window-panes. We would know more in an hour from now. Vieth and Dierk went ahead of me. The bucket was hanging under the scaffold above the rocket. Vieth and Dierk seemed to want to confer over a few details and did not need my presence.

Afterwards Vieth came up to me and said: "We've decided to give our rocket a final loading test. Dierk and I suggest that the best thing will be if you take a seat in the rocket so that we can check everything from the outside."

"You've gone off your head, haven't you?" I said.

"I beg your pardon, Herr Bonifaz?" said Vieth.

"Really," said Dierk, "it's only a matter of a couple of minutes."

"Get on with it, man," said the landlord, who had approached us.

"Why don't *you* get inside?" I asked him.

"I've got a family," he said, puffing up smugly and pointing to his four children standing in the snow with their arms around each other's shoulders.

"I wouldn't mind flying as far as Gundelfingen," I said, "but the moon's too far for me."

"What are you talking about?" asked Dierk. "This is simply a test."

"You're a miserable drip," said Vieth.

"Slacker," said the landlord.

"Chicken," said Dierk.

"Let me fly to the moon," said Ulrike, the landlord's daughter.

"Not a bad idea," said Dierk, and reached out to take her by the hand and clamber to the roof of the shed with her.

"I'll stave both your heads in and rub your guts on the floor if you don't let go of the child," I said.

"If the father gives his consent," said Vieth, "there's nothing at all you can do about it. Ulrike weighs about the same as my friend Dierk. Well?"

I took the girl and said to her quietly: "Go back into the house. Look out of the window. A magic candle's going to fly into the sky. It's much prettier than your Christmas tree."

The landlord stood beside me as Vieth and Dierk went onto the roof, got into the rocket and closed the doors. I tugged at a cord and pulled off the blanket. The snow had stopped.

"Look out!" I shouted to the landlord and pulled the string so that the bucketful of water poured on to the big tin rocket-fish. I threw myself down in the snow beside the landlord. There was a blaze, thunder, and a whistle. Above us there was a rushing sound, a suction of air, a rattling of windows, and when we raised ourselves on our hands, we saw the shed was on fire. It was burning so brightly that we stared in vain at the rocket disappearing somewhere up there among the clouds.

There was nothing left of the shed. The landlord latched himself onto the telephone as soon as he had assured himself that I had no intention of running away. The landlord's wife sobbed into her apron. As soon as the children saw her, oh, how their faces fell!

"Yes," said the landlord, "Brennecke here. I've got a firebug here.

No, not the Christmas tree. Are you drunk? A man here has just fired a rocket to the moon and my outhouse has been burnt down as a result. Stop laughing! The man's standing next to me. No, I run an inn. What d'you mean by 'Is that so?' I'm in no mood for humour. My outhouse has burnt down, can you get that?"

With his unoccupied fist, the landlord beat on his left thigh and bellowed: "Unless you come immediately, I'll never pay another tax! No, it can't wait till tomorrow. D'you think I want to keep the bastard in my house any longer? All right, then."

He hung up the receiver and looked at me mistrustfully. I sat down at the parlour table.

"Shall we have a beer for our nerves?" I asked, but he just went on drumming on the zinc-topped bar. We had quite a long wait before we heard a motor-cycle outside. The gendarme had had to come all the way from Tittingen and he was caked down the front with snow, so that in any other mood I would have taken him for the abominable snowman in person.

"Who are you?" he asked me as the landlord served him a grog.

"I am a neutral," I said truthfully, presenting my document.

"Doesn't apply here," he said, and tipped the hot fluid into his mouth. "Did you set fire to the shed?"

"No, that was the two gentlemen, the ones who invented heavy water and have flown to the moon."

"Don't try to talk to me like that. Just because it's Christmas eve, you needn't think you can allow yourself any liberties. Well, then, now, what happened?"

"Three men arrived here yesterday," said the landlord. "They wanted to fly to the moon."

"I didn't," I said.

"Go on," said the gendarme. "Were the men drunk?"

"I don't think so," said the landlord. "They had a rocket with them."

"A—what?" asked the gendarme.

"I told you: a rocket—a sort of fish made of metal."

"Aha," said the gendarme. "Do you often get fish like that?"

"Very rarely," said the landlord.

"You are under arrest," said the gendarme placing his hand on Herr Brennecke's shoulder but at the same time knocking his glass over and scalding the landlord's belly. The landlord leaped up, shouted to his wife, his wife burst into tears again and the children dashed out of the parlour.

"Just a minute," I said, "it really isn't Herr Brennecke's fault."

"I see," said the gendarme. "So you confess. Then you are under arrest."

"Oh, who is it now?" I asked.

"You," said the gendarme, pointing at me.

The landlord breathed deeply, the gendarme pulled handcuffs from his satchel and placed them on the table. "I have a pistol as well in case you offer resistance."

"I think in the circumstances we can dispense with that," I said.

"So much the better. We shall now go and inspect the scene of the crime."

We went out again and in the moonlight the gendarme walked twice around the concrete foundation where the shed had stood. He was not fully sober.

"And where did you obtain this heavy water?" he asked.

"I met the gentlemen on my way here. I don't know any further details about it. One of them also mentioned helium."

"Sounds highly suspicious. The master-mind, I shouldn't wonder, eh? We'll get *him* in the net all right."

We went back into the parlour, the gendarme had another grog and drew the outline of the shed and the position of the inn on a sheet of paper, like a story in pictures. Then I put on my cap and preceded him out of the door.

"Goodbye," I said to the landlord. "If you hear anything from the two gentlemen, please let me know."

All the landlord said was: "You clear out!"

And I had only wanted to give his children a little fun.

"We'd better walk it, eh?" I suggested to the gendarme, after we had come unstuck on a curve and had shaken off the snow.

173

"Out of the question," he growled. "Do you think I can't ride a motor-bike?"

"Oh sure," I said, "you're a good pilot, but you fly a bit low."

"Can you ride?" he asked.

"Yes," I said.

"Well then, ride!"

"Would you perhaps mind taking off the handcuffs first?"

He unlocked them, which was not a simple operation, as we had to make a long, long search for the key. Then he clambered on to the pillion, clasped his arms around me, and I put my foot on the starter. When we got to Tittingen I had to carry him into the police station, as he had gone to sleep.

57

THE examining magistrate, a man in his thirties, had dandruff. Whenever he went out of the room for a moment I looked behind him as I felt he must be leaving a trail of lost hairs in his wake. He was not unfriendly, but so formal that I could not possibly accuse him of the slightest degree of unseemly indulgence towards me. He knew his way about the law, fair's fair, and now I understood why we have so many bald-headed lawyers.

"You'll have to make up your mind about it," he said at my second examination. "The best outlook for you is nice straight-forward arson. Then you'll get away with twelve months. You don't have to worry about a fraudulent insurance claim, as the policy had expired. My advice to you is this: don't insist on having seen two people in a fish on the roof. That would get you certified, and in the unlikely event of your being believed you'd be in for Section 222: manslaughter with criminal negligence; 226: grievous bodily harm; or 307, Paragraph One: arson and premeditated homicide; not to mention the fact that as you seem to think you've propelled these persons at the moon, you could be liable under Section 139A: failure to halt while in charge of a vehicle, or even section 221, namely, endangering the safety of an infirm person, since according to the landlord's statement one of the two gentlemen can't have weighed more than fifty pounds."

"Fifty-six," I corrected him.

"Well all right," he said. "I won't argue over six pounds."

"Do you think there's possibly any section I didn't break?"

"Hardly. You have imperilled aviation, section 315; committed a public nuisance, 360; and you are a habitual vagrant, 361, Paragraph One, Subsection Three. It is to be presumed that you were also intoxicated."

"No," I said, "that I certainly wasn't."

"You are not in possession of an identity card."

"But I am. I'm neutral."

"Look, my dear fellow," said the magistrate, "what sort of world are you living in?"

"I can tell what sort at times," I said, "but mostly I live in my own."

"Perhaps you really ought to go into a mental home."

"I'll try to mend my ways," I said, as someone in the cell had given me the tip that it pays to show contrition.

At the hearing I was sentenced to eighteen months' imprisonment. I did not appeal.

58

THE prison guard enjoyed conversing with me on the subject of torture. Admittedly the whole prison contained not a single thumbscrew and no amount of searching would have brought either stocks or sticks to light, but it may have been the very fact of these humane surroundings which provoked him, for he would spend hours expatiating on a precise schedule of torture: hot water treatment, shock treatment, monotony with interruptions, promises, arm and leg dislocation, and kindly persuasion. The result he really wanted to achieve was not so much a penitent confession as a man's transformation, so that he should come to perceive his own worth through the jailor's eyes and in this way be induced by self-knowledge to claim the appropriate punishment for himself. The guard had subjected his method to a long period of experiment on his wife, with whom he had registered unique success. It had thus become the custom at home for her to pronounce sentence on herself without having to go into details about the delict of which she sensed herself to be guilty. In place of bed-time prayers she would say "Two months," or, somewhat more rarely, "Sixteen months," and so on. It was only when the sentence exceeded twelve months that he would look admonishingly at her and perhaps threaten her with a wagging finger. One winter evening, however, when she said: "Life," he choked over his soup and tried to laugh. But she was perfectly serious. She had a lover, a crossing-keeper on the Ebersalm-Gundelfingen line, and she had killed him with a meat chopper, after which she had cooked the dinner and put the children to bed.

"My method had been triumphantly successful," said the screw, "you rarely get a case like that."

"It was scarcely preventive, though," I said.

"That's just it," said the guard. "If I'd put her inside a bit earlier, for six months, or twelve months, by God she'd have had to let her crossing-keeper get away and then it wouldn't have hit her so hard when he married the stewardess on the Orient Express."

"What I meant was, preventive in general," I said.

"What! Do you really believe, Herr Bonifaz, that you could ever get people so ironed out by whipping and psychiatry, from the time they were kids on, that they'd actually go to prison of their own accord?"

"It depends on the method," I said.

"No," he said, "it all comes too late. You see, as a prison officer I'm not only a civil servant but also an educator. Not in the sense of simply helping the prisoners to while away the time they spend in our institution, but rather by my being able, as a result of my detailed knowledge of every single case, to hold before their eyes what is reprehensible about their deed. At the same time I point out to them the way in which they can avoid similar transgressions when they are at liberty again. That is the task I have as guard. It is difficult, it is responsible, it requires diplomacy and imagination. Nevertheless, in some cases it has turned out that even these outstanding personal qualities do not in themselves suffice to make a successful correctional officer.

"There are two cases that come to mind, they are some time back now, and they will illustrate what I mean. I will tell you at the start exactly what I am asking for: the judiciary should decide that for every law, and for that law alone, a certain number of officers should be allotted who do not have to concern themselves with any other law, and will only supervise delinquents who have broken that particular law. Let us suppose that parliament passed a law laying it down that bicycle bells must be fixed on the right-hand handlebar; this would mean that the prison administration would quickly make available a sizable number of officers who would be assigned exclusively to taking charge of convicted left-hand bicycle-bell-ringers. You may think this is too minor an example, and we could just as well quote parricide or arson. Basically, the way I see it, it's not the gravity of the crime that counts, and certainly not questions of justice, but rather the inward struggle within a guard, especially if he should ever find himself faced with cases like the two about which I am going to tell you.

"In Cell Seventy-Eight, here in this institution, a two-bunker on the second floor of the left wing, we had two convicts. Both had been bakers. They argued with each other the whole livelong day and I must say that I had to force myself to go near them, whether to bring them their food or to fetch their pails.

"Baker Dammann had been sentenced four and a half years before to five years imprisonment under the Food Acts, as even after the war he had continued to mix bran with the flour and had thereby accumulated considerable wealth. For four and a half years I visited convict Dammann twice a week to convince him of the shamefulness of his deed. I described the sufferings of people with stomach complaints who had unwittingly eaten his bread. I described the miserable wasting away of infants, the agonised screams of the aged and infirm in the hospitals, the puzzled head-shaking of workmen and office employees over their unwonted bowel activity. Not only that, I told him about the godly gift of the wheat in our fields, about the mowing and the threshing, about the hard journey to the mill, about the industrious miller sorting out the husks and setting them aside, if not as rubbish, still, for some lesser purpose. For years I poured the rustling of the cornfields into his ear, opened his window—far wider than regulations permitted —so that he could drink in deeply the scent of the fields in all their verdant freshness under the morning sun. Nature itself with its colours and smells was to have brought about his inward stocktaking and contrition. However, immediately before our final success (convict Dammann was already going on his knees and solemnly promising amendment) it happened that one afternoon, when I fetched the pail from his cell, he didn't come up as usual and ask me about the state of the harvest, but in reply to my astonished inquiry pointed to his bunk where his breakfast was lying almost untouched. He picked up the bread, broke it apart and showed me chaff and bran baked in our otherwise irreproachable loaf. I promised to investigate this, and went down to the yard deep in thought. The same evening the convict Reczoreck was delivered and conducted by the governor personally to Cell Seventy-Eight in the main block, on the second storey of the left wing. One of the clerical staff informed me that Reczoreck had been sentenced to five years' imprisonment under the new Food Acts. After the Right-Radicals had come to power, Parliament had voted, among other emergency measures, an amendment of the hitherto prevailing legislation regarding foodstuffs with the result that henceforward it would only be a crime to fail to mix bran with the dough. Naturally it wasn't called bran but supplementary nutrients, but it came to the same thing. The new convict Reczoreck, who had not complied with this legislation, had received a well-merited sentence in the lower courts. Utterly opposed in his professional outlook to convict Dammann, he was nevertheless lodged in the same cell with him. Even if that had not been the case, it would not have altered my situation as a correctional officer.

"Could I go to convict Reczoreck now and expatiate to him on the degradation of his deed, by telling him—in accordance with the commentary accompanying the new Act—that it was an absolute necessity to supplement the dough with bran in order to preserve the nation's health? That bran in particular—thanks to its prophylactic qualities and in accordance with the commentaries accompanying the new Act—was the source of vital food values for mankind, especially for children? That from bran alone, that is to say, from supplementary nutrients alone do we obtain those body-preserving substances which are lacking in ordinary bread? And all the time I would have my own words ringing in my ears, the words with which I had depicted to convict Dammann the catastrophic effects of bran.

"I have no doubt that objectively speaking convict Reczoreck was the more admirable of the two in human terms, while the trouble I'd taken on behalf of convict Dammann now seem to have been doubly ridiculous. But at the same time the fervour with which as a guard, I love and honour the law prevents one from picturing convict Reczoreck as any sort of martyr, since after all he incurred his penalty in the full consciousness of what he was doing and not as the result of a casual mistake. I feel sure that the rest of convict Dammann's sentence will be commuted in some form or other, although I do not believe—in so far as I, as a servant of the state, have any right to express myself on the subject—that the Right-Radical government of our present prime minister intends to reverse previous legislation in its entirety. For in this paradoxical situation—two bakers guilty of offences that cancelled each other out, sharing one cell—the interesting point emerges that the present government, in declaring itself to be the legitimate successor of the previous one, thus automatically accepts the basic legislative theses of its predecessor. Having acknowledged the logic of this and at the same time taking it into account that a sentence of five years imprisonment had very patently emphasised the fundamentally anti-social nature of convict Dammann's deed—especially as it was not a case of individual parricide or arson, such as I previously mentioned, but an act directed against the state as a whole—it would therefore not surprise me in the least if our chancellor's administration deliberately refrained from issuing a pardon.

"So now we find ourself in a position from which I, a jailor who desires to be not merely a jailor but an educator as well, saw no way out. I could no longer enter Cell Seventy-Eight in the main block without pangs of conscience. Nevertheless I respect, as I said before, the intentions of both laws. Only—how was I to explain to convict Dammann that bran induces diarrhoea, and at the same time to convict Reczoreck that bran builds up the marrow?

"Hence, you see, my recommendation that the authorities should set up a training college for adaptable officers of the law, whose inmates could be prepared for each statute without individual confusion, whether it was to be a case of bran-adulteration, of parricide, of arson or of bicycle bells.

"Admittedly I have my apprehensions regarding this proposal. New measures usually indicate war in the offing. Before my proposal reached the hands of the minister of justice, I might be filling sandbags again. And if the government set eyes on it then, they might easily regard it as treason.

"So I went straight to Cell Seventy-Eight on the second storey in the left wing and asked Dammann and Reczoreck what they thought we ought to do if the worst came to the worst again."

"And what happened then?" I wanted to know.

"They were both pinched again."

"What for?"

"For political activity while under sentence."

"That means somebody must have denounced them."

"Of course. I did."

59

A big ship needs a deep draught and many a time the walls closed in on me. After three months Sepp, the oldest man in our cell, died of a stroke. We had all been together beforehand and he had said, "Then, won't the coaches and the mouse-marriage parties be allowed to drive up to heaven any more?"

Sepp had been a real old soak, which was why he always had mice going round inside his head. For quite a while I made myself unpopular with Theo and Richard by eating garlic, but it agreed with me and I could not afford to be considerate.

Every evening Theo said: "All I'd like to be is a teeny tiny dachshund pissing in all the corners, running round the trees and so full of beans it can't stand still."

Theo had been a salesman for a detergent firm and had defrauded the factory of twenty thousand marks.

Richard was always talking about a blonde with long hair and if he'd told her to she'd even have trodden on it, just for his sake. He could still kick himself, he said, for not having told her to.

Towards the end of the first year the warder took me out to the visiting parlour. There sat Kreti, in a silk scarf and smelling of perfume. His nails were cut to a point and his thumbnails were over two inches long.

"Well, old chap," he said, shoving over a packet of cigarettes which the warder snatched and put in his pocket.

"Well," I said.

"Yes," said Kreti, "that's the way it is, it's cold out there. I've had a lot of bad luck, and if it goes on like this I'll soon be keeping you company. I don't know how I'm going to pay all the mainten-ance."

"How many have you got now?"

"A good thirty," said Kreti.

"Surely Fräulein Händle can't have managed all that on her own . . ."

"Oh, her," said Kreti, "I'm now in a refugee camp where I'm the only male."

"How do you stand it?"

"Sometimes I wonder myself. Of course they make a big fuss over me: breakfast and coffee and lunch one after the other. The only thing is, I really have to keep at them."

"Visiting time over," said the warder shaking his head as Kreti placed another box of cigarettes on the table.

"The Kaiser of Germany is what they call me in the camp," he said and stood up. "By the way, just so that you know: Pulle's having a baby, too. Won't be until the summer, though. You ought to go over and see her. She's living at Mierstedt. Perhaps she'll write to you. You can come and see me too, of course, although, well, you know how it is —I don't have much time . . ."

"So long, your majesty," I said and the warder led me out, and Kreti adjusted his silk scarf in his reflection on the window. Revolting fellow, I thought. Used to be my friend.

In the spring I got a letter from Pulle saying she wanted to arrange things so that she would have the baby when I came out of prison.

I wrote back and said that I would come and see her in Mierstedt as soon as I was free. The jailor's children supplied me with pencil and paper. I wrote on the back of the pages in their exercise book. Bertram had given me his biology book. In it I read: "Hares live in railway embankments. They sleep on the rails. Sometimes the freight trains pass and run over them and kill them."

I sent all this to Pulle and added underneath: "Children have principles, grown-ups have intentions," and for Bertram and Lucie I interpreted the physical formula for work:

$$\text{work} = \frac{\text{distance}}{\text{effort}} \times \text{time}$$

by singing it to them like this:

$$\text{work} = \frac{Tipperary}{Heave\text{-}ho} \times Roll\ on,\ tomorrow$$

In the spring and early summer I spent a lot of time sitting with them. I wove baskets and told stories and when July came and it was my birthday I told Bertram and Lucie, the jailor's children, the miraculous tale of Ah and Oh, and next day I was released.

60

You'll be pleased as porcupines and amazed as armadillos when I tell you the miraculous wonder-story of Ah and Oh. You haven't yet forgotten how to feel wonder, have you? Look around:

The sun's shining, the cow's calving, the cat's lapping the milk, there's a storm blowing up, the cock's crowing, granddad's nodding off over his lunch, the soup's on the boil, the pot's going to crack, the mountain's toppling into the lake, the moon's missing, bread costs too much, fellows are putting on steel helmets, it's snowing in Africa, an Eskimo's planting banana-trees in Lapland, a policeman's blowing on the flute, the midwife's having a baby—you're having the surprise of your lives, and the surprise of your lives is what your life begins with.

You'd open your mouths and your eyes would pop and you'd be astounded if you ever saw the table laying itself, the golden ass spouting sovereigns, and the cudgel in the sack jumping out and whacking the landlord. And you'd shout "Ah!" and you'd shout "Oh!"

And do you know why? No? Well, I'll tell you—

Once upon a time there was a king of the Clods, and it was a long time ago. The king's name was Kalibum, which means "dog". He and all his people lived between two big rivers. Like the rest of them he used to get up very early in the mornings, rub the sleep out of his eyes and go down to the river. All day long the Clods sat by the river and fished. Some sat on the bank of the right-side river and some sat on the bank of the left-side river, and as their capital city lay exactly in the middle, they all had the same journey home.

Several hundred years passed like this. King Kalibum grew old and began to think about handing the regency over to his son Tsukakip, which means "scorpion". Tsukakip, who was two hundred and thirty-four years old already, was to take charge of the half of the Clods along the right-side river on his own, while Kalibum would look after those on the left-side river as before. And it duly came to pass.

Tsukakip was lucky with his fishing and in the evenings when the little fires were smoking away under pans and cauldrons, he had the best stories to tell. It seemed as if the fish must have jumped out onto the sand for him, so round was his belly and so oily were the hair and faces of the right-side Clods. Encouraged by his prosperity, he took to himself fifty extra wives, who in the course of a year had babies one and all.

The following year, however, was poor in fish. Kalibum and likewise his son Tsukakip often came home empty-handed, and when all they brought back was a couple of tiny perch or stickle-back from the rivers, they got a very peculiar look from their wives, and the gesture with which the cooks tossed the fish into the frying pans was far from kindly. There would be none of the usual story-telling at nightfall.

King Tsukakip on the right side, however, had heard from a passing camel drover that only a few miles farther south the two rivers in which he and his father with all their people were fishing formed a single broad stream, which just at that point divided to flow past Clod-land in two streams. Tsukakip, with the good of his family and of his people uppermost in his mind, did not hesitate. Two thousand right-siders were mustered as diggers.

"I say," observed King Kalibum, which means "dog", to his son Tsukakip a fortnight later, "for the past two days there's been considerably less water in the left-side river, although we've had plenty of rain lately—how is it with you?"

"The same with me," replied Tsukakip, which means "scorpion", "I, too, have noticed a lowering of the water level."

And Kalibum asked again: "Where are your people, Tsukakip? Have you had casualties?"

"A few, oh father," lied Tsukakip, "collapsed by the river from exhaustion, but I hope that within a few days they will be sufficiently recovered for me to be able to return them to our capital."

But that night Tsukakip was not watching the moon over the city or listening to the baying of the camels, and the howls of the jackals did not daunt him. With a smile he walked to the right-side river and stood barefoot on the bank. By morning he could feel the water rising around his knees.

When King Kalibum and his left-side Clods went fishing they found the river was no longer there. There was neither water nor fish far and wide. Although some of Kalibum's people threw themselves down on the sand and uttered the sacred cry "Yo-yo!" in the sly hope of pinning the blame for the loss of their river on some deity, the water did not return.

"Well, what do you know?" said King Kalibum, turning tail with his people and setting out to seek counsel with his son Tsukakip.

Tsukakip and the right-side Clods returned to their capital long after dark. Marching at their head was Tsukakip himself with a forty-pound pike. The rest panted along behind, staggering with whole sacks and armfuls of river fish.

The eyes nearly fell out of the heads of Kalibum and the left-side Clods.

"Ah!" they exclaimed. And then again "Ah!" and yet again: "Aaah!" and their astonishment and joy knew no bounds.

But Tsukakip and the right-side Clods put their catches down at their feet, raised their fists against their brothers and shouted: "Oh!" and again "Oh!" and yet again "O-oh!"

"Ah!" sounded from the left, "Oh!" sounded from the right, "Ah" and "Oh" and "Ah" and "Oh", until even the camels realised that something was wrong. Glittering pike, silvery stickleback, grey-gleaming perch and slimy eels darted and slithered on the sand. But that was all that happened: the left-side Clods shouted "Ah!" and remained empty-handed. The right-side Clods replied darkly with "Oh!" and stuffed away to their hearts' content. And Tsukakip mocked the left-side Clods and his father Kalibum more than all the others. Now and again he threw over a piece of tail or a clean-licked spine. accompanying it with a thunderous "Oh". Kalibum and his people had stopped letting out their "Ah's" by now, for they had at last tumbled to the fact that they were going to get nothing.

The right-siders did not forget the shouting, however, and from that time forward they called their hungry fellow countrymen the Ah-

Clods. It was only fair that the left-siders began to call the fat-bellies on the other side of the river the Oh-Clods.

Although these names didn't last for long, the division between them has remained roughly the same, since one lot have (as they like to call it) channelled the river, while the others have to do without any water at all. Miracle upon miracle!

King Tsukakip could not long tolerate the sight of his poor old father and the Ah-clods wasting away to skin and bones, so he let them have a little fish, although on condition that they built solid houses for the right-siders in return, as Tsukakip's wives had long been complaining that they had to have their babies in the open air. King Kalibum, hungry but with his wits about him, accepted the offer. Ah-Clods built houses and Oh-Clods lived in them.

Nobody really knew what a proper house was supposed to look like, but the underfed left-siders set about their work without hesitation. They felled cedars, sawed them up, dug foundations and propped beam against beam and plank against plank at a sharp angle, closed in the open ends with strong bars and daubed the walls with damp clay.

When Tsukakip and his Oh-Clods came back from fishing, their new dwellings were handed over to them with a certain amount of grinning. However, the right-siders didn't take any notice, but lay down with their wives in the houses with their A-shaped entrances, just like the Ah-shout of the left-siders.

Now you are going to ask me why it was that the Ah-Clods put up with all this. Why didn't they have a share in the right-siders' catch from the very beginning? Why didn't they look for the reason why the water had stopped flowing through the left-side river?

And this too I shall explain to you.

On the day when Tsukakip and his people returned home with their great catch of fish, a man named Maresda, which means "gazelle", took him aside and warned him. "Great king Tsukakip," he said, "the problem will be keeping all the fish for ourselves. We've got to get the others to see it our way."

"You are right," said Tsukakip, "but how are we to do this?"

"Leave it to me," replied Maresda, and so when they arrived back in the city it was he who first raised his hands and bellowed "Oh" at the left-siders.

"We of the right-side river," he began, before the assembled people, "have a sign of grace. We are the elect. The sun, the great O in heaven, has taken away the river from you and has given it to us. The right-side river belongs to us. Whosoever wants to eat shall earn it by serving us."

And, because all the Clods were impressed by the sun, the Ah-shouters had to abide by this.

So it is to this day, and there are still many who shout "Ah" and "Oh" without knowing the reason why. The Ah-Clods, who had been looking forward to their fish, eventually forgot about shouting "Ah". Today it's only children who still remember how to. And so when the sun shines, or a cow calves, or a cat laps the milk, or a storm is blowing up, or a mountain topples into the lake, or a policeman blows on his flute, the children all shout:

"AAAAAAAAAAAAAH!"

The grown-ups, however, and all the people with possessions, stretch their hands out in front of them and cry:

"OOOOOOOOOOOOOH!"

And what happened afterwards?

I can tell you that too.

Not long ago some good folk set out in the direction of the great noonday sun, that is to say, up-stream. It won't be long now before they reach the place where many thousands of years ago King Tsuka-kip built his dam. They will sit down on top of the great barrier and see the water that has been flowing to the right only for so long. They won't wait there for night to fall, but will hasten back to you with the wonderful news. And it's up to you to receive them with jubilation when they come!

> *Ah! Ah! Ah! Ah!*
> *Slop the nasties into the pail,*
> *Tuck the nicies under your arm,*
> *Lock the nasties up in jail,*

Keep the nicies cosy and warm,
    Oh! Oh! Oh! Oh!
Fiddlers, swindlers and toffee-nosed spinsters,
Snoopers, seducers and services ministers,
Nostalgia-dampers and travel-restricters,
Pulpit chiders and red-tape tiers,
Panders, landlords and stock-exchange twisters,
Cine-sexsymbols and tele-break pluggers,
Birdsnesters, bombers and Lord's Day Observers,
Growlers and grumblers and sneakers and snubbers,
Caneswinging boneheads, respectable drivellers,
Own-axe-grinders, other folk's business minders,
Defeatists, despisers, spoilsports and sneerers—
    Oh! Oh! Oh! Oh!
You there! Into the pail! Into the jail!
    Oh! Oh! Oh! Oh!
Who's tucked in my arm? Who's cosy and warm?
    Ah? Ah? Ah? Ah?
Magicians and children and rainbow-riders,
Favourite uncles, dancers and tumblers,
Architectural toytown constructors,
Daredevil space-captains, post office workers,
Dashing and elegant champion skaters,
Kindly and punctual omnibus drivers,
Swimming instructors and organ grinders,
Explorers, inventors and house decorators,
Tramway conductors, plumbers and plasterers,
Turners and joiners and carpenter-masters,
Anglers and gardeners and highway menders,
    Ah! Ah! Ah! Ah!
You there! Under my arm! Keep cosy and warm!
The rest in the pail! The rest into jail!
    Ah! Ah! Ah! Ah!

61

It was summer again, the great bleach season, the river banks and meadows had made up their bed with a hundred thousand sheets, and perspiring women hopped about in it like fleas, shaking out and smoothing and sprinkling water over their white dowry. Bicycles rang on the highways, loaded with rucksacks and children. I had to walk eighty kilometres to Mierstedt: the land was now rolling, bridges placed themselves in my path, planks rumbled, resin-scented and clean-swept forests of fir stiffened their virgin necks, and around midday I lay down in the shade of an elder and ate some of the white wheat bread that the jailor had given me for my journey.

I walked all the afternoon and all the evening, refusing to accept a lift, letting every passing car go dust-billowing on its way. I slept for the night in a haystack among mice and owl hoots. I set out again after dawn through two or three interminably long villages, drank from every fountain I passed, splashed water under my shirt but did not take the time to wash.

Mierstedt lies on the Mierstedter lake, through which two rivers flow, the Miere and the Muthe. And the Muthe rises in Tesch, the birthplace of the high-and-dry mariner Bonifaz, seeking the ocean and a white four-master.

There is a monument in Mierstedt to Faithful Jack. He is an old man made of bronze with a raised forefinger and a dog at his feet. In their lifetime, both belonged to Duke Wolfgang. The dog had saved Jack's life before he was quite so old and had fallen into the Miere. Whereupon Duke Wolfgang had demanded of his serf and servitor Jack that in gratitude he should teach the dog to speak. Jack did his best, but as after three years the dog could still not even say "Your Grace", Duke Wolfgang had Jack's head chopped off. The dog died soon afterwards, being already fourteen years old and dragging his back legs. Duke Wolfgang died too, and his successor plundered the church coffer and put up the monument.

I sidled around the market square for a time before I found the courage to ask for the Lying-In Home, a depressing title which suggested to my imagination something like a birth-mill or baby-factory. I took off my cap and enquired. It lay on the Mierstedter lake, in a small, quiet street where the only sound was the rustling of broom in front gardens and now and again a shriek, but then that told the neighbours: there it goes, they've laid another, one more mouth for the world to feed, and grandpa's off to the savings bank, opens a savings book, deposits the first hundred, three and a half per cent per annum, but the granddads of the squawkers born here usually don't know anything about it. This was a home for fallen girls, you could see that at once from the outside.

The winner in the contest for the most repulsive barracks ever designed must have been qualified to build the Lying-In Home at Mierstedt. As it went upwards it grew wider and longer, standing on red, black-jointed spider legs, bulging out in a dropsical belly with narrow slits, pulling sunblinds down its sightless eyes and folding over its head a slate roof covered with mansard tumours, scabbed and mossy. It would not have surprised me in the least to see it begin grinding its teeth.

Inside were lying the sort that had chilled their bottoms on the grass after hot dance-floor nights, don't do that Erwin, but the moon looks so lovely and Erwin's wet harelip nudges a small cold ear: Let yourself go, Yvonne, it'll be all right.

Instead of legs the matron had character, short and thick. Amethyst is a charm against drowning, but is there anything to save us from the unfriendliness of women?

"Reverend Mother," I began. Wrong, completely wide of the mark: urban-nondenominational. There had been green beans for lunch, she wiped mutton from her face.

"Wassthe matter?" she asked, as if I were waking her from a three hours dream.

"Excuse me, doctor," I said. Naturally she did not correct me, but led me into the parlour instead. The first thing the girls saw on arrival here was this sort of *Après-midi d'un Faune*, framed and glazed—a sturdy bourgeois sitting on a cliff by the sea pursing his lips, tapping in time with his round hoof and leering out of his picture frame at the adjoining wooden plate with its poker-work inscription "SELF-HELP".

"What I've come about is this . . ."

"You needn't tell me," said the matron, "you're the grandfather and you don't care for the feeling. What's the girl's name?"

"Greifenhagen."

"Will you speak to her yourself, or do you want me to do it for you?" asked the matron, sitting down in a sombre leather armchair that had crochet-work protectors on the arms.

"About what?"

"Well, about the child. She'll be foaling tomorrow or the day after," she said with a laugh. "Please don't take any notice of the expression. If you have to see it every day, you can't keep up the reverence. It gets to be just the same as turning out rolls in a bakery. It'll cost you twenty marks a month and it won't get any further. Though you can't expect me to be able to help you when later on it comes to custody claims. My job is simply to patch things up for the sake of morality and smother the voice of nature."

She was so fat and greasy, I thought she would need to look out of the window on getting up in the morning to convince herself there were other people left in the world. When she started walking, it was like a monument on the move. She left an imprint on the linoleum.

She had an effect on me like roast pork and red cabbage: they always remind me of my mother's favourite song—*Still as the night, deep as the sea, so shall my love e'er for you be.* She always sang it at confirmations, and at confirmations we used to get roast pork.

"I would rather have liked to speak to Fräulein Greifenhagen," I said.

"We don't bargain. Twenty marks a month or nothing doing. It wasn't like this before."

"Sure, sure," I said, "nothing's the same as *that* any longer."

She pressed a button on the desk near her and asked the sister who promptly came in to fetch Fräulein Greifenhagen.

"She'll want to get changed first," she said. "Have you seen our garden yet? Your little grandson will be able to enjoy it right up until he's fourteen."

We walked to the window. She drew the net aside and let me look at the garden.

"Tell me, why have all the children got green trousers and green shirts on?" I asked.

"Surplus uniforms of the frontier corps. They're the gift of a textile factory."

"Couldn't you at least have dyed them something else?" I asked.

"Do you mind! On twenty marks a month?"

"But you needn't have cut all the children's hair off . . ."

She pulled the net curtain in front of my face.

"Nobody's forcing you to leave your brats here. But we do you the favour of de-lousing them for you."

"Do you mean it's so filthy here?" I asked but never heard the answer because at that moment the door opened and Pulle came in. She greeted the matron first and then me.

"Hullo, Pulle," I said and looked everywhere except in her eyes, which were so big you could have dived right into them.

"Had any contractions yet?" enquired the matron.

"No," said Pulle and smiled at me.

"Taking his time, isn't he, the little earthling?" said the matron reproachfully, as if a foetus required a written excuse for coming into the world three days later than expected.

"I wonder whether . . ." I said.

"Naturally," said the matron, "exercise will do no harm. But see that you're back in time for dinner."

I shook the matron's hand, and Pulle walked out in front of me. When we were in the street I saw what an enormous belly she had. Pulle looked down at herself as if noticing it for the first time.

"What was it like in jail?" she asked and blushed at the same time.

"Not at all bad. We were able to have a shower twice a week, with spiritual consolation on Sundays, which made it a lot easier for us all. I can even sing the Mass, and loudest of all the Credo, that's to say, I believe."

"Why don't you know for certain?"

"Credo *means* 'I believe'—and that's what I can sing loudest."

"Oh I see," said Pulle putting her arm through mine. "I don't know any French."

We turned off in the direction of somewhere or other, towards park and city wall, bushes and playground.

"Your old dragon thinks I'm the granddad," I said, nodding at Pulle's belly.

"Granddad?" she asked, getting into a kind of roll which I had only seen done before by parsons' wives on their way out into the garden to cut parsley, wearing mules and holding a little knife.

"What do you think of that?" I asked.

"Funny," said Pulle.

"Aha," I said.

We went on stepping over the roots for a bit without speaking.

"Heard anything from Kreti?" I asked when we sat down on a small bench.

She shook her head. "He's got troubles enough. He's supposed to pay out a couple of hundred marks maintenance every month. Where's he to get the money from?"

"He ought to have thought about that first," I said.

"Oh," was all she said, looking at me from the side.

"How many is it now?"

"It said in the paper that the forty-first had just been delivered. You know I really thought he was going to stop at forty. But he's got no self-control. That's always his way, exaggerating."

"Yes," I said, "and you'd never think he was like that. He always seems sort of diffident."

"I oughtn't to be sitting down for so long. Frau Melde said I was to keep walking, then it comes quicker."

"Has she got children, too?"

Pulle laughed. "Lord! Nobody's ever managed to get at her."

"What are you going to do when it's arrived?"

"I'll go back to Berlin."

"We could get married," I said.

"But you're married already."

"Oh yes, so I am," I said. I had really and truly forgotten.

At about seven I took Pulle back to her baby factory, but took care to avoid running into Frau Melde.

Pulle didn't turn to watch me go, her thoughts were probably entirely centred within. No blind twitched as I left, and in the hostel nobody spoke to me when I entered.

I pulled off my shirt and trousers, a boy shone a torch down my seams, sniffed up his phlegm and said to the card players: "No bugs."

I lay on my back on a sack of wood-shavings. It was like being home in jail again.

"My name's Ollrich," said an old man on the same row of bunks as mine.

"Screw you," I said and went to sleep. But at about midnight I woke up as this creature next to me had started singing. *To thee my heart I wholly offer, Enter Lord, my saviour, come.*

On the opposite wall, under the screened light, hung Pius XII. *Habemus Papam.*

"*I will give me to thee utterly,*" sang my neighbour, "*though I to thee am small enough, Oh, yet shalt thou to me alone Be more than earth and heaven could.*"

He had a good, high voice for the soprano aria, but a bit throaty, as Senhora Golvão, who knew quite a bit about singing, would have said.

"My name's Ollrich," he said again. He must have noticed that I was awake, or perhaps he was used to saying it to anyone who might be listening.

"I'm on the road," he said, "I'll get a job in Trier. I'm an organ builder." He suddenly laughed. "But you're all too cracked to care!"

"Quiet!" shouted someone from the other row.

"*I will stand beside thee, then,*" he intoned softly, going on to the chorale, "*Condemn me not before.*"

"Turn it up for goodness' sake, Emil," shouted the same voice from over there, but my neighbour sang on: "*I shall ne'er abandon thee When thy great heart shall break.*"

194

I turned over on my side and went to sleep again. In the morning, it was still before six, I saw him. He snapped his braces on his blue shirt, pulled a grey jacket over and for a moment looked at me through thick lenses. He picked up his kitbag and went out of the door. Pale Pius hung on the wall, with a look of holding off doomsday single-handed and of already feeling nauseated by the din of trumpets, the stench of corpses and the endless petitioning.

I gulped corn coffee from a sky-blue enamel mug, declared: "May the Lord reward you!"—although it nearly tore my tongue—and went into the street.

62

THE best whistling tunes are the ones my grandma sang. When she put me to bed she used to sing *Wo Tann und Fichten stehn am Waldessaum, verlebt ich meiner Jugend schönsten Traum*. At the same time she would be pulling the hairpins out of the coiled plaits on top of her head and once I saw her sitting on the edge of the bed with her long grey hair down and heard her sing right on through the rest of the stanzas about the poor innocent little roe deer and the bold bad huntsman. I recited it to Pulle when she came out of the shaky house one day after breakfast, but the thing that sent Pulle swooning was *The Isle of Capri*.

"I didn't sleep well, anyhow," she said as if it was my grandma's fault.

"Did you dream?" I asked.

"Yes," she said, but would not tell me what.

"The thing you really mustn't dream about is a deer, and on no account let yourself get a fright from a deer, otherwise the child will be born with antlers on its head."

"Things like that can't happen," she said.

"They can," I contradicted, "everything can happen. There are some children, for instance, with keys and little hearts on their chests, like a sort of birthmark. Keys appear on those whose father isn't married to their mother."

"What about the little hearts?" asked Pulle.

"Women who conceive without love give birth to children with little hearts on them."

"It was love with me," said Pulle.

"Then you've nothing to worry about," I said, and went down to the Mierstedter lake with her. We hired a rowing boat and went out into the middle.

"No fear of me feeling queer," said Pulle, "you know, I've never been seasick."

"Don't give it a thought," I said, taking off my jacket and laying it on the plank so that Pulle could sit more comfortably.

"Have you got a name already?" I asked.

"What for?"

"Pulle, Pulle Pulle," I said, "where's your head? The child's got to be called something. Do you know what it says in the statute book, which I read through while I was in clink, under Section One? Legal responsibility in the individual commences upon completion of delivery in childbirth."

"Oh," said Pulle, "d'you think there'll be trouble with the cops straight away?"

"God knows. But a person's got to have a name."

"Hm," went Pulle and kissed herself on her left shoulder.

"Shouldn't I be doing that?" I asked and drew in the oars, but she was not even listening.

I began to feel rather superfluous; she was now kissing herself on her right shoulder.

"Pulle, for heaven's sake," I said in a muted voice, "What about me?"

"What?" she said, jerking her eyes open and blushing, which went very well with her brown dress.

"All I mean is . . ."

"Why aren't you rowing?"

"I am, I am," I said, catching a crab out of sheer nerves.

"If it's a girl I'll call her Heidemarie."

"Are you nuts?" I asked.

"Or Iphigenia," said Pulle.

"You have some ideas! For all I care you can call her Clotilde."

"That doesn't sound decent," said Pulle and put her hand into the water.

She suddenly bent forward, screwed up her face and said: "Bonifaz, quick, go back!"

"Is it starting?" I asked.

"I think so."

I turned around and pulled away full speed ahead.

"And what if it's a boy?" I asked, out of breath.

Pulle made a face long enough to do for three funerals.

We had already paid for the boat; I flung the chain to the boatman, lifted Pulle onto the jetty and hobbled away with her. Every twenty paces we came to a stop. Pulle made a deep bow with the pain, and I followed her halfway down each time, partly out of anxiety and partly because I could not see what else to do. The school was straight ahead and the little snot-noses took a bit of time before they had all cottoned on to what was happening. The boys smirked as if they had seen it all before and the girls hitched their plaits back to stammer encouragement into each other's ears. Pulle was not crying, but she groaned as if she was actually making the baby. I held onto her shoulders and her arms and was not far from thinking it was almost harder for me than for her. When we reached the Lying-in Home, Frau Melde, the matron, was standing in the front garden and weeding round a couple of late radishes, or, truer to say, weeding was going on around them, since her size was such that it was impossible to see whether her arms were moving.

"Are we there now?" she asked.

I just nodded.

"Gwan in," she said and tapped the earth off the hoe against the fence. I was not sure that I had grasped the whole of her speech, but supposed that she knew what she was doing.

"That makes three today," she said behind us, as though it was quite a liberty for babies to arrive in her house. Pulle was going to leave me behind in the vestibule but I went on with her through the reception room into a whitewashed corridor where we were received by a woman in a nurse's bonnet whom Pulle called Sister.

Sister looked at me kindly and removed my cap. She must have been the first person here to take me for the father, and she had long since resigned herself to the ways of absent-minded, overwrought men.

"It'll take quite a while yet," she said to me, put her arm round Pulle's shoulders and led her away through the second door on the right.

I stood there a little longer, wondered why Pulle had not turned round to give me another look, in the end put it down to her pains and retired into the reception room.

Frau Melde was sitting in her leather armchair with the crotchet-work protectors and grinned.

"Like a nip?" she asked.

"Wouldn't mind," I said.

"Rum, sixty per cent," said Frau Melde. "Cracks the glass."

"Really?" I said, swallowed and blew out a breath fit for a T.B. test. "Not bad," I announced.

"A drop a day wears the Rockies away," said Frau Melde and poured out another.

"Shall I deal?" she asked, lifted the lid of her desk and took out a pack of cards.

"As you will," I said.

She shuffled by dividing the pack into two, raising the corners with her thumbs and riffling them together. But before she dealt, each of us knocked another one back.

She dished out three for me and three for herself, flipped up the next card and laid it on the table, the queen of clubs, gave me another three, herself the same and covered the queen of clubs with the remainder.

"Shall we play for fun?" she asked and settled me in my chair as comfortably as possible.

Frau Melde arranged her hand and watched me with one eye over the top of the chequered backs. For the first time it struck me that the other one was glass.

"One mark for every ten games I win," she said. "If I lose ten I'll stand you a Schnapps."

"Trying to stamp out alcoholism, are you?" I enquired.

"Your turn," she said, "and always follow suit." I played the ace of hearts, which she took with the ten of clubs. We both helped ourselves to a new card from the pile. She played the ace of spades, to which I had to surrender my king. She grinned. "Thought you'd call 'twenty', eh?"

I shook my head, although I had the queen of spades. Before we got down to the last cards she turned up the queen of clubs, which doubled the stakes, took my trumps, showed the ten of diamonds and queen of hearts and won. Very contentedly she poured out a Schnapps and tipped it down. I shuffled, dealt and won. She made a tick.

"I'm keeping track in my head of what you lose," she said.

I laid the cards on the table when I heard screams behind me from the corridor, but Frau Melde reassured me: "That's the other one. Your daughter-in-law's not due for ages."

I lost that game.

"Let's hope we don't get a rupture," said Frau Melde while she shuffled the cards again.

"Ah, no," I had replied and only then got what she was talking about.

"Can be nasty," she said and dealt me my cards. "All sorts of things can happen: forceps, caesarian. All depends on how your little grandchild's lying. I call 'forty'."

She let me see her queen of hearts and king of hearts, followed this up by offering an ace of clubs, but I was able to take that with a ten of trumps, and I also had the knave of hearts and the ace of hearts and took all the other tricks.

"D'you think it'll be twins, perhaps?" I asked. Frau Melde had her mouth full of rum and could only shake her head.

"That's an expense you don't need to fear," she pacified me. I lost the next seven games and had to shove her a mark. Unfortunately I noticed that she was cheating. Every ace whatever that I played she trumped, I worked it out that she must have been able to make a pretty packet on the side if she played sixty-six with everyone who came here waiting for a baby to be born.

Frau Melde downed her ninth rum and twisted her glass eye round so that she won one game after the other. Behind my back things had quietened down, now and again a pregnant girl crossed the room in felt slippers, quietly closed the door behind her and somnambulated on her way. A huge grasshopper was sitting trapped in the glass chimney of Frau Melde's desk lamp, and every few minutes it leapt up against the cardboard lid the matron had placed on top. The plop was like treading on sorb-apples. Then there was the slapping of the cards on the table, the sisters in the all-green kindergarten outside shooing the three-year-olds to bed in their pairs, buck up or the bogeyman will get you, but who's afraid of bogeys if you've already started life clad in uniform? Frau Melde's left eye, the false one, was studying her cards while she observed me with her right one: spades or diamonds, clubs or hearts. I was having a run of luck and made it up to ten wins. I would have liked to take back my mark but Frau Melde poured me out a Schnapps and shook what was left in the bottle into her own glass.

"I'll go and have a look at how things are getting on, shall I?" I asked, as we had not exchanged a word for half an hour. Frau Melde shook her head, pressed on the button and said to the sister: "Seed bag popped yet?"

"Yes," said the sister. "On the way now."

"Carry on," said Frau Melde and played the queen of diamonds although she had the king, which showed how tight she was. I won ten games and now she was obliged to give me the mark back, having finished up the Schnapps. I put it in the fob pocket by my flies as a souvenir.

I took one game after the other. When my wins had brought me up to another mark, she said: "We'll have to notch that one up. I'm out of

Schnapps. Money too," she added quickly. "Perhaps we'll set it against the expenses here," she suggested.

"I'm not the grandfather," I said.

"Oh, so," said Frau Melde. "The father?"

"No," I said, "I've been in prison for the past year."

"Well, then you ain't," she said.

The next we heard was screaming through two doors: Pulle.

"I'll have to go and see now," said Frau Melde and there was not a trace of intoxication about her any more.

"It's a boy," she said an hour later, "and he's got nothing on his chest. Come again early tomorrow morning. Everything's O.K. She's asleep now."

I went to the door and saw that she was back in her leatherwork armchair with the crochet-work protectors. But her face was grey and sweat glistened under her hair.

"Whadda you waiting for?" she asked, without turning round.

"I'm going," I said.

"How much did I lose?" she asked.

"Nothing," I said, "nothing," and crept away.

63

I went back to the hostel, borrowed a knife and went hunting for some soft wood in the outhouse; but all I could find was a splintered cart-shaft. I spent half the night sawing and boring and chipping. The bowsprit had a leftward bias, but luckily there was some unused emery paper sticking out of a can on my bed so that I could even out her waist, and my four-master finally looked as if she were bearing to port, though with a full wind astern. I rounded off the masts, polished the keel, tightened the yards with shrouds and stays made of twisted cotton until everything was shipshape except for what really mattered, the sails. My blue shirt wouldn't do, and my collar was no longer white, but a four-master has to have sails. This was a ship for putting to sea and not for lying reefed at anchor. I could have done with a bit of the Reverend Leverentz's sheets, a strip of his nightshirt, the one in which he had floated on the gentle breeze up to heaven, where the Moravians can at last say "Goodnight" to the Jesuits and they pull away together at big bottles of Jamaica rum, gurgling toasts to the Council of Trent and the dogma of papal infallibility. Wasn't it he who once threatened me with the day that would come when I was to lean my head against the window and look out into the dark street and know nothing any more, not even the sea? Me, who was going to be loved by a seamstress after I'd given my last shirt away? Where had she got to, my Singer-Beloved, my buttonhole Desdemona, my cuff-turn fairy? Masts and yards are set, but next door it's the skat-fraternity thumping their cards, scraping their boredom across the table, in the Lying-In Home Pulle is in bed with a suddenly empty belly and perhaps crying for joy. To the high seas, to the far ocean—where and whither away? What good are we when we've got no sails, those patches of hemp and jute with their hard weave and their double ply? For on your own account there's no crossing the sea, and that's why one takes friends with one, or women, and Senhora Golvão used to say that Don Quixote couldn't have kept going without Sancho Panza, because he needed someone to share his secrets with, one ear being as good as the whole human race for the purpose. What's become of Kreti? Where's Pulle? Was I back in the depot, just minus sardines and staff maps—only a model ship in my hand sailing the voyage of my dreams, a four-master with a broad red hull-line and a full wind astern and let it blow any way it likes so long as she gets going again?

I took my wallet out of my coat: Pulle's letter, my ticket of leave, a provisional identity card and my neutrality certificate. No repatriated person shall be employed on active military service. Article Seventy-Four of the Geneva Convention of July 27th, 1929.

The captain, officers and members of the crew, when nationals of the enemy state, are not made prisoners of war on condition that they make a formal promise in writing not to undertake, while hostilities last, any service connected with operations of the war. Chapter Three, Article Six of the Hague Convention on the right of capture in maritime war of October 18th, 1907, published in the German *Reich-Gazette*, 1910, Number Two, page 316.

Good strong paper with a wavy watermark, fine typing with no spots or dirty margins, just a bit frayed at the edges from being got out and shown so often. It's about time I gave my soul a retread like a worn motor tire. Old skin is worn off every seven years, the old Adam is made new. But to show his colours, he reaches out for the same old hat as before and, hey presto, it still fits! And how well, that sweat-stained band and crumpled brim! I mix with people, me with my paper —look, what's bothering you? I've got it black on white: I'm neutral. I'm a Swedish match, a Swiss cuckoo clock—whizz-fizz, tick-tock. A ship has no conscience, a bosun's pipe has no conscience. The wind hasn't got a conscience either, it shifts from right to left. It blows the Trades, it blows monsoon and when it blows up big it blows typhoon and devours one and all, good and bad.

Only man has a conscience and so for that reason I cut eighteen little white sails out of my document and gummed them to the yards and gave my ship to Pulle and her son, whose navel cable she had just cast off and who still knew about nothing.

64

FRAU MELDE let me in herself and went ahead of me, bending the staircase beneath her. "The little lad weighs nine pounds," she said and opened the door to a lightly-papered room with six beds. Three girls were playing cards, one was pointing her sharp belly-prow at the window, and Pulle lay radiant on the pillows and had done her hair up with an elastic band. The girls looked up from their cards and observed me as I crossed the linoleum and the bedside rug to Pulle and laid my ship between her knees. For God's sake, kid, please, please don't start weeping now, where am I supposed to sit down? Your arms are terribly thin.

"I . . ." I said.

"Yes," said Pulle and moved over a bit towards the wall to give me room to sit on the bed, which I didn't dare do because of my dirty trousers.

"You could put down a piece of newspaper," said Pulle, but I shook my head.

"You'll be needing a lot of rest now," I said.

"But I am resting," said Pulle.

"I mean—altogether," I said but I wasn't really sure now what I meant.

"He's got black hair," said Pulle.

"Was it bad?"

"Very. I yelled. He's got such a big head, but nothing went wrong. I've got an ice bag on my tummy now—want to see?"

I could hear the girls turning to peek at us behind my back.

"I'd rather not," I said.

"Is that for him?" asked Pulle and pointed to the sailing ship.

"Yes," I said, "and what's more I'm bequeathing him all my real estate lying between seven degrees four minutes seventeen seconds east and fifty-two degrees eight minutes nineteen seconds north."

"Where's that?"

"Not far from Osterode, where my aunt lives. It's all water, but you can fish in it and swim, all that sort of thing, eh?"

"Thanks ever so much, Bonifaz. And what are you going to do now?"

"Me?"

"Yes."

"Oh, I'll find myself something. Is there any way I can help you?"

"You? Help me?" Pulle laughed. "But Bonifaz, I've got a son now. He'll help me."

"All the same, he's still a bit young," I said.

"Had you been thinking of setting up with me or something?" asked Pulle.

"No fear. I just thought that, as you'd written to me, there must be something behind it."

Pulle twisted up a strand of her hair and brushed her nose with the bunch. "You don't manage too well on your own," she said.

"I was thinking about it last night," I said, picked up a newspaper from the table and sat down by her on the bed. "We could go to some place where I could find work."

"Where you could go to sea . . ."

"Well, yes."

"Do you really like me at all?"

"Yes."

"Bonifaz, it wouldn't work." She laid her left hand on the sleeve of my jacket and looked at me just as she had on that evening between the Jerusalem church and the Otto Platz when the soap bubbles bounced around us. "I'll manage all right," she said, "and you'll manage without us, too. We'd only be in your way. The kid needs somebody who won't just promise him the moon, he needs somebody who's always there, not just for today."

I stood up and twisted my cap in my hands.

"He's being brought in now," said Pulle, "you'll have to go."

I nodded and wanted to shake her hand; but the sister, who I hadn't heard coming, was already laying the child in her arm. Pulle unbuttoned her nightshirt and shoved him at her breast. He looked like Rumpelstiltskin, only without the beard, refusing to open his eyes and moving his mouth fast with smacking noises.

"A prize boy, eh?" said the sister. "We'll pump off what he leaves, Fräulein Greifenhagen."

Pulle closed her eyes to show her that she'd understood but didn't want to speak. The sister took the playing cards away from the others and went out.

"I'm going now," I whispered.

"Come here," said Pulle.

I bent over her.

"Closer," she said.

I laid my ear to her mouth.

"Goodbye," she said quietly, "Hajji Halef Omar."

I straightened up, my heart kept thumping and the sun shone on the linoleum, and without looking right or left I walked out of the room. On the staircase I put on my cap, and in my eyes as I stepped into the street a tiny four-master sailed over the endless white wastes of a bed.

65

THE fir trees clamber up the slope, the earth revolves and the thought of it is enough to make you dizzy. A young man with a radio lay on his belly in the grass next to me and the radio said: "Good health and all God's blessings are wished by Aunt Tutti and all her friends and relations to Herr Alfred Rutschke, who is obliged to celebrate his ninety-second birthday in the Eastern Zone." I could feel how my mother's face was spreading out over my own, how I was becoming more like her, as if the crust were breaking off me. I touched my forehead and could feel her narrow eyebrows, her thin nose was cutting out of my skull, my mouth was diminishing to a pale slit and my eyes were creasing up until my face was one big wrinkle. I tore at the grass for dandelions and blew memory away, over the boy and his radio.

Adam, the first baby, was a hermaphrodite, and at the age of one hundred and thirty begat a son and named him Seth and lived another eight hundred years and begat and begat. When did Cain die, and did they bind his feet together, as they used to do to dead vagabonds, to prevent him from coming back and haunting them?

We are the average-tempo people. We strike out at a pace somewhere between sauntering and scampering. We hasten along, a couple of inches too far and at the same time too short. The train is already at the platform, but what is the point of dashing and panting, only to miss it anyway? Why ask to be disappointed? We don't rush, we don't stand still either. Ours is the average tempo. In between indolence and enthusiasm. Neither yesterday nor tomorrow. Hallelujah, Neither ebb nor flood.

The moon still shines tonight. A soul rising from heaven through the shining gate.

What is it that the British Prime Minister's grandson wants to become?—A German—Well done, my boy, says the gentleman into the microphone.

Can you spare me five minutes? asks the woman's voice. Doesn't matter what I talk to my husband about, complains a listener in Baden-Baden, in half an hour we want a divorce. The moment after committing a crime may be the most exquisite one in a person's whole life, says Kleist in *Die Familie Schroffenstein*, and what would your comment be on that, professor, from the purely medical point of view?

The fir trees clamber up the slope, the earth revolves, and the thought of it is enough to make you dizzy. Time, at any rate, for me to go.

66

TESCH-WARDS lies the town of Gremmen, fifty-thousand inhabitants, through which, following the course of the Muthe, I had to go. I did not want to go all the way to Tesch on foot, and looked around in Gremmen for a job that would get me there by car. It was also in Gremmen that I became aware of the first black and yellow posters announcing the Tesch horse-market lottery with associated bomb-show. The official opening, the gala procession and the bomb-fair had been arranged for August 28th, that is to say the following day. So it ought not to be difficult to pick up a lift.

I kept my ears open and a man to whom I am indebted to this day gave me the tip to apply to the civil defence centre, as it was partly responsible for the bomb-show in Tesch and was looking for a driver.

I went to the civil defence office, showed my identity card, was engaged by a personnel officer in a state of anticipatory intoxication, and was assigned to deliver a hundred and fifty manual fire-extinguishers to Tesch by truck. Now it struck me as unusual, compared with how things used to be, for a horse-market lottery with nags and cows as prizes to be linked with an exhibition of bombs, which were in any case considered sufficiently unsafe to require garnishing with a hundred and fifty manual fire-extinguishers, but there are no pockets in your last shirt, and if somebody comes and offers to sew them on all over and put in a little something in them besides, what I say is: With gold you're bold, and if you haven't any, get the hell out of here.

The personnel officer, who was unaware that I knew more about getting around Tesch than driving a motor vehicle, described to me where the exhibition was going to take place, which was next to the castle, and sent me on my way with the driver's papers, but unfortunately no licence, although that might have come in useful, and a petty cash advance of ten marks.

I went round to the garage and asked the attendant for the truck and the fire-extinguishers. The attendant also seemed to have wetted his whistle, but no doubt that is part of a conscientious fire-fighter's training. He showed me where the extinguishers were, foam-jets with a range of eight to ten yards, and I loaded them onto the van, taking my time and stopping to smoke a cigarette. Then I threw a chain over them, clapped up the boards and fixed the pegs.

"Have a nice trip," said the attendant.

"Who am I actually supposed to deliver the stuff to?" I asked him.

"To Director Vieth," said the attendant.

"Who?"

"Vieth," he repeated.

I put in the ignition key and backed out of the garage. Vieth; well, what do you know?

I had thirty kilometres ahead of me and trailed along the highway as slowly as I could. But even at a walking pace I would still be in Tesch by evening, and I did not want to arrive on the eve of the festivities but on the day itself, regardless of what the Gremmen civil defence boys expected.

I stopped at Senkau, where geese flew across the street and pressed web-patterns in the mud and the cottagers lived who worked in the Tesch biscuit and hand-grenade factory. I parked the truck. I ate and drank at the Green Tree and nobody recognised me. In the evening I stretched out in the cabin of the truck and slept soundly until morning, when my feet got stiff and cold, for they were sticking out of the window. I locked the truck and went the rest of the way to Tesch on foot. I did not travel alone.

The road was full of dark suits and green and white country bodices. Children ran around the walking sticks of the men; families, pressed and ironed on every side, advanced separately, like little colonies through the dust, which on arrival on Tesch's first paving-stones was flicked from shoes with handkerchiefs. Brooches and watch-chains glittered in the sun, hats were doffed hither and thither, best coats still covered shiny trouser seats, only the few in a summer sweat dragged their necks free from collar and tie, and then in the shade of the town gate there was a tugging and a combing, the women straightening their men's jackets and their children's ears, examining their own finery in a neighbour's eye and then entering in upon the merrymaking.

Civic pride was bursting out in Anhalter brain-pudding and bitter beer. Under the black- and white- and red-pennanted tents capons flew onto the grill, an ox was turning beside the square-based tower, spit-pierced by the butchers from neck to rump. The Shooting Company swayed over the town square in march time, having discharged their tommy-guns at pigeons earlier in the morning, and when I got to the castle green a formation of jets screamed over the town, dropping chocolates, lametta, and pork sausages. All this seemed cause enough for me to turn around and go and bring the truck with the fire-extinguishers after all.

On my way down the main street past the Guinea-fowl gardens on my way to the station I had difficulty in making my way through the crowd, and broad, thick people, their hats pushed back over their ears with *joie de vivre*, were thrusting against me; women with thick red arms and tiny black watches threaded round them pushed me aside when I got in their way. The older children jumped down from house porches and banged me on the head with cardboard slapsticks. I hurried out of their reach, but felt drawn back to them at the same time. I knitted my hands on top of my head, ducked at every blow, and made it as far as Chestnut Avenue, where I knew a bar I could shelter in.

"Excuse me, would you mind telling me," I asked the tavern-keeper, "is there something the matter with me that puts people against me?"

"Your nose," said the tavern-keeper. "We don't care for your nose."

"My nose?" I asked and looked round me. All the men had squashed noses, broken nose bones, smashed noses with enlarged nostrils.

"Which way were you going?" asked the tavern-keeper.

"I want to get to Senkau," I said. "My truck's there. I've got a load of fire-extinguishers. For the horse-market lottery."

"You'd better stay here. You don't seem to be quite familiar with what's going on among us . . ."

"What's everybody had their noses bashed in for?" I asked.

"You don't know?" The tavern-keeper looked round cautiously. Only when he was sure that nobody could overhear him, did he say: "Everyone who's got a bashed-in nose—as you put it—actually they're called the N.F.N., that's for New-Form Noses, is a government supporter."

"Marvellous!" I said. "Having badges and banners used to be good enough . . ."

"Cha, used to be," said the tavern-keeper. "For today's great horse-market lottery they're giving everyone an N.F.N. who hasn't got one already, provided he has been proved acceptable."

"A New-Form Nose?"

"Exactly. And I dare say that in your case people had decided you were trying to dodge it."

"Aha," I said. "Now there's just one more thing I'd like you to tell me: What's the reason for their having gone for noses in particular? You could cut off an ear just as well, or shave heads?"

The tavern-keeper gave me a shocked look. "Shsh—watch your

tongue. Our New-Form Nose is derived from our Chief. He was the first to have that sort of nose."

"And who bashed his in for him?" I asked innocently.

"Hush," said the tavern-keeper. "There are three versions of the legend.—One's in the school books, another circulates among his supporters, and the third is true, but can't be told."

"You tell me," I said.

"Well, the first merely says that he was born with a button nose which made him the loveliest child on earth. The second says that he broke his nose on a field-gun while fighting against our country's enemies; probably because he was very short-sighted. And the third . . ."

"Well, get on with it," I urged.

"But you musn't let it go any further! Well, the third isn't a legend at all, because as a matter of fact, once when he was drunk, when he was still a waiter, he slipped in the w.c. and cracked his nose on the toilet lid. That's what did it."

"What do you think I ought to do?" I asked.

"The simplest thing for you is to get hold of a pint pot and swipe it in your face yourself," the tavern-keeper advised. "It's the most widely practised political activity around these parts. Of course you've got to bleed nice and heavy, otherwise you don't get the full effect."

I touched my nose, stroked it between thumbs and forefingers, tested the calibre of the nostrils with my little finger, took out a handkerchief and blew into it.

"I'll think it over," I said then. "At all events, I'd like some roast pork beforehand."

While I was pressing the potatoes into the gravy and seasoning up the sauerkraut with some mustard, I asked myself whether it was really worthwhile bringing in fire-extinguishers for people like this. Wouldn't I be laughed at for my pains? Wouldn't I have to break my nose first so as to join their gay and glorious fellowship of the mutilated?

But I stuck to my principles. The tavern-keeper came and brought the bill and said: "If you hurry you can get over to Senkau now. Around noon they're all in the taverns. Between one and two the procession will form at the tower, and that'll make it easier for you to bring in your fire-extinguishers. If it's any help, I might even take one off you, if they're for sale . . ."

"O.K.," I said, "but take it as a gift."

I made my way past the station out to Senkau. The truck was behind the barn where I had left it.

I returned over the hot asphalt road without a stop. I handed the keeper of the Chestnut tavern one extinguisher out of the truck and drove on into the town. However, the road was closed at the tower for the procession. It was going to pass the law courts and on to the castle grounds, past the saluting base and up to a raised wooden stage, where the nose-cadets were to have their noses broken.

The colour bearers had been selected for the particularly deep scars on their noses. As they inserted the heels of the colour-shafts in the leather buckets hanging on their uniformed bellies, their nostrils dilated, their eyes shone with that inward fire that is called optimism, vitality and the killer instinct. Flags and uniforms of rich, mossy green. Only at collars and cuffs was there a gleam of red complexions and white gloves. One solitary standard bearer, some five yards in advance of the others, was holding a gigantic gold-green standard.

The colour party were waiting for the ensign's command, and at its sound raised their left feet in unison and slammed them on the pavement. At the same moment the massed kettle drums of the 1st Regiment of Flatnoses crashed into a march which tickled one's martial appetites most pleasurably, and the backing of two hundred big drums made it an easy job for the band to keep time and the people to keep step.

Following close on the heels of the brass were about a hundred whole-nosed youths. They marched with heads drooping, ashamed of their nasal bones. Those with bigger beaks covered them with their hands. A broad green banner fluttered above their heads with the inscription: HURRY UP AND HAMMER OURS! The bottom right-hand corner was embroidered: NOSE-CADETS OF GERMANY—SUB-AREA TESCH. Behind the eager nose-cadets who could hardly wait for it marched the Old Guard, long since seasoned to hullaballo, stern-faced and pointing their marching tempo with a rhythmic jolt of the head. They were the only ones allowed to wear moustaches, behind which their nostrils completely disappeared. The ends were brushed up to their eyes like tangled, unkempt brambles growing on their weather-beaten faces. Two fuglemen carried a broad green cloth stretched between poles over the heads of the formation, and on it stood in gold letters:

BRING ROSSBACH HOME TO THE REICH

Crowding behind the veterans came the people of Tesch with slogans including:

ROSSBACH—LEST WE FORGET

ROSSBACH IS OURS

FREEDOM FOR ROSSBACH

REMEMBER ROSSBACH

UNION IN FREEDOM

FREEDOM IN UNION

WE'VE GOT IT GOOD—WHAT ABOUT THEM?

and many times repeated:

BRING ROSSBACH HOME TO THE REICH

I turned in with my truck and drove through the crowd. I wound down the cabin window and said to a cross-looking man with a broken nose: "Look, where is this Rossbach?"

He studied me and my nose very carefully and replied: "Over there. Across the border."

"In Germany?"

"Where do you think?" he said, and if he had had a real nose he would have turned it up at me.

"Does this mean war again?" I asked.

"It's about time," he said. "Do you imagine that our Herr Vieth is having a bomb-show here for nothing?"

He quickened his pace so as not to have to go on talking to me. I stopped the truck and pressed on the klaxon until I thought I was bursting my eardrums. A few people, particularly in front of me, stopped, turned round and approached.

I got out of the seat and clambered down.

"Ladies and gentlemen!" I shouted, but they all laughed.

"My dear fellow countrymen!" I shouted, but the ones who had stopped first went on again.

"Friends and colleagues," I shouted.

"Speeches from over there," said a young girl and pointed to the tribune by the castle.

"I have something to tell you," I shouted. A policeman came over from the other side of the street. "I'm the same as you. Listen to me, I'm seaman Bonifaz, the friend of you all."

The policeman elbowed people out of the way. He had approached to within twenty paces.

"If you go on like this," I shouted, "there'll be fireworks. I've got a hundred and fifty fire-extinguishers. Come and get them and squirt your Chief off his platform! I'm giving them away. Help yourselves!"

I lifted up two of the extinguishers and held them out to the marchers. But they had eyes for nothing else but green and gold and their Chief, who was now addressing them over loudspeakers, and although he was muted, calm, with a slight cold, yet he sounded more assured and louder than I was. The policeman took the fire extinguishers out of my hand and pulled me out of the truck.

"No parking," he said. "Would you be so good as to take your truck and park it in a side street?"

"I'm awfully sorry," I said, "I've been talking through my hat."

"No objection," said the policeman, "you can please yourself. Down there, please, in the side street. We've got freedom of opinion here, you know, but I have to keep an eye on the traffic and make sure it's moving freely."

"Sure," I said, "where's the bomb-show?"

"We're having no bomb-show here," he said.

"But I'm supposed to bring these hundred and fifty fire-extinguishers to Director Vieth."

"I take it you're referring to the new Pan-German Security Organization which is putting on a defence exhibition?"

"That could be it."

"Well then," he said, "I'll dig a path for you," and laughed at his own joke. I started the engine and moved forward again and the policeman strode ahead of me and bellowed, so that I got through without hooting and without disturbing the Chief's speech, which had now turned into an urgent whisper. For one moment I saw the Chief through my right-hand window, a tall, lean type, looking like an embittered prohibition-era waiter serving whisky in lemonade glasses and slipping his tips into a waistcoat pocket. I took no further notice of him and drove behind the policeman by the back of the tribune, past the castle, up to the octagonal wooden pavilion.

"I'll go and inform the director," said the policeman and went inside through a glass door. Two minutes later he came out again, followed by Vieth, the rocket expert. I let him come close and wound down the window when he was right outside it.

"Hullo, old chap," I said.

Herr Vieth shook his head. "I'm sorry," he said, "I don't know you."

"I'm Bonifaz, the sailor who sent you to the moon."

"I've never been to the moon."

"So I see. How far did you actually get in your fish?"

Herr Vieth turned to the policeman in disgust: "Constable, I hope you've heard everything this man said."

"Certainly, sir. He enquired whether you had flown in a fish."

"Exactly," said Vieth and gave me a challenging look, as if to see whether I would go on and finish tying my own noose.

"And what else do you know about me?" he asked, as I remained silent.

"Oh, but sir, you aren't going to take a little joke seriously, are you?" I said, and realised why Vieth looked different: he too had had his nose broken. "We've been downing a few this morning on account of the festivities—sheer anticipation, you know."

Vieth smiled, and the policeman said: "He's been talking through his hat during the parade—in that condition you're unfit to be in control of a vehicle, understand? But I'll shut an eye at it for once, shall I, sir?"

"Certainly," said Vieth, "we'll both shut an eye. Now get the extinguishers unloaded. The exhibition is being opened in half an hour."

He turned and went back into the pavilion with laughing shoulders while I started up the engine again and drove the truck to a door which was pointed out to me by the policeman before he made off. Presumably I was expected to hang the extinguishers on the brackets on the walls, but I was too curious and wanted to see the exhibition.

The octagonal hall, glass-roofed and air-conditioned, was draped with grey velvet. Glass cases and tables were placed round a raised platform in the centre and on the walls I could see charts and photographs to illustrate statistics of actual and estimated victims, ballistic trajectories, mushroom clouds, the evacuation of casualties, and happy-faced, sweating gunners firing tactical nuclear warheads. Puffs of vapour from bacteriological projectiles hung over mountain villages; a man wearing a panama hat and white football stockings was serving his private battery of poison-gas mortars under some peach trees; a twenty-four centimetre anti-tank shell bore the painted inscription BALLS TO YOU, neatly hand-lettered—as the label explained—by the seventy-two-year-old, near-blind backwoods-artist Gunzinger; while the young people of Tesch had spelt out the words TOTAL DEFENCE in twelve-centimetre shell cases.

I suddenly thought of Emma, my wife, and how she would look with a broken nose—I had no doubts about her loyalty to the régime—and how she would manage to make her glasses stay up, under the bows of which, to my disgust, she kept tucking her hair. The exhibition accounts would surely have been entrusted to her, who had once been decorated for her work in the Winter Help as a dead-accurate bookkeeper second to none.

Maps were also displayed on the walls, broad black arrows pointing at Rossbach, which—according to the legends—was the principal strategic objective of the Tesch forces, especially the artillery. The situation of Rossbach constituted, as the Chief had once been recorded as saying at breakfast, the arch-enemy's threat, and if he was not prepared to climb down in peace and freedom he would have to be completely erased with a very big rubber. If the Rossbachers were even then unwise enough to try to hit back, there was no need to worry—the new pan-German Security Organisation had taken the necessary measures. An ultra-comfortable shelter had already been constructed for the Chief, equipped with coarse-sand filters and ventilation pumps capable of an intake of six hundred litres of air at thirty-five strokes per minute. Professor Sporrel had, however, calculated that a capacity of five hundred litres of air per minute would suffice for the Chief. Now and again he would spend a night in his shelter and the whole country watched through his slumber at their loudspeakers, which relayed the ruler's high-pitched wheezing from eleven p.m. to seven a.m. He would then be awakened by the playing of the national anthem and only after he had brushed his teeth would the nation proceed, with a sigh of relief, to go about its daily tasks.

"Get a move on in here with your contraptions!" bellowed someone above me. It was Herr Dierk, the featherweight pilot. He was standing on the platform, his hands on his hips, and fairly bursting at the seams. He must have tipped the scales at ninety-eight pounds.

"Seems to have thoroughly agreed with you, that space-flight."

"I'll put a bullet through you if you don't shut up," said Herr Dierk.

"Oh, you're *hot* at that, I know."

He pulled a small revolver from his pocket and pointed it at my head.

"Are you moving?" he asked.

"Yes," I said and went out to the truck. I unloaded the extinguishers and lugged them up to the platform. From the castle and the tribune I could hear the first commands of the guard companies; the Chief was already on his way. I tugged an air-raid warden's armband on my sleeve and picked up the reserve petrol can which was under the passenger seat. I went round the pavilion and copiously sprinkled each of the eight corners with petrol. I could be generous, I had twenty litres to spare. Policemen, wardens and snoopers were standing all over the place, but because of my armband, no one stopped me or asked me what I was doing. I would have liked to get up onto the roof as well, but I wanted to play safe and take no risks which might spoil the success. When the Chief arrived I stood up straight and raised my hand to my capband. He did not notice me. All round him was a rout of mayors, aldermen, lawyers, headmasters, flag-waggers, cheer-leaders, youth-leaders, jingo-journalists, dialect poets, house-wives, tarts, priests, pettyfoggers, queers, officers, and girls with red ears and frilly white collars. They all went inside and I closed the door behind them. Through the window I could see how they grouped themselves: dinner-jackets and uniforms and long dresses in front, and the rest of the riff-raff behind. As soon as I was sure that Herr Vieth had begun his speech, I went to the eight sides of the pavilion, turned the keys in the locks and struck a light. There were marvellous shooting flames which singed my eyebrows, and I could hear the applause from inside, where they took the blaze for a good start to the gala fireworks. When the fire had taken hold of the wood at four points, I went into the pavilion by the tradesmen's entrance and squeezed my way up to the platform where the fire-extinguishers were still lying on the floor. The temperature rose and a few people began to look around for the exits. Herr Vieth hesitated and fell silent but was obliged to go on speaking again, as the Chief's eyes were upon him.

I waited until one of the side walls had scorched through, then I jumped onto the podium, pushed Vieth aside and shouted into the face of the Chief and his gang:

"Fire!"

But the Chief laughed. Vieth pulled himself together, seized me in his arms from the back and was about to throw me off the platform. I bit him in the hand and got free.

"Hoorah!" I shouted. "Fire! You're going to blow up with your own bombs and bullets, you shower!"

One of the burning side walls collapsed inwards. Suddenly they all shouted: "Fire!"

"Out of here!"

"Help!"

"The doors are locked!" a woman screeched, banging on the handle. Emma perhaps?

218

The officers swiped at the window-panes with their sabres. They had forgotten the way to open a window. Two soldiers dragged the Chief, scarlet in the face, to the nearest door but nobody let them out. I took over the microphone and bellowed at the top of my lungs: "Come over here to me! I'll save you! I'm Bonifaz, who'll put everything right! I'm Captain Bommalaria!"

They turned around to look at me, but were too scared to be capable of understanding my shouts.

"Come up to me! Come up to me! I'll help you!" I picked up the nearest extinguisher, smacked down the plunger and sprayed the mob that was beating at the windows. The foam hit them on the backs of their necks, ran down their backs and slopped spumily to the floor. I stood five extinguishers in a row, gave each a blow on the plunger and threw them down among the glass display cases. A jet spurted towards the glass roof, swished back onto me, splashed my face and blinded me. But in the darkness I reached out for the microphone again and yelled into it: "Come to me! Pick up the extinguishers! I'll help you! I'm Seaman Bonifaz!"

I wiped the foam from my face, got my sight back in one eye. The roof fell in, the glass shattered, the burning timber struts fell among the seething Pan-Germans as they tore off their coats in the heat, slapped their hands over their faces to save their lives, squeezed their puny souls through the windows, and I threw the spouting extinguishers at them, aiming the foam at their heads so as to blind them, so that they would crash into each other, fall into the glass cases, down onto the bombs, onto those smooth, cold bodies and warheads. I spotted pilot Dierk before he did me. I caught him at four yards distance with a jet as thick as my arm. He staggered and stumbled against a burning wall, which collapsed over him. The more courageous ones leapt through the flames into safety. I hurled my cap into the fire, then my jacket. Sweat was tickling my chest and I reached for more and more extinguishers, knocked them in and threw them into the crowd.

"You're not to burn!" I shouted. "You're to stay alive! But you've got to learn what your war means! There's no one else to help you, Flatnoses!"

But they did not hear me, they hit, scratched and bit each other, trampled over fallen bodies and ducked away from my squirts.

A smouldering joist glanced off me, my trouser bottoms were on fire. I reserved the two last extinguishers for myself. With one I sprayed myself, with the other I fought a passage to the exterior. Apart from Dierk, everyone escaped. Even the Chief.

67

I stopped the truck and sneaked away. I ran around the castle pond but nobody came after me. I did not go home but straight into the woods, over the Reuthen highroad, continuing for quite a distance parallel to the Rossbach road. It was afternoon. My face was burning. When the fir needles pricked my brow the pain made me clamp my tongue to my teeth. I was close to the border. I had not seen the soldier and he had not heard me coming. I collided with his shoulder and threw myself on top of him as we fell. His pupils were right in front of me, and his small broken nose. He rolled up his eyes and then closed them. I let go of his throat but kept my knee on his chest and threw his rifle away. He looked at me again. "What do you want me to do?"

"Me? Nothing. I thought it was you . . ."

He shook his head. "Keep running. Beat it. What do you want here anyway? You haven't got the right sort of nose."

I took my knee off his chest and stood up. "Your gun's over there," I said and pointed at it. But he stayed on the ground, not even moving his eyes.

"I'm Seaman Bonifaz," I said.

"So what?"

"If anyone asks about me, I'm on my way to Rossbach. I've got a friend over there. He's called Bogumil."

"Bring Rossbach home to the Reich," said the soldier.

I turned, did not look round again, took off my shoes, threw them into the undergrowth, and ran over the border in my vest and my singed and spattered trousers. In half an hour I'll be at the tram terminus, I said to myself. Perhaps they'll let me on even without any money. I had nothing left of my own any longer. Just my nose.